P9-BXZ-671

A Carrot for the Donkey

Also by Les Roberts

Saxon Mysteries
Not Enough Horses
An Infinite Number of Monkeys

A Milan Jacovich Mystery
Pepper Pike

A Carrot for the Donkey

Les Roberts

St. Martin's Press
New York

 For information, address St. Martin's Press, 175 Fifth Avenue, New York, N.Y. 10010.

Library of Congress Cataloging-in-Publication Data

Roberts, Les.
A carrot for the donkey.

"A Thomas Dunne book."
I. Title.
PS3568.023894C3 1989 813'.54 88-30544
ISBN 0-312-02554-8

First Edition
10 9 8 7 6 5 4 3 2 1

To
Robert J. Randisi,
whose dedication and generosity
made it happen

A Carrot for the Donkey

1

I suppose I should have been flattered. Any actor would be. Flattered and excited and all atwitter that Mark Evering, one of Hollywood's most successful producers, a heavyweight with development deals at three major studios, had called and left a message. And if he had called my agent I probably would have been thrilled to death. But he had called instead my own number—the number of the private investigations agency I opened five years ago to supplement my income and support me between acting jobs until that big break came along. I became a private detective the way some actors take out a real estate license in the San Fernando Valley. It was something to do besides sitting around in La Scala Boutique every day at lunch lying about what parts I was up for. And it allowed me to live in the style to which I had decided to become accustomed, i.e., traveling to San Diego or San Francisco or Napa for the weekend, having a nice place to live, full of paintings I liked and jazz records I loved, and eating the foods I enjoyed—Szechuan Chinese, northern Italian, well-poached seafood, and chunk-style peanut butter. The two careers combine to give me a relatively decent income.

And now the call from Mark Evering. I had been out wrapping up the loose ends of a rather messy divorce case I'd been working on. My client was the husband's attorney, who had a suite of dark paneled offices in Venture City and wouldn't dream of soiling his pristine French cuffs digging up the evidence to prove that the wife in question was carrying on a lesbian affair with a conceptual artist in El Segundo. Instead, he hired people like me to do his dirty work.

I came back to my little office in Hollywood where my assistant, Jo Zeidler, was reading one of those self-help manuals that urge you to take care of your own needs and to tell everyone else in your life to bite the big one. I guess reading the books made her feel better: she was married to a sweet New York Jewish intellectual named Marshall, who had come west to write the Great American Movie and wound up waiting tables somewhere in Westwood.

"Mark Evering called," Jo told me as I walked in the door. "I've been absolutely dying all afternoon to know why."

"Any other calls?"

"God, aren't you excited? I mean, *the* Mark Evering!"

"He probably has a sob story about the discreet abortion he wants to arrange for some kid from the Paramount typing pool, or an even sadder one about how the twenty-year-old bimbo whose rent he pays on Doheny Drive is making it with Bruce Willis's stunt double."

"You're a cynic," she said.

"I'm a realist."

"Same thing."

I went into my little private cubbyhole and dialed the number on the message slip. The man who answered sounded like the maître d' at the Mon Kee Seafood House, but I managed to convey to him that my name was Saxon and that I was returning Mr. Evering's call. He put me on hold, which put me immediately into a lousy mood, and then the great man himself got on the line.

"Saxon, I need to talk to you on a matter of utmost delicacy," he said without much preamble. The Doheny Drive bimbo scenario seemed likely. "Whyn't you come out to the house about nine or so this evening, and we can talk."

"Mr. Evering, I prefer working out of my office, and I also prefer working during the day unless it's absolutely necessary."

"I'm having a party," he said, as if that made it all right.

"Look, come on over, have a couple of pops, talk to me for ten minutes. Chrissake, won't hurt you to take a meeting."

"Take a meeting" is vernacular unique to the film community. Elsewhere one goes to meetings, or holds meetings, or attends meetings. But in Hollywood one "takes" meetings; it's the official sport. The usage amused me when I first came here from my native Chicago ten years ago. I thought "take a meeting" sounded suspiciously like "take a shit"—except in the second case you divest yourself of shit; in the movie business, when you take a meeting, you are more than likely about to acquire some.

In any event one simply doesn't say no to people like Mark Evering; they are so unused to rejection that they tend to shatter. So I reluctantly agreed to attend the festivities at his home that evening. I was glad I had worn a dress shirt and sports jacket to work that day; I'm more likely to get caught in jeans or sweats. As I was leaving Jo couldn't resist a final needle.

"You're getting up there with the big boys now, aren't you? After you become a star in Mark Evering's new picture, will you still remember me?"

"I hardly remember you now," I said.

Mark Evering's home is in Beverly Hills. You're surprised, right? It struck me as one of those places people buy for the sole purpose of letting everyone else know they can afford to do so. I can't imagine actually wanting to live in a house whose general size and ambience suggest the Louvre and whose driveway looks like a used Mercedes lot. The door was opened by a white-jacketed Filipino houseman even before I rang the bell. He led me through a large atrium vestibule full of tropical plants and into an enormous room that I assumed was the living room, although perhaps in the Evering household it was referred to as the Crystal Room. It was bigger than my entire house, and at the moment it held more people than might be found attending a high school basketball game. They were mostly young and attractive, all lying around on huge pillows and sprawling sofas, passing pipes and joints back and forth the way I imagine they do in opium dens in Shanghai. The music, which seemed to be coming out of every square inch of wall space not covered with Chagalls and Ben Shahns and Joan Mirós and Picassos, was strictly hard rock, and the bass notes caught me behind the breastbone and made my whole chest cavity resonate. It was that kind of sound system.

All of a sudden there was a blonde standing in front of me, smoking a joint and smiling with a lush, pouty mouth. She was a knockout, all right, somewhere in her very green thirties, and she was wearing a silk kimono that had probably cost my entire income for the year 1985. You'd think for that kind of money they could have put some sort of buttons on it so that it didn't just hang open to reveal that her only other garment was a pair of bikini underpants that didn't completely do the job of covering that which panties are designed to cover. The visible curls were blond, too. The woman appraised me the way a diner in an expensive restaurant might examine the label on a bottle of '68 Montrachet before allowing it to be decanted and said, "Well, hello there. Nice to see some new blood." And she offered the joint to me.

"Thanks, I'm trying to quit," I said. "I'm here to see Mr. Evering."

She looked disappointed. She took a heavy hit off the joint and blew enough fragrant smoke in my face that I could tell it was extremely expensive stuff, probably Thai. She moved much closer to me than was absolutely necessary and said, "Maybe when you finish your boring business discussion you could come back to the party and find me—just to say hi." And then she reached down with the hand not holding the joint and cupped my genitals and gave me a friendly little squeeze that just about lifted me out of my shoes. She smiled, apparently pleased with what she'd discovered.

"Does that work," she said, "or is it just so your pants don't hang funny?" She moved off languidly without waiting for an answer, but then, the question was rhetorical anyway.

I followed the Filipino out into the back yard. The swimming pool was roughly the size of Lake Huron and was ringed with every kind of exotic tree and shrub imaginable, each lighted with its own individual colored floodlight, which gave the area the effect of the Mato Grosso after it had been redesigned by Disney World's Imagineers. The pool itself shimmered a vibrant turquoise, and a few water babies were splashing and squealing, although most of the guests outside were standing around in casual Melrose Avenue chic clinking the ice in their glasses and letting the marijuana smoke drift out over the trees and into the warm and nonjudgmental Beverly Hills night.

On the end of the diving board a beautiful girl was poised for an evening dip. At a pool party, not remarkable. However, I took a second look and realized that what I had perceived as a white bikini was simply her tan lines, and that the girl was delightfully mother-naked. She saw me staring, smiled, waved, and jackknifed into the water. She had the kind of body I was very sorry to see disappear into the deep end.

The Filipino houseman motioned silently at me like the Ghost of Christmas Yet to Come and I reluctantly tore myself away from poolside to follow him. He ignored the nubile nymphs in and around the water, and I wondered whether he was gay or simply used to the sight of beautiful naked women. The thought occurred to me that he might be a eunuch, but I dismissed it out of hand. He led me down to the far end of the pool and into a cabana big enough to house a family of twelve. Its dominant feature was a billiard table with a flaming red plush cover. At the end of that table Mark Evering was preparing lines of cocaine on a small mirror.

He was about fifty, short, stocky, and bullnecked, and he wore a flowing caftan open to the waist to reveal his abundance of chest hair and crisscrossing gold chains. A successful producer with clout equal to Henry Aaron's on a warm Atlanta evening with the wind blowing toward left field, he looked more like your brother-in-law's accountant all dressed up for his first Hollywood party. An extremely self-confident accountant.

He glanced up from his labors and nodded a welcome. "Come on in, Saxon, glad you could make it. You toot?"

I shook my head. I had been in Mark Evering's home less than five minutes and had already been offered hash and cocaine and seen one woman totally naked and another nearly so. Just a bunch of creative filmmakers getting together for a little relaxation. And this was only Thursday. Weekends at the Everings' must have been just a load of giggles.

Several hundred dollars' worth of illegal drugs disappeared through a short gold drinking straw and up Mark Evering's nose, and I waited until the rush hit. He stood there for a moment, his eyes closed, a beatific expression on his coarse features, looking like a little pagan idol. Then he shook his head and snorted like a coach horse. Ill at ease, I took out a cigarette. I almost felt obligated to display some sort of vice of my own. At the sound of my Bic lighter flicking he opened his eyes and frowned at me.

"Do you mind?" he said, waving the smoke from in front of his face. "That's poison you're putting in your lungs. It's okay if you want to die, but don't pollute my air too."

My attempt at not laughing wasn't entirely successful, but I dutifully crushed out the cigarette in a crystal ashtray that looked as though it were losing its virginity that very second, and I watched, fascinated, as Evering began circling me warily, like a mongoose with a cobra. I was sure this was his standard routine with balky writers and uncooperative actors, but why he was doing it with me I'd have to wait and find out.

"I've seen you someplace, no? You've got a class A commercial running on TV, for vermouth or something." I nodded. Of course he knew damn well who I was and what I'd done as an actor before he'd ever picked up the phone to call me. Guys like Mark Evering leave very little to chance, which is why they are so successful. It's known in the industry as covering your ass. "Word is that you're very good at what you do—the detective shit, I mean. Fast, sincere, discreet, loyal. Is that true?"

I shrugged.

"Don't be so fucking modest," he went on. "That's just bullshit. First rule in the picture business is don't be modest. If you're good you tell the world. The second rule is you tell the world you're good even if you stink. Or maybe that's the first rule; I get them mixed up."

"Okay, then. I'm very good at what I do."

"That's more like it," he said, pleased that he'd made me say it. He went to a desk over in the corner that was home to a telephone console the size of a Monopoly board, took a photograph out of an ornate silver frame, and handed it to me. It showed a very pretty blond girl in a typical high school yearbook pose: the V-necked black dress, a string of pearls, expensive orthodontia, and a dewy-eyed, looking-to-the-future-with-hope expression.

"My daughter, Merissa," he said. "That was about four years ago, but she still looks like that. She's missing. Run away, I should say." He began pacing, his silk caftan rustling as he moved, reminding me of the sound Sister Concepta's habit used to make as she walked back and forth at the blackboard explaining algebraic equations. I'd noticed things like that when I was a boy, especially since I'd never given a shit about the value of *x*.

"She had all the advantages, that kid," Evering was saying. "Money, security, position. Two of my pictures are in the all-time top twenty biggest-grossing box office hits, you know." I hadn't known, but I wasn't going to admit it. Why pull the man's world down around his ears? "I gave her everything. Schools in Switzerland, in France. Nannies, tutors, a Maserati for her sweet sixteen party—everything!" The sad thing was that he was deadly serious. "When she was thirteen she lost her cherry. At fourteen she had the first of three abortions. For high school graduation I gave her a detox at Betty Ford's. Why does a girl with all her advantages turn out like that?"

I turned both hands palm up. If he didn't know, I sure wasn't going to tell him.

The naked girl from the diving board appeared in the doorway to the cabana. She was dripping wet, water plastering her feather-cut hair close to her head and beading up tantalizingly on her tanned shoulders and white breasts, her reddish-brown nipples wrinkled and extended in the cool night air. She had put on the bottom half of her bikini. She twinkled at me and said, "Hi," and then to Evering, "I'm sorry, Mark, I didn't know you were busy." She winked and went away, leaving unspoken promises I didn't even want to think about.

"I don't know," Evering said, blissfully unaware of any irony, "you raise a kid, she turns out to be a crazy woman, you gotta wonder where the fuck you went wrong."

He sighed, the weight of the world pressing heavily on his hairy shoulders. Then his manner changed abruptly. Gone was the sorrowing Lear whining about serpent's teeth and thankless children; now he was showing me the barracuda, the movie mogul, all business and hard marble eyes. "Okay," he said, and I think his voice actually dropped half an octave. "Cut to the chase."

I shook my head. More Hollywood shorthand. In an action

picture when the dialogue gets dull and the plot begins to drag and the monosyllabic leading man can't seem to muster up any more than two emotions, angry and not angry, they often do a quick cut to the main action set piece of the film, the one in which so many horses are galloping or so many cars are squealing around corners or so many airplanes are peeling off that no one notices that the plot of the movie is bankrupt. Hence, cut to the chase. As used in the business affairs offices and heavy money meetings around the industry, it means, we're going to stop farting around with all this idle talk and get down to the serious business of the bottom line. Cut to the chase.

"I give you ten thousand dollars to bring Merissa back here, Saxon," Evering said.

I almost hyperventilated. That was more money than I'd seen in one hunk in a long time, and I didn't want to blow it. But I dislike making promises I can't keep. I spoke as carefully as I could. "Legally, your daughter is an adult, Mr. Evering. Maybe she doesn't want to come back, and forcing her to do so would be kidnapping."

"Fifteen," he barked, as though upping the ante would make what I'd just said go away. I simply kept quiet, and I suppose he took my silence as acquiescence. "I don't know where she is. If I knew, I wouldn't need you. The last few months she's been running around with an attorney I've been doing some business with, name of Martin Swanner." He jotted something down on a personalized memo pad, ripped off the sheet, and gave it to me. It was an address in downtown Los Angeles just off Broadway and Seventh. Not exactly the silk stocking district. "He's twice her age, for chrissakes," Evering said, and there was real anguish in his voice. "When I think of that shitburger putting his dirty hands all over—"

"The fee doesn't include my expenses, Mr. Evering," I said, realizing with a start that I'd decided to take the case. "All

I can guarantee is that I'll try and find your daughter and notify you when I do. As for bringing her home, that's between you and her." I breathed deep. "I'd like a little taste in advance."

Evering took a moment to think it over, then laid a finger aside of his nose like a hairy Jewish Saint Nicholas, went back to his desk, and took out a ledger-type checkbook. "Let's do what we call in pictures a step deal," he said as he wrote out a check. "A third up front, a third inside a week, and the final third when Merissa's sitting in the living room."

"I told you—" I began, but he put a hand up like a kindly traffic cop holding back the cars so the children can cross the street.

"Hey!" he said, meaning nothing. "You understand what I'm saying here. I mean, we're guys, we know what's going on."

The non sequitur might have dizzied me had I not already grown accustomed to Mark Evering's inability to link cause with effect. Then he looked somewhere over my left shoulder and said, "Oh, hello, darling," and I turned to see the blonde in the kimono I'd spoken to in the living room. She had crept into the cabana on quiet little cat feet shod in high-heeled leather sandals. "Mr. Saxon, this is my wife, Brandy."

Brandy smiled the smile of a coconspirator. "We've met," she said, and let her gaze drift slowly and deliberately down to my crotch and then back up again. Evering couldn't have missed it, but apparently he didn't care, or chose not to notice. "Have you invited Mr. Saxon to join our little party, Mark?"

He didn't answer her, which made me uncomfortable, so I said, "Thanks, but I've got to run."

"Your loss, my dear," she said in a voice like poisoned molasses.

Evering tore the check out of the ledger and came toward

me with it, waving it in the air as if to dry the ink, although he'd written it with a ballpoint pen. When I tried to take it from him he pulled it back just out of my reach, a favorite uncle teasing his small nephew with an ice cream cone he fully intends to give him anyway. "Find my baby for me, Saxon," he said. "Bring her back safe and sound. My goddamn heart is broken, you know?"

I nodded and reached once more for the check, and this time he actually took a step backward out of touching range. "Don't deposit this till tomorrow afternoon, will you? I've got to shift some funds around to cover it." He finally handed it to me, and I had to wonder what kind of cash flow problems Mark Evering was having, and whether most of his discretionary monies were going up his nose or into Brandy Evering's secret savings account in a bank in Downey.

"Listen," he said after I'd put the check in my wallet, "when this is all over, maybe in another month, you have your agent call the office, talk to my girl, Suzanne. I'm in preproduction on a dynamite script I've just optioned, and there may be something in it for you. No promises, now, but let's us at least talk, okay?"

There it was, like a carrot dangling in front of the donkey's nose, the show business possibility. The nonspecific and nonbinding half-promise that keeps hopefuls hanging in there one more time, one more year, waiting for the big one; the kind of sleight-of-hand hoodwinkery by which guys like Mark Evering acquire the power that make men crawl and women lie down, or at least kneel down, which is the current position of choice in Hollywood. I hated myself for recognizing it as the bullshit it was. Still I was plugging into it the way the bastard wanted me to, making a mental note to have my agent call his office. Visions of sugarplums cavorted unbidden in my head.

I put the check in my wallet and to my enormous self-disgust said, "Great."

When I parked in an overpriced lot half a block from Martin Swanner's downtown office the next morning and walked down Broadway toward his building, it was hard not to notice I was the only non-Latino in sight on the busy street. It didn't particularly bother me; I'm not one of those paranoid WASPs who believe that everyone not a fair-skinned Episcopalian is about to move into my neighborhood, spray it with graffiti, and marry my sister. But most wealthy movie-industry types like Mark Evering usually do business with attorneys who maintain offices in Beverly Hills between Rodeo and Linden on Wilshire, or on Venture City Drive West, and not way down here in taco territory. It wasn't exactly going to keep me awake nights with a rifle trained on the door, but it was something to squirrel away and think about in case things got complicated later.

The towers of downtown Los Angeles cast their shadows on these streets behind the one- and two-story buildings that housed discount appliance stores, cheap clothing shops featuring purple shirts shot through with silver thread, Spanish language phonograph records, and tiny sidewalk produce markets displaying plantains and papayas and dried chipotle peppers, but the glass and steel high rises reflecting the calescent California sunlight might have been a million miles away. The panhandlers and whores and winos and the shop girls wearing the white sleeveless blouses that revealed the sides of their brassieres did not seem impressed with the view. Their crowded little enclave was a world apart.

Martin Swanner's office was on the second floor of a walk-up with a modern glass door at street level that opened into a swaybacked stairwell with peeling linoleum covering the steps and institutional cream-colored paint splashed indifferently on the walls. Somewhere upstairs a tinny radio was blaring salsa music behind a closed door, and somewhere else two men were screaming what sounded like curses at one another in Spanish. I found Swanner's office easily. On the solid-looking oak door, the only one in the corridor not made of cheap pine with frosted glass paneling, was his name, followed by the words A LEGAL CORPORATION and beneath that, ATTORNEY AT LAW and ABOGADO. I went inside.

The reception room was large, cheaply furnished, and populated almost entirely by Latinos. Some of them were chattering animatedly, but most looked pretty glum, sitting with downcast eyes, hands quietly folded in their laps or holding their hats. All the men seemed to have hats of 1930s vintage. There was one large cheap metal desk, and behind that was one of those plump but pretty blond girls who has narrowly escaped the ribbon counter of the five-and-dime but is destined never to be a brain surgeon, a rocket scientist, or the first female CEO of her semiconductor company. She was typing when I walked up to her desk, and she didn't lift her eyes or her head, but showed me she was aware of me by saying, "Take a clipboard, fill out the form, have a seat over there." I didn't move. I bided my time, waiting for her to look at me. She sensed my noncompliance and said, "Do you speak English?" and finally looked up, and when she did I gave her the 150-watt smile and said, "Hi, there."

She blinked sort of stupidly and said, "Oh! Oh, gee!" I am not without a certain charm sometimes.

I said in my best obscene-phone-call voice, "I wonder if it would be possible to see Mr. Swanner for just a few minutes. My name is Saxon."

"Oh, gee," she said again, flustered. I couldn't remember the last time I'd heard anyone say "gee" and mean it. "Gee, I've seen you someplace before. Are you in the movies or something?"

I lowered my lashes modestly. "I've done a few films," I said. "Is Mr. Swanner in?"

"I'm awfully sorry," she said in a way that convinced me she truly was, "he's gone. I mean, well, this is Friday and he's left for the weekend."

"Rats!" I said, all Van Johnson in *The Human Comedy*. "It was so-o-o important, too. Although"—and here I increased the candle power of my smile—"I can't say I made the trip down here for nothing. What's *your* name?"

"Debbie," she stammered, as if she'd had to give it a little thought.

Of course it would have to be Debbie. I admit her reaction to me was a great stroke for my ego, and being in my usual lovelorn condition I could use as many of those as I could get. The poor child, although pretty in a pudding-faced way, had been blessed with neither talent, brains, nor advantageous social position, but from the way her face was flushing and her breath quickening when I grinned at her, I figured whatever higher power it was that oversaw the universal law of compensation had given her the capacity for easy and multiple orgasms, and I knew plenty of women with looks, smarts, and wealth who would gladly have traded places with her. I guess it was love at first sight; unfortunately it only went one way.

But I always play the hand I'm dealt, and I happened now to be holding some fairly good cards. "You don't think it would be possible to give Mr. Swanner a call at his home?"

"Well . . . he spends just about every weekend at his house in Laguna Beach," she said.

"Do you have the address and phone number there?"

"I'm not supposed to give it out."

"Oh, no!" I said. "I'm really desperate to talk to him." I looked downcast and gave her my helpless Newfoundland puppy grin. I'm really a very good actor; I can't understand why I don't work more.

"Golly," she said. Her vocabulary was starting to impress me. She blushed and twittered and jotted down an address on the back of a pink While You Were Out message form.

"Please don't tell him where you got it," she said.

I kissed the paper. "I'll be your best friend," I told her.

The door to an inner office opened and two people emerged. One, an elderly Mexican woman, was dressed all in black and had a sad, beaten look, the hopelessness that comes from grinding poverty and no expectations of brighter times ahead, and she was dabbing at her reddened eyes with a wadded tissue.

The man who escorted her out I had seen before, to my sorrow, and had heard about even more, and he was noteworthy indeed in the Chicano community of Los Angeles. His name was Jesus Delgado, and he spent a lot of his time at police headquarters or in the courts talking to lawyers and bail bondsmen, although to my knowledge they'd never been able to nail him with anything that would stick. Any time there was a racketeering or narcotics beefs in the barrio, whenever anyone was running whores or numbers or a crap game with funny dice or an extortion racket, it was a pretty good bet that Jesus Delgado was either behind it or lurking somewhere around the edges.

He was about thirty-five and looked as if he hadn't bathed since Cinco de Mayo, and his clothes were right out of Damon Runyon, a pearl gray suit and a maroon shirt with a white tie. What he was doing ushering people through the offices of an Anglo attorney like Martin Swanner had nothing to do with me; I was just looking for a spaced-out rich girl who had flown her palatial Beverly Hills coop.

The look Delgado gave me, though, had plenty to do with me. We had met briefly about three years ago when, through a cameraman pal of mine, a little sixteen-year-old Chicana had come to me for help. She wanted to get off the streets, where she had been put by a dope pusher who had hooked her little brother on smack and was making her sell her chubby body to anyone with a ten dollar-bill, to pay for the kid's habit.

I had handled things quietly and efficiently and put the pusher out of business permanently, and out of commission for a while as well, with a mouth full of spaces where his teeth had once lived. But the pusher had apparently been on Delgado's payroll, and Jesus and I had exchanged a few words outside the courtroom. They weren't very nice words. He obviously didn't like me very much, and though his animosity didn't cost me any sleep it did tend to make me watch my back and flanks whenever I was within shouting distance of the barrio. To see him here in Swanner's office was a distinctly unpleasant surprise. He shot curare-tipped darts out of his eyes and nodded his recognition of an old enemy, and then he went back into the inner office again, leaving the old woman to talk to an elderly man in one of the chairs. After a moment both of them began to cry.

"Debbie," I said, "does Mr. Delgado work here too?"

"Not exactly. He's a friend of Mr. Swanner's, and he's here an awful lot. But I don't think he's an attorney."

"You're right, he's not. Debbie, what's Mr. Swanner's legal specialty? Divorce, personal injury. . . ?

"Oh, no; mostly immigration law. You know, getting green cards and stuff."

I put Swanner's Laguna Beach address in my shirt pocket. "Debbie, I can't tell you how much I appreciate your help." I gave her an eye crinkle. "Maybe I'll see you again."

"Gosh," she said, completing the trinity she'd begun with gee and golly. "It was nice meeting you, anyway."

It had been, I suppose. She'd given me more than she could realize, but I think I gave her something in return, a few moments of harmless romantic flirtation with someone who'd actually been on television. She'd remember it a long while, and the fact that I'd no intention of ever seeing her again wouldn't make that memory any less precious to her. The Debbies of this world often ask for little and get considerably less than that, and I was glad to have been a small part of brightening her day.

2

So much for a quiet weekend in town. The Dodgers were playing at home, a three game series with the Mets, and I had hoped to catch at least two of them. Now I was going to have to drive down to Laguna Beach in traffic that was always bumper-to-bumper from Friday to Monday, and I didn't know when or if I would make it home in time for one of the games. That was disappointing, and it was going to be doubly so for Marvel.

I never quite know how to explain Marvel, which he pronounces with the accent on the second syllable. If I introduce him as my son people look at us doubtingly because Marvel is black and I'm not. If I tell them he's my roommate we get even stranger looks, since he's only fifteen and looks younger. Every time I say he's my ward, which is the truth, I feel like we're Batman and Robin.

Marvel came to my attention while I was working on a case, and when I was faced with the choice of sending him to a facility for homeless children, turning him back out onto the streets, or looking after him myself, it seemed like no choice at all. Since that case caused me to be evicted from my apartment anyway—the landlords seemed to have an aversion to bombings in their parking garage—I rented a nice house in Venice with a view of the canal, a room for me and a room for Marvel, a small den, and enough space in the driveway for a little one-on-one basketball. I had yet to cave in to Marvel's request for a dog, a wall-size TV, a pool table, or a housekeeper to pick up after him, but other than that we were a regular, albeit atypical, family.

When I arrived home from Swanner's office it was about one in the afternoon. It was July, summer vacation time for the kids of the world, but Marvel had never really gone to school before this year and had a lot of catching up to do, so I had hired one of the little girls in the neighborhood, a straight-A honor student named Saraine, to come in five mornings a week during vacation and tutor him in his reading and math. The two of them were sprawled all over the living room, loose-leaf papers scattered, books tossed randomly around on the floor, pencils rolling on the rug, the dead bodies of a six-pack of Pepsi strewn about haphazardly, and what seemed like more than the requisite number of sneaker-clad feet sticking up over the tops of sofas and hooked over the arms of chairs. Marvel was laboriously reading aloud from a textbook about Jeff and Jennifer, who are the modern-day equivalents, I suppose, of the immortal Dick and Jane.

"Hi, Mr. Saxon," Saraine said. Saraine and her family lived four houses down and across the canal. Her mother was Caucasian, her father black, and she herself was absolutely winsome with a café-au-lait complexion, green eyes that seemed to sparkle all the time, and that kind of rangy, sixteen-year-old cheerleader figure that makes dirty old men of us all. Marvel adored her in a mute, stoic fashion, which manifested itself in his never speaking to her directly unless the course of his lessons necessitated it. She seemed to understand this, and managed to bear up under the burden with a display of unflagging good humor and patience.

"Hi, Saraine," I said, riffling through the mail on the table near the door. "How's he doing today?"

"*He* doing fine," Marvel said with a little heat. "If you wanna know how *he* doing, whyn't you ask *he* instead of *her*?"

"Somebody put battery acid on your cornflakes this morning?" I said, and Saraine couldn't suppress a giggle.

The mail consisted of a get-rich-quick scheme that would only cost me thirty-nine dollars, an announcement from the Church of Scientology which had mistakenly placed me on their mailing list and refused to remove me despite phone calls and letters begging them to do so, and a cute-as-a-button postcard with a picture of a gorilla from my dentist, reminding me it was checkup time. I went out to the kitchen, dumped the mail in the trash, and opened a John Courage beer. I was looking forward to my trip with a sort of resigned bitterness, and I disliked having to disappoint Marvel. Not too many good things have happened to the kid in his short fifteen years on this planet, and when it comes time to say no to him about things like baseball games and weekend outings it isn't always easy for me. The world doesn't owe anyone a living, but somebody owes Marvel a little something, and a caprice of fate has chosen me to pay the debt.

I went up to my room and packed two shirts, a tie, underwear and socks for three days, and gray slacks and an extra sports jacket into an overnight case, along with the usual razor and toothbrush. I was hoping I'd get back to Los Angeles late that night, but I always like to be prepared. I hate getting up in the morning and putting on yesterday's clothing. I also packed my .38 Colt Trooper in its brand new ballistic nylon holster. At one point in my life I had kept one gun in my office and one in my automobile in a specially designed holster under the seat, but when my last car got blown to smithereens I decided I'd either carry or wear my gun, or else leave it at home. I was just finishing up my packing when Marvel wandered in, casting a narrow look at the overnight bag.

"Where's Saraine?" I said.

"Went home," he answered. Marvel was a man of few words. "You goin' someplace?"

"Look, pal," I said, "I'm going to have to run down to Laguna Beach tonight. I might be back real late or I may have to stay down there a day or two."

"I guess that means no Dodgers." It was a statement.

"I'm sorry," I said. "This is a big-money gig. If I come back tonight we'll go tomorrow and Sunday, how's that?"

He shrugged, his handsome young face an impassive ebony carving. "Tha's cool," he said.

"There's a pizza down there in the freezer," I said. "Just stick it in the microwave. And there's ice cream and stuff. And if I don't get back tomorrow and you need anything you can call Jo. Or Paula."

Paula Avery was the guidance counselor at the Bishop School in Westwood where Marvel was a student during the academic year. She was also a sometime lover of mine, and had been since about three weeks after I had enrolled Marvel in the school. She has soft brown hair and gray eyes and a ready laugh and a compassionate nature, loves good music and old movies and adventures in cooking and dining and serendipitous weekends, and is terrific in bed, and I wished very much that I could be in love with her, but I wasn't. I felt vaguely guilty about Paula, but it was simply one of those things. It takes me a long while to get over shattered love affairs, and Paula just had the misfortune of coming along too soon after the last one, or too late, depending on how you looked at it. But she was a good friend, she was very fond of Marvel, and I knew that if I were held up in Laguna Beach for a few days she would come over to the house with a sack of groceries and make sure Marvel was brushing his teeth.

"Look," I said, digging into my pocket. "Here's twenty bucks. Why don't you and Saraine go to a movie tonight and then out for a hamburger? On me?"

"Me an' Saraine?" he said, as if I'd suggested he stuff his pockets with rocks and attempt a cross-channel swim to Catalina.

"What's the matter with Saraine?"

"Man," he whined with that upward inflection he always affected when he was being put upon.

"I think she's cute."

He shook his head. "Mud shark stink pig," he pronounced, and went downstairs. I noticed he took the twenty, however. Could be Marvel protested too much?

I called Jo at the office to tell her what was happening, and then called Paula. She wasn't home, so I left a message on her recorder telling her Marvel might or might not be in need of assistance over the weekend. It was just as well she wasn't home, because lately whenever Paula and I talked she always got around to the subject of Us, which seems to be some women's favorite topic, and Us was a conversational area I was just as happy to avoid, laced as it was with land mines.

Marvel was shooting some baskets into the hoop I had erected over the garage door when I came downstairs. He had gotten over his disappointment about the Dodgers, I guess. When you compare that to some of the things that had already happened to him in his short lifetime, you could see why he took the loss of a ticket to a ballgame in stride. I made a feint at taking the basketball away from him but he faked me out and came up with a pretty little hook shot. I slapped him on the back, which was about as much affection as a fifteen-year-old boy can be comfortable with. "I'll call you if I'm going to be any later than tomorrow morning," I said.

"Tha's cool."

"Stay out of trouble, okay?"

He dribbled past me on the way to the basket and skillfully used the backboard for his shot, shouting "Kareem!" as it went in. I took that to be the equivalent of good-bye.

The gold-colored Le Baron convertible that a grateful client had leased for me when my own little Fiat had been consumed in a fiery explosion made the trip more pleasant than it might otherwise have been. The drive south from Los Angeles to

Laguna Beach always strikes me as schizophrenic, as if it can't make up its mind whether to be squalid or beautiful. The San Diego Freeway bisects southern Los Angeles, with its endless car lots and factories and urban blight, and a huge oil refinery with two flaming towers of burn-off that is as close to a vision of hell as I ever want to come. Then, once past the aging city of Long Beach, the road meanders through flat green fields to the east and rolling brown hills separating the freeway from the Pacific to the west, a monotony broken irregularly by Johnny-come-lately industrial parks and upper-middle-income housing tracts until some seventy miles south of Los Angeles. There it reaches what is laughingly known as the Laguna Freeway, in reality a winding canyon road through the hills that emerges in a pitiless burst of sunlight at the ocean in the calculatedly quaint village of Laguna Beach.

Tucked into one of the lovelier coastal crescents, Laguna was once a mecca for artists, writers, and other bohemian types, until its white sand beaches and cliffs and crags proved irresistible to the moneyed interests from up north, and surfside real estate began selling in the seven-figure range. In the summertime the Festival of Arts draws enormous crowds on weekends, and the camera-laden out-of-town visitors rub elbows with the tanned teenyboppers running around the Pacific Coast Highway in their minikinis, the blond fuzz on their arms and thighs contrasting tantalizingly with the gold of their skins. I've never figured out why all Caucasian children in Southern California are blond. Perhaps it's a seldom-talked about state law.

From her school picture, Merissa Evering was no exception, a pretty kid. Guys like Mark Evering always had gorgeous daughters, whom they managed to screw up through indifference and neglect. Now, at the age of twenty-one, she had run off with a shady lawyer twice her age and her father had hired me to find her, a California golden girl whose glitter had tarnished from overuse.

The address Debbie had given me cost me a trip up a steep, serpentine road into the hills. Martin Swanner's home proved to be even more impressive than Evering's, though not nearly as ornate and imposing. What made it so spectacular was its location, high on a bluff above the Pacific at its most beautiful and sun-drenched, the wide crescent of beach trimmed with lacy surf breaking onto the sand. I imagined sitting behind the glass walls of the house with a drink in my hand and a George Shearing record on the stereo, watching the annual migration of the California gray whale through the glittering sheen of the coastal water. I could really get behind that kind of life-style.

But I wasn't whale-watching today, I was heiress-hunting, and so I rang the doorbell and waited a very long time before it was answered by a plump Mexican housekeeper who managed to let me know that *el patrón* was *no en la casa* but could not or would not tell me anything else, perhaps because my Spanish was so rudimentary I couldn't make her understand what I wanted. I was frustrated and annoyed at having made the long drive for nothing, but there didn't seem to be much I could do except poke around town for a while to see if I could flush the elusive Swanner from wherever it was he had gone to ground.

I drove back down the hill to the antiquated Hotel Laguna, perched right on the beach. I went through the old-fashioned lobby to the cocktail lounge and sat down on the terrace to have a drink and watch the sun set over the water. I always feel aloneness more keenly when I'm near the ocean. Perhaps it's because the sea itself is so vast and lonely, but more probably it is my incurable romantic streak, which makes me yearn to walk arm in arm with someone in the wet sand with our pants legs rolled up and our shoes and socks in our hands, stopping occasionally to kiss, squealing when the icy surf breaks around our ankles. I hadn't had that with anyone for a while, and I missed it.

The waitress was a cutie in her little tunic top and matching panties, and she was all smiles and personality, but I correctly read it as a play for a bigger tip and nothing more. When she came back to ask if I wanted another drink I told her no, but that she might be able to give me some information. I asked if she knew Martin Swanner.

Her hair bounced appealingly as she nodded. "Everyone in town knows Marty Swanner. You take away the summer people and the tourists and this is a pretty small community."

"Do you know him well?"

"I see him now and then. He hits on me every time he comes in, but that's a reflex action with Marty. He'd fuck a snake if he could figure out how to get its legs apart. He's charming and funny and sexy, but I'm not about to be just another notch on anyone's gun, especially someone old enough to be my father." I tried not to let that one sting. "Besides, I've got a boyfriend."

"Any idea where I might find Marty today? I've been to his house but I couldn't get much out of his housekeeper."

"This isn't Marty's kind of place. It's too tame for him—mostly couples staying at the hotel. But when he's in town and on the loose he usually goes to The Three Coins up the street. It's one of his hangouts."

The Three Coins. Tossed into the fountain to find a true love. That didn't much sound like Marty's kind of place either. True love apparently wasn't his style. But I thanked the waitress and tipped her accordingly. It was fairly early, so I wandered down the highway to a favorite out-of-the-way restaurant on the sand. I was a sucker for abalone almondine, especially when Mark Evering was paying the freight, and The Beach House does it as well as any restaurant south of Carmel. I even splurged and ordered a good Chardonnay with dinner, although I rarely mix drinking and long-distance driving. I calculated I'd have lots of time to sober up before heading back to Los Angeles. Both the dinner and the wine were worth it, accompanied by the soothing murmur of the waves breaking on the beach.

When I finally got to The Three Coins it was well after nine o'clock and the jazz trio was just beginning their first set. I'm no slouch at a piano keyboard myself, but I'm not good enough to play the true jazz rooms and too good to work at a piano bar where a bunch of elderly drunks do a sing-along to "Shine on Harvest Moon," so I just play as a hobby. It's also a great way to meet women. How many guys can sit down and dash off a relatively decent rendition of "All the Things You Are"? I keep meaning to get myself a piano for the house but haven't gotten around to it. Maybe with Evering's fifteen thousand dollars.

I was fairly critical about other players, though, and I had to admit this guy at The Three Coins was pretty good in a road-company Bill Evans kind of way. The place had not yet filled up with its Friday night crowd, so there was a vacant stool at the bar, which I commandeered. The bartender lifted a supercilious eyebrow at my grapefruit juice order, but since he charged me two seventy-five for what must have cost them about eight cents, he really didn't care that much. He probably just worked there, anyway.

One of the other men at the bar was giving him a pretty hard time about something. I couldn't tell what it was, but they seemed to know each other better than bartender and customer. Finally the barman snapped, "Listen, Larry, I've been working my butt off during the festival this summer, and they don't pay me enough to take your crap. So get out of my face!"

When he brought my change I asked casually if Mr. Swanner had been in yet that evening.

"Marty the Fucker? No, I haven't seen him since last weekend." He looked at me closely. "You don't look like you'd be a friend of his."

"Why do you say that?"

He sniffed. "Mostly because he doesn't have any friends, he's such an asshole. Besides, you're too good-looking, and Marty hates competition. Look, it's none of my business. I'm sorry." He lasered a toxic look down to Larry at the other end of the bar. "I'm a little overwrought this evening."

"No, wait a minute," I said. "I'm not a friend of Mr. Swanner's. I don't even know him." I separated a ten-dollar bill from the change he'd given me and pushed it almost imperceptibly toward him. "I would like to find him, though."

He hesitated, his hand hovering. "Irate husband?"

I laughed and shook my head. "Doesn't much sound like he's a friend of yours either."

The long, delicate fingers moved quickly to the ten-spot and palmed it. "Look, I don't care who does what to who. I'm gay. You want to know about Marty Swanner? Ask that blonde over there at the table. She used to run around with him."

I turned and looked in the direction of his nod. She was blond, all right, and slim and leggy, and had probably been attractive once, before too many vodka tonics and Quaaludes and Tuinals and one-night stands had dimmed the luster in her gray-green eyes. She was sitting alone at a table near the wall, listening to the jazz and trying hard to give the impression she wanted to be left alone, so that whoever eventually picked her up and laid her would think he was something really special instead of just an anonymous body to make her forget she was pushing thirty and pushing burnout and caught up in the sleazy singles scene that perpetuates itself like an itch that only gets worse when scratched. I rolled off my barstool and took my drink over to her, and she looked up and smiled as though she was seeing me for the first time and hadn't already checked me out thoroughly when I walked in the door. I smiled back.

"Hi," I said. "Mind some company?"

"Ordinarily, yes," she lied. "But in your case . . . well, it's the least I can do for a stranger in town. Pull up a chair. I'm Sharon."

I introduced myself and handed her my business card. She read it, and it seemed to pique her interest even more. "A private detective. I don't think I've ever met one of those before. I'm disappointed. You don't look anything like Humphrey Bogart."

"I know. It almost kept me from graduating. What are you drinking?"

"Gene knows," she said with a nod at the bartender. I waved at him to bring more drinks, and he rolled his eyes heavenward, put-upon once more. Sharon and I bullshat back and forth for a few minutes, all the standard do-you-come-here-often stuff that I found so dreary and demeaning, that I had outgrown several years ago when I'd awakened in a strange bed once too often and the self-disgust had knifed through me like a physical pain. After what I thought was a decent interval, I casually mentioned that I was looking for Martin Swanner, and her whole body stiffened, almost jerked, as though from an electric shock. It was very quick, and she tried to cover it with a sardonic laugh, but I had noticed. Her composure had very definitely been shaken.

"I'm a little irritated," she said. "I thought you came over to talk to me because you were in heat."

"I did, and I am. But I'm also trying to find Swanner. The two aren't necessarily mutually exclusive. Gene said you know him."

"Gene has a big mouth," she said, "and you can imagine what from." She looked off into the distance for a while and we listened to the trio swinging through an up-tempo "Hello, Young Lovers." Finally she took a deep breath, as though inhalation was painful. "Marty moves around a lot. Los Angeles, Tijuana, or here in beautiful Faguna Beach." She seemed to relax a little, and smiled. "That's part of Marty's appeal. He's one of the few unmarried heterosexuals in town. He's kinky as hell, but at least he likes to do it with women."

Gene appeared behind me with the drinks, having overheard the last few sentences. "Don't be so smug, Sharon," he snapped. "We're an oppressed minority. One of these days they're going to qualify us for federal aid." He put the glasses down, a bit peevishly, I thought, and went back to the bar. He didn't exactly flounce, but I don't recall Clint Eastwood ever walking like that.

"About Martin Swanner," I said, aware I was pushing a bit too hard, "how do you mean, kinky?"

She waved a hand as though brushing away a mosquito but I realized she was brushing away my question instead. I let it go for a while. "Prosit," she said, and we tinked glasses. "What is that stuff you're drinking anyway?"

"Grapefruit juice."

"Ugh. Why? Are you an alcoholic?"

"Sometimes I think so. But no, I just have a long drive back to Los Angeles tonight and I don't want to have to do it shitfaced. The highway patrol takes a dim view of things like that." I glanced over at the trio. "Those guys are pretty good. I play a little bit myself."

"I'll bet you do," she said. She put half her drink away in a single swallow. "So how do you know Marty?"

"I don't. We have a mutual friend."

"What will you do when you find him? Beat him up?"

I laughed. "I hope not. I just want to talk to him. Do I look like the kind of guy who goes around beating people up?"

She thought about it for a while, then said "I'll bet you handle yourself pretty well. Marty's not a fighter, he's a lover."

"That would be my first choice, too." The group was doing

"Skylark," now, Hoagy Carmichael and Johnny Mercer. I said, "This tune's a favorite of mine. Want to dance?"

"That's what I'm here for," she said.

We went out onto the tiny parquet floor and she moved into my arms, pressing a lot closer than a first dance would call for. The lady was nothing if not direct.

"You feel good," she said, her face warm against mine. Since we were the only couple on the floor I was a bit self-conscious about the unabashed eroticism of her dancing, but I did want to find out about Martin Swanner and, let's face it, I was enjoying myself, too. Her body was firm and lithe through our clothes.

At the end of the song I put four singles into the brandy snifter that served as the trio's tip jar, and said, "Know any Jerome Kern?"

The piano player nodded and went into a spirited "Pick Yourself Up," which was my national anthem. I went back to the table, where Sharon was finishing up her drink and looking as if she might want more.

She said, "Now, let me get this straight before you order another round. If you didn't have to drive back up north tonight you'd break down and have yourself a real, adult drink?"

"Absolutely."

She winked at me. "Drink up, sweetheart," she said.

I wouldn't exactly say that the earth moved. That only happens, apparently, in Ernest Hemingway's sleeping bag, and it is one of the two literary conventions that have blighted male-female relationships in this century, the other being the image of a fatuous, pluperfect Prince Charming—something that modern women always fault their men for not being. But white horses are impractical in the city, and unless you happen to live in California atop the San Andreas Fault, your chances of finding someone with whom the earth will move are pretty slim. So I blame Papa Hemingway and the brothers Grimm for screwing us all up by making us set our sights too high to ever find true romance.

Sharon knew what she was doing between the sheets, though, and she was damn good at it—adept, inventive, creative, and eager, all designed to make me think I was the world's greatest mattress athlete. But it seemed to me to be a conditioned response: those were the things she did automatically when she climbed into bed with a man, hoping he'd be enchanted and charmed and excited enough to come back for more. Eventually there would be a moment when he decided he couldn't live without her long red fingernail gently scratching that place between his anus and his scrotum while she was sucking him off, and then Sharon would have found her prince at last, followed by the inevitable happily-ever-after. She was apparently going to stick with that formula until it worked. It was the kind of sex one should never take personally.

We had finally finished—we had finished a couple of times, as a matter of fact—and were lying side by side in her water bed in a little apartment over a garage about half a block from the ocean, listening to the thrum of the surf and the whirring of the little wheel in the cage in which she kept her pet white mouse. The perspiration cooling in the breeze from the open window felt good.

She reached out for a sip of her drink and said, "You're really something else."

"So are you." It sounded lame even as I said it, but I never seem quick enough with postcoital compliments; I often find myself in a me-too mode.

"You get down this way often?"

I laughed at her inadvertent obscenity and she slapped my bare stomach playfully. "You know what I mean, you bastard!" She left her hand where it was for a moment and then moved it lower. "You have an open invitation. Any time you're in the neighborhood. I haven't been turned on like that since . . . I don't know when."

"Not since Marty Swanner, maybe?"

Her hand stopped moving, and then she took it away. It was a churlish, even cruel thing to have said, but pleasant as the evening's festivities had been, I could have stayed in Los Angeles and found that kind of entertainment. I was in Laguna to find Martin Swanner, and I wasn't about to forget that. It was the main reason I'd gone home with Sharon in the first place. I was sorry, though, that I'd had to hurt her feelings. There are times I don't like myself very much.

She said, "Were you expecting a virgin?"

"Just asking."

She got up and went across the room to her dresser and went through the familiar ritual of the cigarette. Her body looked great in the brief sulphur flare of the match. I heard her quick, angry exhalation and the cigarette end glowed orange as she took another puff.

"Okay," she said in a flat tone. "I got what I wanted, now I suppose I owe you what you want."

"That's putting it pretty cold."

"Let's not kid each other, my friend. You're no pickup artist; you've got too much class for that. It's my fault for not figuring it out in the first place."

"Sharon, I'm—"

"Save it. So you want to know about Marty Swanner in bed, huh? Okay. Sure, Marty's a great lover. He gets enough practice. But sex is his only hobby, and I guess when a guy screws as much as he does it gets old after a while."

I tried to envision a scenario where a surfeit of sex would bore me, but sometimes my imagination lets me down.

"So he got where he liked to spice it up a little," she went on.

The next sound was the bastard child of a laugh and a cigarette cough. "A lot." I waited. Whatever she wanted to volunteer would be fine with me, because this was a subject one didn't pry into, especially under the circumstances. She said, "He liked games. Scenes. Fantasies. You know, spanking and bondage and things like that. Sometimes he liked being dominant and sometimes he was very submissive. It's all the same to me; when I really care for someone, whatever happens to be his turn-on, I'm usually game. But Marty comes up with some pretty off-the-wall stuff.

"I remember once we were driving down to Tijuana. He has a lot of business contacts down there, spends at least one weekend a month. Anyway, I was wearing kind of a miniskirt. It was really more of a tennis dress, but it was pretty short. So while we were still on the freeway Marty told me to take off my panties, and he was fooling around with me while he was driving. Then we stopped for gas, and when the kid came around to clean off the windshield Marty made me open my knees and give him a beaver shot. The poor kid, you should have seen his face. He was about sixteen, really dorky-looking, with greasy fingernails and acne, and he'd probably never seen a woman that way. It made his day. It made Marty's, too, I guess, really got him hot, because when we started driving again, he asked me to—"

"Cute guy," I said. I was regretting my question.

"I went along with that stuff for a while because I was really crazy about him, you know? But everyone draws a line somewhere. Even me." The self-hatred in those words was sandpaper across the heart. She took another hit from the cigarette and sat down on the edge of the bed, her back to me. She had a dime-size purple birthmark almost in the middle of her back that I hadn't noticed before, almost glowing in the light from the arc lamp outside the open window. "Marty wanted to watch me do it with another guy."

I put out my hand and touched her gently but she moved away. Whatever intimacy we had shared had evaporated along with the perspiration. "There's this bullfighter he hangs around with down in TJ. A gorgeous-looking kid, too. I might not have minded under different circumstances. But it would have made me feel like a whore, you know? In a sex circus." A silence while she smoked, thinking about God knows what. Then she said, "What do you want with Marty anyway?"

I rolled off the bed and went to where I'd slung my jacket over the back of a chair. I took Merissa Evering's photo from the pocket and showed it to Sharon. "I don't want the best part of Martin Swanner," I said. "I want her."

She turned on the lamp beside the bed and examined the picture, and there was deep hurt in her eyes as she looked at what she considered to be her replacement, a younger, fresher, prettier version of herself. Sharon's makeup was smudged from our exertions, the little lipstick she had left was all over her chin. She had dots of mascara on her cheeks and green eye-shadow smeared almost into the thin blond hair at her temples. She shook her head, whether expressing a negative answer or sad resignation I didn't know. "I've never seen her," she said finally, "but that's Marty's speed. Young, vulnerable. He's probably giving her a lot of shit."

She handed back the photo and I replaced it in my pocket, and all at once I realized we were naked and there was an awkwardness. It is rather curious that two strangers can meet and come together in the dark and explore each other's most intimate places and yet be uncomfortable when the lights go on and their nakedness is revealed under the searching shine of a sixty-watt bedside lamp. Sharon turned the light off quickly and I stood there for a moment, not knowing whether to get back into bed or put my clothes on, but she made the decision for me by donning her robe, leaving me the only one in the room naked.

I put my shorts on slowly, feeling like a louse. We had used each other, and I don't suppose either of us had any illusions about that. It was unrealistic for her to think that if she met someone at nine o'clock and was sitting on his face before midnight, something warm and wonderful and special would come of the relationship, but my old-fashioned morality was giving me the guilts. I've gone through my sport-fucking periods like everyone else, but I always feel a little empty and cheap and cheated afterward. I guess I'm a romantic at heart.

She got up and fed the mouse and gave it fresh water while I buttoned my shirt and wished there was something I could have said to make her feel less like a one-nighter, but of course that's what she was, what we both were, what we'd set ourselves up to be. It didn't make me feel much better about using her to get information, but I learned a long time ago that life is a lot like the National Football League—if you want to survive you have to learn to play when you're hurt. Sharon, me—even a slime like Martin Swanner. So I try not to make too many judgment calls about what it takes certain people to get them through the long nights. In my business there's no percentage in that.

3

I headed south down the Coast Highway. I could have used a shower and a few hours sleep, but when I pulled away from the curb in front of Sharon's apartment there was a pink light in the eastern sky and I thought it would be pretty foolish to rent a motel room for just a few hours. I took my time, enjoying the oceanside scenery of Dana Point and San Clemente and San Juan Capistrano, and by the time I hit San Diego I was ready for breakfast, which I enjoyed in a little chowder house on Harbor Island. Then I called Marvel.

"Hey," he said.

"Hey," I said. "How's it coming?"

"Awright."

"Looks like I'm going to be a couple of days. Did you call Jo?"

"Nun-uh." I think that meant no.

"How about Paula?"

"Nun-uh."

"Well, call them, okay? Tell them I'm going to be away awhile."

"Awright."

I said, "What'd you do last night?"

"Watch TV and stuff."

"What other stuff?"

He paused. "Saraine come over and watch with me."

I said, "Did you study?"

"Nun-uh. Man, it was Friday night, okay?"

I smiled. "You behaved yourself, didn't you?"

He sounded exasperated. "Yeah, man, what do you think?"

"Did the Dodgers win last night?"

"Nun-uh. They got shut out."

"They're going to have to start hitting pretty soon." He didn't answer. "What are you going to do tonight?"

"Don't know," he said. "I guess I'll call Jo. Maybe she'll take me to the movies."

"Sounds good," I said. "Get some money from her if you need it, all right?"

"Awright."

I sighed. Extracting conversation from Marvel was a lot like squeezing blood from a turnip. "Okay, Marvel," I said. "I'll call you as soon as I know what's going on."

"Tha's cool," he said.

I guess it was. Ordinarily I wouldn't leave a fifteen-year-old boy alone for so long without supervision, but Marvel grew up on the streets and can handle himself a lot better than I ever could. I hung up and returned to another cup of coffee.

I knew finding Martin Swanner in Tijuana on a crowded bull-fight weekend was a long shot at best, but I was still operating on Mark Evering's money, and I figured I'd have a pleasant enough weekend across the border before heading back to Los Angeles to confront Swanner in his office on Monday.

Since Southern Californians have been raised and nurtured on the atrocity stories about what can befall a *norteamericano* in Mexico if he has an auto accident without benefit of Mexican insurance coverage, I stopped at a motel near National City and purchased sixteen dollars' worth from a lady who had the orangest hair and bristliest eyebrows I had ever seen on a female. I always thought the Turkish-prison stories about Mexican border-town jails were exaggerated, but it cost very little to be on the safe side, and again, it was Evering's money.

At the border checkpoint the Mexican official asked me if I was coming to Mexico for business or pleasure, and I was hard put to answer. I finally told him business, because that was the truth. But there was certainly a perverse pleasure, too. I enjoy walking on the wild side once in a while. Some people race cars for fun, some rappel down the side of a cliff. My way of taking risks is to poke around in the personal affairs of people who sometimes don't want me to be there. I suppose I got into the private investigating racket in the first place because of a certain fascination with turning over rocks to see what's crawling around beneath. The underbelly is not my favorite part of the body, but it's never less than interesting, and more often than not it gives me a rush that Mark Evering's cocaine can't even come close to.

Even though my natural habitat is more civilized and sophisticated, an excursion down Tijuana's back streets promised to be an exciting, almost dangerous high. If you scratch away the tourist rip-offs like the genuine imitation leather goods and the full-breasted nudes depicted in tempera on black velvet and the photographs taken of tourists astride pathetic little donkeys with painted-on zebra stripes, there is a moral stink over Tijuana, hanging in the dusty air, overpowering even the odors of cheap meat cooking in grease and outhouses that are never cleaned. The place smells of poverty and corruption and despair. It is not my favorite city in the world, but once in a great while I enjoy a day there precisely because it's the cesspool that it is.

On this Satúrday morning as I drove across the international boundary and into the town itself, the dirt hung in the breezeless air and made little crunching sounds between my teeth. My car wheels bumped and jostled over enormous potholes that had been gaping in the asphalt since before the Second World War. The marines furloughing from Camp Pendleton cruised the streets in pairs and threesomes like advance infantry patrols, looking for whores, their crew cuts and stiff backs and hard, tight bodies marking them like a Semper Fi emblem. Many of the stores had music blaring from loudspeakers that had sounded terrible even when they were new in 1952, and urchins ran up and down the sidewalks entreating visitors to buy gum, souvenirs, candy, bodies, or a tip on where to go for the dirtiest show in town. All the border towns are alike, and yet each—Mexicali, Ciudad Juárez, Tijuana—has its own specific character. Tijuana makes the biggest pretense of respectability, to cater to the Los Angeles and San Diego tourist trade, but it doesn't quite succeed, and its efforts are pathetic.

The traffic was horrendous, as I suppose it is just about every weekend of fair weather. I was struck with the number of uniformed police on the street, taking care of the trucks, trailers, campers, vans, and cars rumbling over the border checkpoint and heading for the Avenida de la Revolución. At one point a cop forced me into a left-hand turn I had no desire to make, so I just followed the vehicular stream. There were no clearly marked lanes on the street; people just sort of drove willy-nilly. As before, my only impression of the town was of squatness, with few buildings over three stories, and almost all painted in shades of brown and yellow. A lot of auto body and upholstery shops lined the streets, and a remarkable number of Chinese restaurants—don't ask me why.

While I paused at a red light a little boy ran up and cleaned off my windshield with a filthy rag, making it harder to see through than before. I didn't give him any money, and he called me a cheap cocksucker before running off to the car behind me. I continued in the traffic flow without the vaguest notion of where I was, mainly because there were few signs bearing street names. On several corners were posts or stanchions where someone had made off with the street markers, though who would want one I couldn't imagine. Many people were out on the sidewalk with beer bottles in their hands. The decibel level on the streets from the music and traffic and loudspeakers was shattering. Even the drivers played their car radios at full volume, and one, stopped at a red light right next to me, had a

Beach Boys cassette in the tape player of an antediluvian Chevrolet. The salsa and mariachi music blended strangely with "Surfin' Safari."

Since the only thing I knew about Martin Swanner was that he had a kinky friend who fought bulls, I drove to the tourist hotel nearest the bullring. It was one of the tallest buildings in town, about seven stories high, and still under construction from the looks of it, reminding me of photos I had seen of bomb-pitted luxury hotels in Beirut. However, the desk clerk who signed me in was wearing a blue suit and an almost clean white shirt and was more than pleasant. He also demonstrated an excellent command of English.

"We are delighted to have you, Señor Saxon. Will you be staying long?"

"I'm not sure," I said. "A day or two."

"*Bueno*. My name is Nacio. If you need anything, please call me."

"*Muchas gracias,* Nacio."

"You go to the corrida tomorrow?"

"Maybe. Actually I'm here on business." I made the decision to take a wild swing, figuring it couldn't hurt and it might help. It *was* one of the nicest hotels in town and it was just a few blocks from the arena. "I'm here to see Mr. Martin Swanner."

It turned out not to be a bad guess. Nacio's friendly, open face slammed shut like the automatic sliding door in a supermarket, and he became all business as he rang for the ancient bellhop. My swing had made contact, and I decided to run it out.

"You know Mr. Swanner, Nacio?"

"No, señor," he said, not meeting my eyes, and then he barked at the bellhop, *"Número cinco cero ocho, pronto!"* The old man took my key and overnight case and gripped my elbow firmly with a wizened claw. I knew Nacio had dismissed me. I also knew he had lied.

"Are you sure? He's a *norteamericano,* a lawyer. He comes to Tijuana often."

"Enjoy your stay, señor," Nacio said, and disappeared into a back room somewhere.

The bellhop led me to my room, which was fairly clean and well appointed, although no one would think he was in the Beverly Hills Hotel. From my jacket I took Merissa's picture and showed it to the bellhop and he murmured dutifully that she was *muy bonita.* I put a five-dollar bill in my hand so that it partly obscured the girl's face, and he reiterated his extreme admiration for her, although he was staring not at her face but at Lincoln's. "You ever see this lady?"

He looked longingly at the money but shook his head. "No, señor. A beautiful lady like that, I would remember."

"She is beautiful," I agreed. "She is a friend of Mr. Martin Swanner."

The admiration in the old man's eyes abruptly became something else, and he shook his head, not in negative response to my question but seemingly as a denial of the question's very existence. He said nervously, *"Con su permiso,"* and turned and went out without the customary bow, without turning on the lights or pulling up the shade, and without waiting for his tip, leaving me standing there with the picture and a five-spot in my hand. Apparently Martin Swanner was a fairly well-known fellow down here in Tijuana. The old man knew who he was, and so, I thought, did Nacio, and they were both obviously frightened. But of what? And why? I sighed, supposing that I was probably going to find out and that I wasn't going to like it much.

I figured I would cover a few more bases. I picked up the telephone and told the hotel operator that I would be in the bar in case Mr. Martin Swanner called and I listened to the tiny gasp before her polite, "Sí, señor," and the sound of a quick disconnection. It struck me that mentioning Swanner's name in Tijuana provoked the same reactions one used to get inquiring after Mr. Sam Giancana on the West Side of Chicago.

I decided then that my best ploy would be to spread myself all over town letting people know who I was looking for, and perhaps word would get back to Swanner and he would contact me. Tijuana had to have a grapevine; every place else in the world certainly did. I unzipped my overnight case on the bed, took out my extra jackets and slacks and shirts and hung them in the closet. I also removed the .38 Colt packed snugly in its holster. Reasoning that if I were to meet up with any of the local constabulary they might take a dim view of my walking around their town that well dressed, especially since I had literally smuggled the weapon across the border, I put the gun back in the case and put that on the floor of the closet. Then I went out for a walk.

I spent the next three hours visiting the various bars and hotels in the downtown area, putting out the word that I was looking for Marty Swanner. Half the people I talked to, mostly room clerks and bartenders, seemed genuinely unfamiliar with the name, but in many instances I got the same reaction I'd had from Nacio and the bellhop. Nobody wanted to talk to me very much, and in one place, a really raunchy saloon on a side street, when I gave the bartender a slip of paper with my name and my number at the hotel on it and asked him to give to Swanner if he saw him, the guy tore it up and put the pieces carefully in an ashtray right in front of me. Then he leaned against the backbar with arms folded, incinerating me with his eyes.

I finally tired of the game and headed back to the hotel to wait for someone to take the chum I'd cast onto the waters. On the way two street kids bounced up to me, their eyes dancing with the exuberance of being boys in the summertime. Each carried the kind of cigar box we used to keep our pencils in back in grammar school; theirs were full of packs of gum and miniature rolls of Life Savers, rubber iguanas, pencils. The old Yankee peddler, with a twist.

"Hey, mister! Want some gum? On'y twenny cents."

I shook my head and tried to move on, but the two of them were everywhere, under my feet and between my legs like gamboling puppies. "Come on, don't be no cheapskate. On'y twenny cents." I smiled a no. The twenty cents would not have busted me, but had I given in and made a purchase, every kid on the avenue with shoelaces or postcards or sharp-edged tin ashtrays that said HELLO FROM TIJUANA would have been all over me like sharks in a feeding frenzy. I was having enough trouble with just the two of them.

The little one pulled on my sleeve, raised up on tiptoe, and lifted his sweet flower-face up to tell me something, and I bent down so he could say it into my ear. "Hey, mister, you wanna see a dirty show? Naked women, everything."

My recoil was involuntary. The kid couldn't have been more than seven years old.

"Come on, mister," he said, glancing at his companion, an older, wiser nine. "Bare titties, everything. Fi' dollars, mister."

Now I know we have similar depravity in the good old U.S.A. I've seen more than my share of it during my years in Los Angeles. I wasn't shocked, exactly, or even terribly offended. I guess I just felt sad, looking down into those enormous brown eyes that were so old and jaded in that cherubic little face, knowing that in ten years he'd be a pimp or a pusher or, at the very least, a punk, and if I'd had three wishes right then the first would have been to zap him magically off the streets and into some empty field in the state of Chihuahua where he and his brother could throw a baseball around so that maybe he could become the next Fernando Valenzuela and hold out for two million bucks a year instead of hustling tourists for five dollars to look at bare titties. My second wish would have been to zap myself off the street so I wouldn't have to think about him anymore. My third would have been to find Swanner.

When I got back to the hotel I asked Nacio if Martin Swanner had called for me. With downcast eyes he shook his head, and when he finally did look at me it was as if he were holding me personally responsible for the U.S. annexation of Texas. When I crossed the lobby to the elevator I could physically feel everyone in the room looking at my back, a sensation like the lightest, gentlest touch of a sharp stiletto. I recalled a short story by Steve Allen in which fifty thousand people got together in a baseball stadium and hated a man to death. The prickles at the base of my backbone gave me some idea of how the poor bastard must have felt. At least he knew why they were hating him, which made him one up on me. I got into the elevator and turned around, and in that split second before the automatic door slid closed you never saw so many pairs of eyes being quickly averted in your life.

I'd papered the neighborhood with messages for Swanner, so I didn't want to be out of my room for fear of missing his call. I hadn't the foresight to bring anything to read, and even though the TV set in the room picked up the signal from nearby San Diego, turning it on wasn't much of an option. I never watched TV anyway, except for baseball, old movies, and the news, and the Saturday afternoon fare was mostly golf matches. The view was something less than fascinating, my window looking out as it did over the back parking lot, so I decided to nap. One of my last thoughts while I dozed was that I had no idea what Martin Swanner looked like.

I awoke at dusk, since sleep had been brought on by boredom rather than exhaustion. I've reached that age where I no longer require my eight hours, and I only take daytime siestas when I'm bored, ill, or unhappy. I've always found sleep to be the best escape from the blues, and if I could ensure only good dreams it just might work better.

I stripped and turned on the shower, noting with relief that the water was hot and plentiful. A few years back I'd spent a weekend at another Tijuana hotel and had been forced into a cold rinse because of a woeful shortage of hot water. I love long showers with plenty of hot water. The fact is, I have been known to masturbate in the shower. If that strikes anyone as a radical confession it's only because not many men would admit to it, but lots do it. It's a natural. You're warm and relaxed and unhurried and alone and the water feels good and sensual and there are no visual distractions to keep your mind from a truly delicious fantasy. I suppose it depends on the individual's imagination, but my sexual fantasies are terrific. Fantasies never have bad breath, or headaches, or forget to shave under their arms. And they never want to talk about Us.

I walked around my room toweling myself dry with the thin, worn hotel towel, wondering if any place close by sold magazines or books. I heard footsteps on the tile floor outside my door but I paid little attention, since I'd been hearing them all afternoon. These particular footsteps stopped outside my room, however, so they did manage to get my attention. Quickly I wrapped the towel around my middle. I didn't know what was coming, but there is no more vulnerable human state than total nudity. The towel made me feel about five percent better. I gauged the distance between where I stood and the closet, where my gun was doing me no good at all zipped up in my suitcase. There was a rustling outside the door, and one sharp rap, followed by the sound of footsteps again, this time receding. I leapt to the door, yanked it open, and rather stupidly stepped out into the hallway.

The corridor was not well lit and I sensed rather than saw a figure disappearing around the corner; I took a few steps in that direction before I realized I was wearing only a hotel towel and a smile. Besides, the envelope at my feet was of more interest to me than its courier. It had been propped up so it would fall inward when the door was opened, a manila envelope with nothing written on the front, sealed across its flap with cellophane tape. I took it back into my room, making sure the door was locked behind me, and went to the window to see if anyone interesting was in the parking lot, but no one out there looked like the deliverer of mysterious messages. I ripped open the envelope, which contained one sheet of lined paper torn from an ordinary steno pad. On it was printed in an almost childlike scrawl:

M. Swanner
El Portal Hotel, rm 17
9p

People who write 9p and fail to add the *m* irritate hell out of me, but here the content was more important than the style. The words had obviously been written by the left hand of a right-handed person, and in soft lead pencil. All very mysterious, very amateurish. But apparently my fishing expedition that afternoon had gotten me the nibble I wanted.

What I still didn't know was whether or not Merissa Evering was with Swanner. I wondered what I'd feel when I finally had the pleasure of meeting him, knowing all the things about him that I now knew or had figured out. It was hard not to be judgmental about a sexual sicko whose very name inspired such fear and loathing in an entire town.

I dressed in my dark blue jacket and a white shirt with an open collar and had a bland dinner in the hotel dining room, which evidently catered to U.S. visitors who weren't interested in the local cuisines and customs but were too rich or too embarrassed to eat at McDonald's. At eight thirty I left for my indefinite meeting, and when I arrived at the El Portal Hotel I saw at once I was overdressed. It was not your basic tourist or commercial hotel, unless the scraggly whores hanging around the entrance could classify it as commercial. They all spoke to me and grabbed at my privates as I ran their gauntlet into the lobby, which was so dingy and flyblown it lacked only Elisha Cook Jr. behind the desk to make it a Warner Brothers *film noir* come to life.

The desk clerk was so fat his belly nestled on his hams as he sat, and the thunderous sounds emanating from the vicinity of his nose told me he was probably asleep. An old table radio played bad mariachi music and the clock over the desk ticked merrily away in a loud off-rhythm. My instincts pointed me to a grimy hallway off the lobby and I headed down it, peering at the numbers almost obliterated by dirt and grease on the doors.

I found number 17 down near the end of the hallway and played a paradiddle on it with my knuckles. The door was made of plywood and the sound it gave off when rapped on lacked resonance or conviction. It opened a crack and a gruff voice grunted something I couldn't quite catch, and I answered that I was there to see Mr. Swanner.

The door opened wide very quickly. I was seized by a pair of hands that could only have belonged to a full-grown orangutan, and I felt myself mysteriously airborne, sailing across the room and making a three-point landing face down on a chenille bedspread whose nubby pattern began to imprint itself on my cheek. My arm was twisted up behind me in a painful hammerlock. Someone very large and heavy knelt on the small of my back, and I felt those huge hands patting me down none too gently in search of the gun I had wisely left in my hotel room closet.

When it was ascertained I wasn't armed I was yanked upright, turned around, and hurled like a throw pillow against the headboard, which separated itself from the bedframe from the force of my head battering it. Little black opalescent dots that seemed to be all the notes of a Bach fugue danced on my eyeballs, and I shook my head and squeezed my eyelids together, hoping they'd go away. I opened my eyes. Hovering over me was the biggest Mexican I'd ever seen, well past six and a half feet tall and weighing in at about two sixty. He had one of those skimpy adolescent mustaches affected by half the Chicano population of Los Angeles, and it looked very foolish indeed on a man large enough to play offensive tackle for the Raiders.

There was a man in his middle thirties sitting on the edge of a dresser across the room, one leg dangling, the heel bumping insolently against one of the drawers. He wore a lightweight blue suit with a blue shirt and tie, and he was pointing a gun at my stomach. I calculated how very much it would hurt were that gun to go off.

The man with the gun had a soft voice, and he said, "Start talking, señor," but before I could begin the large one slapped me on the side of the head, and in my left ear the Mormon Tabernacle Boys Choir began the simultaneous singing of every song ever written, and I knew how it must feel to be hit by a bus. I think the son of a bitch enjoyed it, because he was preparing to do it again when the man with the gun stopped him. I said a silent prayer of thanksgiving. I was about to demand to know the meaning of all this but I feared any show of belligerence might bring the bus back again, so I kept my mouth shut and hoped the big guy wouldn't want to hurt me anymore.

The man with the gun said "I am Sergeant Ochoa of the Tijuana Metropolitan Police. This is Officer Cruz."

His accent stirred a childhood movie memory of Alfonso Bedoya and Humphrey Bogart, and all that is perverse and off-the-wall in my nature came bubbling to the surface. Nothing could have prevented me from saying to him, "Let me see your badges."

Ochoa looked at me through the two slits he used for eyes and curled a contemptuous lip. I guess he'd seen the movie, too, and knew he was being put on and didn't much like it. But he was not about to inform me that they didn't need no stinking badges, so he took his silver shield from his pocket and flashed it at me. Wearily.

"And you?"

"My name is Saxon. I'm a private investigator from Los Angeles. Here's my license." I reached into my pocket for my wallet and felt Cruz tense beside me, and I hoped he wasn't going to hit me with those human catcher's mitts every time I tried to move. I took a photostat of my PI license from my wallet and handed it to Ochoa, who read it carefully and returned it without comment, looking at me expectantly. It seemed to be up to me to carry the conversational ball. "I just arrived in town this morning. I'm looking for a man named Martin Swanner. I was told I could find him here at this hotel. In this room."

"By whom?"

With a wary look at Cruz I delved into my other pocket for the note and passed it over to Ochoa. He read it, sighed, and put it in his pocket. "Somebody's been seeing too many lousy movies," he said. He holstered his gun. "Come in here."

He stood up and motioned for me to follow him. I did so gingerly, taking pains to stay as far from Cruz as I could, and went after Ochoa toward the bathroom, halting when I reached the threshold. The floor was sticky with fresh blood, and the stench of that and bodily excretions made my stomach turn over. Cruz shoved me in the back and I did a buck-and-wing into the bathroom, joining Ochoa, who swung the door shut. I thought I was going to faint. I knew that passing out or throwing up would be looked on by these two macho Latinos as less than manly, so I fought to keep my throat closed, cursing the dinner I'd had at the hotel, which was battering at my gag reflex to get out again.

Hanging on a hook on the door, the kind usually used for towels and bathrobes, was the body of a man.

He seemed to be in his late thirties, and from what I could see above the gag tied around his mouth he might have been good-looking before terror and unspeakable pain had twisted his face into a grotesque mask. He was wearing a long-sleeved black leather outfit, square at the neck and about the length of lederhosen, with metallic studs all over it, and a set of snaps at the crotch was open and his genitals were exposed. Though I had never seen one before I reckoned it to be a bondage-and-discipline outfit, worn by those whose sexual proclivities ran along the lines of master-and-slave. His hands were bound behind him with leather wrist restraints that probably had come from the same mail order house as the suit.

The special alteration in the ensemble, one not put in by the designer, was a large hole that had been cut in the stomach of the suit, presumably to facilitate a corresponding foot-long incision in the man's stomach. He was nowhere near my first corpse, but he was the first who had been disemboweled. If there is a supreme power who watches over the Saxon clan, he'll be the last. The Yves Saint Laurent leather belt around the corpse's neck had simply been used to fasten him to the hook, but from the look of him, he had not died of strangulation. That would have been too easy.

Ochoa said, "Señor Saxon, Señor Swanner."

I knew he was waiting for me to vomit or keel over or both, but I was damned if I'd give him the satisfaction. Finally he allowed me to escape back into the other room, where even the sight of the hulking Officer Cruz was an improvement. I explained why I had been looking for Swanner, and even showed them Merissa's picture, but the whole truth didn't buy me a thing. Ochoa still invited me to accompany them to police headquarters to talk some more.

"Look, that's all I know," I said. "You can let Godzilla here slap me around all night. I can't tell you any more."

Ochoa smiled but his eyes were dead. "This is Mexico, Señor Saxon, not Nazi Germany."

That somehow did not reassure me. I sat down in a sagging upholstered chair, still shaky from the one-two combination of Cruz's enormous hands and Martin Swanner's horrifying appearance. I glanced down and saw a pack of cigarettes on the table beside my chair, and a book of matches that looked vaguely familiar. I lit one of the cigarettes with a hand that was trembling as badly as I'd ever remembered, and quietly put the matchbook in my pocket. The taste was ghastly; they were not American cigarettes. "Give me a minute, okay?" I said, and Ochoa nodded. I took a deep puff and blew enough smoke through my nose to camouflage the acrid stench that was starting to permeate the room. A disemboweling might have been just routine for Ochoa and Cruz and the El Portal Hotel, but for me it was a shattering experience. Besides, I knew I was in for a long evening at police headquarters and I wanted as much time as possible to get myself together so I wouldn't make any mistakes. Sergeant Ochoa struck me as the unforgiving type.

At the police station, after I had told my story five times in Ochoa's office, Cruz came in with a computer print-out and conferred with his superior for a moment in rapid Spanish. It was the first time I'd heard him speak. Then Ochoa sat down on the edge of the desk and looked at me the way a biology student might study a frog before getting out the scalpel. "The border guard remembers you from this morning," he said. "Says you were kind of a smart guy. The clerk at your hotel recalls you left at about eight thirty. So your story checks out. Lucky for you."

"Have I done anything illegal?"

"I can't hold you. I can request politely that you stay here in Tijuana for a while so I can reach you if I need you. And I do request that." He sighed. "Don't give me a reason to have to arrest you, Saxon. You won't like it."

"I don't know how you can say that, Sergeant," I said. "So far, Tijuana's been a little slice of heaven." I gave him my most offhand wave and walked out of his office, and there was no way he could know that the armpits of my shirt were soaked and there was a small lake of sweat in the hollow near the base of my spine. Some things never change. No matter what it is that gives them the indigestion—fettucine or corned beef and cabbage or tamales and chiles rellenos—a dyspeptic, mean-spirited cop is the most frightening thing in the world, because most of us learn when we're little kids that when you get in trouble you call the cops. So when your trouble *is* the cops, there's no place left to go. I knew Ochoa was just doing his job, and I also knew the job was necessary, but I was innocent of any wrongdoing and still sweating like a pig from the close call of near arrest and maybe even worse, and along the line someone ought to come up with a system that protects innocent people from feeling like that.

When I got back out onto the street into the relatively fresh air, and well away from police headquarters, I remembered the matches in my pocket and fished them out. I knew taking them in the first place might be construed as withholding evidence, but the Tijuana Metropolitan Goon Squad showed no eagerness to help me, and doing my job was still foremost in my thoughts. I looked at the name on the cover. The matches had seemed familiar at first glance, and now I knew why. They advertised the Pajarito Beach Hotel, a seaside resort some twenty miles south of Tijuana on the Baja coast, old and uncomfortable and always in a state of disrepair, and I thought it the most wonderful and romantic place I'd ever seen.

Perhaps it had been the company, but forever the mention of Pajarito Beach will conjure up memories of the time I'd been more than willing to talk about Us, when I'd romped on the beach and drunk tequila with lime and salt and made love all day and night to a magical girl whose face and eyes and voice and touch were never really completely out of my consciousness, even though she was long out of my life.

Now that memory was smeared with the blood and offal of one Martin Swanner, and I felt an unreasonable anger that even in death Swanner had managed to dirty whatever he touched. I didn't want to go back to Pajarito now and sully the memory further, but I had to find Merissa Evering, not only because it was my job, but because I sensed she was now very much alone in this foreign country and needed to be found. Pajarito seemed to be the next stop on her own personal Yellow Brick Road. So I went back to my own hotel, changed into my remaining clean shirt, and headed south down the Baja Peninsula.

There were road signs posted all along the toll road reading 60KM, but since I'm not very good at math I've never been able to translate kms into mph, so I kept to a steady sixty on the speedometer and hoped I wouldn't land back in Ochoa's lap for speeding. There was hardly any traffic, and I regretted having to awaken the toll collector, who was snoring happily in his little collection booth. The night was cool and I had raised the ragtop and rolled up the windows. I pulled off the highway at the Pajarito exit and started down the wide dusty road that was the town's main drag—its only drag, as far as I knew. After another few kilometers I drove under the large stucco arch that served as the hotel's entry, jounced down a heavily pitted drive, and parked next to a mesquite bush. Saguaro cactus plants stood with upraised arms guarding the front door.

The lobby was huge and high-roofed, with heavy wooden vigas supporting the ceiling and a terrazzo floor. The somber dark brown of the wood was enlivened by slashes of color from the hanging piñatas and the serapes and massive murals on the wall. From somewhere far away inside the hotel I could hear a strolling mariachi ensemble, but the only sign of life in the lobby was the desk clerk. I was getting tired of talking to desk clerks. This one had dirty blond hair and didn't look particularly Mexican, and he seemed surprised to see me. He was even more startled when I asked for Mr. Swanner's room.

His face went into a zone defense. "You are from a newspaper?"

The grapevine, it seemed, was even more efficient than I'd thought. I decided a newspaper reporter was as good a thing to be as any, and I told him that I was.

"The *policía* are making the arrangements," he informed me rather haughtily. "Until then, Mr. Swanner's room is sealed off."

"I can't tell you how that disappoints me," I said. I took a ten-dollar bill from my pocket and waved it under his nose.

"Please!" he said, offended at the thought. He shook his head.

"Sorry." I put the ten back in my pocket. He seemed to regret seeing it go. "Well, long as I'm here I might as well grab myself a drink." I went around the front desk to the cocktail lounge.

It was almost midnight, but that was no excuse for a hotel bar to be totally deserted on a Saturday night. Well, I was grateful not to have to deal with a crowd of merrymakers. I nodded to the bartender and went on through the lounge and into the residential section of the hotel. The corridors were deserted—until I turned a corner and almost bumped into a big man wearing an off-white suit and a straw hat. He was standing stiffly in front of one of the room doors. I gave him a dazzlingly innocent smile, but he didn't smile back, and I couldn't help noticing the bulge of a pistol butt under his arm beneath the suit. Thank you, Officer, for letting me know which room is Swanner's, I thought, and went past him down the hallway and around another corner. He seemed uninterested in me, and that was all to the good. When I was out of his sight I moved quickly to one of the glass doors that led from the Spanish-style corridor to the outside of the hotel.

It took my eyes a moment to adjust from the lit hallway to the darkness, and more than a moment to get used to the chill breeze blowing off the ocean. The moonlight made the breakers a phosphorescent blue about a hundred yards from where I stood. It was a yellow moon. I doubled back, counting windows, to what I sincerely hoped was Martin Swanner's room. The hotel had dormer windows, and this one was closed and latched, but it didn't pose much of a problem for me. I didn't even need the set of lock picks I often carried, nor the stiff piece of celluloid I sometimes used for discreet breaking and entering. I used a simple nail file from my pocket to diddle around with the window for a few seconds before flipping up the latch. I opened it and climbed over the sill into the room, closing the window behind me.

Like the rest of the hotel the rooms were large and a little seedy, with hardwood floors and high beamed ceilings. There were two double beds, neatly made up with faded Mexican spreads, and some rather tacky occasional tables and chairs. Swanner could obviously afford better than this, and I wondered why he would be staying here rather than in one of the more modern hotels back in town. Maybe for all his whips and boots and chains he had been at heart a simple soul who'd wanted to be close to the sound of the ocean. I noted the Louis Vuitton valise on the luggage stand and it looked absurdly pretentious in these humble surroundings. Using my handkerchief to avoid leaving fingerprints all over the place, I opened the case and examined its contents. There were the usual items for weekending, socks (cashmere), underwear (Jordache bikinis), a few silk hankies and the normal complement of shaving and grooming aids.

There were also several obscene photographs, somewhat out of the mainstream of the usual suck-and-fuck variety. The charm of a nude woman shoving a banana or a zucchini or a cucumber up into herself somehow escapes me, but then I already knew Swanner's erotic tastes were a bit more arcane than mine. The photos were not of Merissa Evering, but of a very young Mexican girl, possibly not more than thirteen years old. It was hard to tell; in the pictures her face was contorted by what might have been passion or pain or humiliation.

Under the photos were a few blue-covered legal briefs and affidavits, all having to do with immigration, but none of the names on the papers meant anything to me. I jotted them down in my notebook, however, just for the hell of it.

I heard voices from outside in the corridor, and from beneath the crack in the door I could see the shadows of two pairs of feet where only one had been before. Then a key was inserted into the lock. I looked around in a panic. Ochoa already half suspected me of eviscerating Swanner, and I could imagine what he might make of my breaking into the victim's room. I didn't even want to consider the consequences. There was no time to get back out the window, so I performed what used to be known in my army days as a field expedient: I stepped into the closet. My timing was split-second. Just as I got the closet door shut, the door to the room swung open, flooding the place with light from the hallway.

I peeked out through a hairline crack in the closet door, not daring to move. White Suit had come in with another man. I was acutely aware of the scent of expensive men's cologne, which permeated the clothing hanging all around me. I stood there, estimating how many quarts of the stuff had been bought with the meager savings of poor Mexicans trying to get themselves a green card to stay in the promised land of Los Angeles and live on the run. They'd go from job to job until finally the Immigration Service descended on them and packed them back across the border on a bus so they could work some more and save up enough money to give to Martin Swanner or someone like him to bring them back again.

I didn't know how long I'd have to stay hidden in the closet, until I heard the unmistakable tinkle of urine hitting the water in the toilet bowl and I knew my visitors were simply making a pit stop, proving once again that cops are human too. I waited until they had finished (they apparently both went at the same time—cute, huh?) and gone back out into the hall, noting with distaste that no one had bothered flushing. I gave it a few more seconds for safety's sake, then inched the closet door open.

The room was once again dark save for the moonlight coming through the window. I decided to check the pockets of Swanner's clothing and came up with a few more matchbooks, but one was from the hotel, one was from Von's Markets, and one from The Three Coins back in Laguna. Then I found a small white envelope in a white silk Bill Blass jacket. Inside were two tickets, and when I moved to the window to read them by the light of the moon I saw they were for the bullfights the next day. Quickly I put them in the pocket of my own inexpensive C & R Clothiers sports jacket, gave the rest of the room a cursory tossing without unearthing anything even mildly diverting, and left the way I had come, through the window. Before I went back into the hotel, through the corridor and past White Suit, I had the presence to brush from my shoes the sand I had picked up from the ground outside Swanner's window. There's no such thing as being too careful.

I went back into the lounge and ordered an Armagnac, just in case anyone was looking. I wanted to have a legitimate excuse for being in the hotel. Besides, after getting swatted around by Cruz, discovering a mutilated corpse, answering a bunch of dumb and repetitive questions at police headquarters, and hiding in a dead man's closet, I felt I owed myself a drink. I sat there at the bar, the snifter cupped in my hands, warming the delicious pruney brandy and letting the memories flood over me, remembering who had been with me the last time I'd been at that bar when murder and bullfights and runaway junkie heiresses had not been on my mind at all, and then I became aware of someone watching me and I turned and realized I was no longer the lounge's only customer. The woman who sat alone at a table near the window almost but not quite made me forget all the other things that had happened that night and all those other nights at Pajarito. And almost everything else that had ever happened to me.

She was Mexican, about twenty-five, dressed elegantly in a black dress and an exquisite black lace mantilla, and her eyes were the color and size of Hershey's Kisses. She was the most classically stunning woman I'd ever seen in my life. Her hair was long and inky blue-black, thick and wild like the mane of a wild horse, and I didn't even check out the rest of her because it would have taken several years to really see and absorb and fully appreciate. She was looking directly at me and not smiling, and her nonsmile almost took my breath away. There was no seductiveness in her look; it was as if she was boring through my head with those dark brown eyes, seeing into my thoughts.

I ventured a tentative smile at her. She didn't smile back, neither did she look away. Almost unsteadily I got to my feet, still holding the snifter in both hands, and went over to her table. Beyond the window the waves broke softly on the beige sand. I had no idea what I could say without sounding like a lounge lizard moving in on a stewardess in some Manhattan Beach watering hole. I finally settled on, "Don't you hate drinking alone?" and immediately loathed myself for the banality of it. There are times when I'm smooth and easy when approaching a woman; at other times, like this one, I'm a thick-tongued Reuben.

But she answered my question anyway. "Sometimes," she said. Her voice was low and musical and somewhat breathy.

I agreed, "Sometimes." And I waited.

She said, "And sometimes not."

The invitation was tacit, but it was there. I sat down across from her. "I suppose you get awfully tired of being told how beautiful you are?"

"No," she said, and for the first time a hint of a smile appeared. "I never get tired of it."

I lifted my glass and toasted her beauty, to which she graciously inclined her head. The Armagnac warmed me all the way down, and when it hit bottom it spread slowly and comfortably. I felt a thin film of perspiration at my temples that wasn't completely from the effects of the brandy. I didn't dare reach up and brush it away. I said, "I wonder why you're alone, then, on a Saturday night."

"Perhaps because I choose to be."

"Do you think you could choose not to be?"

She frowned as slightly as she had smiled. I was afraid for a moment I'd blown it, and for some reason it was awfully important for me not to have. She thought it over, and then she said, "You're very direct." There was nothing pejorative in it, just a simple observation of fact. I was relieved I hadn't offended her.

"Why shouldn't I be?" I said. "I hate games. I don't see why I shouldn't say what I think. And I think you're absolutely breathtaking. You live here at the hotel?"

"Sometimes."

"And sometimes not?"

She didn't want to laugh, but she did anyway, and I told her that she had a nice laugh. "But I suspect you don't use it nearly enough," I said.

She sobered quickly and turned away from me, looking out the window at the water.

"I'm sorry, did I say something wrong?"

"You dig too deep," she said, and I accepted the rebuke. Then she said, "It's late in the evening. Am I the first you've told tonight that she is beautiful?"

"Señorita, there are a million pretty girls. But you are much more than that, and I don't know how to say it to make it sound as sincere as I mean it."

She just looked at me with that direct gaze of hers, and the air between us fairly sizzled. Finally we both became uncomfortable with the intensity of it, and she stood up. "I must go."

I stood up too, wanting to do something, anything, even something silly just so she wouldn't go away. I said, "Perhaps we could see each other again. Would you like to go to the bullfights tomorrow?" which was about as silly and rash as one could get, considering the tickets in my pocket belonged to a man who was hanging on a hook on the inside of a bathroom door with his large intestine reaching the floor.

"I hate the corrida," she said, looking away again. "It is cruel."

"Well, how about if we go and not look?"

She shook her head almost sadly. "I am sorry," she said, "but this is not the right time."

"Another time, then, perhaps."

She shrugged her shoulders very slightly, which made the rest of her body do wondrous things, and then she put one hand quickly up to the side of my face and her touch was cool, but I understand why it left a burning place on my skin, and then she disappeared quickly down the corridor of the hotel and I sat down in the chair she'd just vacated and finished my drink, keenly aware of the ocean and the lonely feeling it brought. The sensation on my cheek almost made me forget for a while about Sergeant Ochoa and Sharon and the bullfights and the butchered Martin Swanner, and that somewhere in Swanner's wake was a frightened and used little girl whose father had a thousand-dollar-a-week cocaine habit, and that he was paying me a great deal of money to find her.

I finished my drink and drove back up to Tijuana, where I once more ran the gantlet in my hotel lobby. I fell asleep as soon as my head hit the pillow. My dreams were not pleasant ones.

4

There are certain places I have seen, certain streets or buildings, that immediately fill me with a sense of dread and foreboding whenever I look at them. There never seems to be a particular reason for it, but these places make the skin on the back of my hands prickle with some nameless fear. For instance, baseball fan that I am, I never found Yankee Stadium in New York to be festive or fun; it somehow makes me uneasy. In Chicago, the city of my birth and upbringing, the famous Buckingham Fountain figured in many of my childhood nightmares. The peculiar full-size copy of the Greek Parthenon that sits incongruously in the middle of a municipal park in downtown Nashville gives me the collywobbles every time I think of it. Now to these I would have to add El Toreo de Tijuana. At least I could figure out some logic to this one, for the *plaza de toros* is a place of death.

The sun was westerly and still hot and the air was dry, and I hadn't been outside for more than ten minutes before the dust in the air was clogging my sinuses, and as I looked around at the eager aficionados streaming into the arena I realized that a bullfight crowd is very different from, say, a mob of Sunday afternoon baseball fans. For one thing they are, not surprisingly, ninety-five percent Latino, but this isn't the main difference, because when Valenzuela pitches in Dodger Stadium English is almost a second language. The significant difference is that baseball fans have the comfortable certainty that no matter what else happens, Valenzuela is in no danger of being gored to death by a bull. The Cincinnati lineup might rough him up, but he certainly ought to survive to pitch another day.

At El Toreo de Tijuana Death was the third party down in the ring, which was completely encircled by the rickety wood and steel structure. It seemed like an old-fashioned minor league ballpark someplace in the Midwest, only specifically designed for its bloody purpose. Death was as much a participant in the proceedings as the torero or the bull himself, and the screaming crowd knew that Death would visit one or the other before the dust in the arena had settled. That's what they had come to see, just as most baseball fans come to see home runs. As beautiful and artistic and ritualistic and symbolic as is the corrida, bullfight fans come to root for Death, and finally that was the difference between the two crowds. I just moved along with this one, another sheep in the flock.

Swanner's reserved seats were excellent, down front, with a perfect view of everything. I settled in and took off my jacket, revealing a new shirt I had bought at a bargain store that morning, which was eighty percent silk and was being added to Mark Evering's bill. It was a soft lustrous pink, and I'm sure it made my skin glow as the bright midday sun refracted the light onto my face. Perhaps my ego is a trifle overhealthy sometimes, but I do know when I look good, and I looked good this bullfight Sunday. I felt lousy, the way one might if one had seen what I saw hanging on that bathroom door the previous evening. But I looked good, and sometimes that's even more important than feeling good.

The empty spaces around me began filling up, and I noticed I was in an enclosed box of eight seats. Most sports arenas in the United States are built that way, so I didn't think anything of it. Not until my box-mates began filing in. Then I thought a great deal about it. A large, expensively dressed Mexican man wearing a beautiful cream-colored raw silk suit and a Panama hat came to the end of the row and looked at me through his blue-tinted glasses. He must have been about fifty and weighed close to two hundred thirty pounds, many of which had undoubtedly been added to his large frame by fine wines, rich foods, and never getting off his ass to burn up any calories. He moved with the authority found only in the rich and powerful, certain that whatever obstacles stood in his way would be cleared from the path. In contrast, Mark Evering moved like a man who somehow knew he would wake up one morning to find that the mansion and the servants and the nymphets and the drugs were gone and he was once more plain old Murray Eisenberg from Bensonhurst, Brooklyn and had to go back to being a suit salesman. But this man walked with every confidence that the waves would part before him and that his lizard-skin shoes would touch only dry and safe ground. This man exuded power—and danger.

Then he stepped aside and I saw the lady with him. Today she was dressed completely in lemon yellow, looking for all the world as if she were in an air-conditioned restaurant in Paris or San Francisco and not in a hot, dusty bullring in an ugly little border town. Instead of being the Dark Lady of the Night, she was all sunshine and dandelions, but there was no mistaking that incredible mane of black hair and those Hershey's Kisses eyes, and when she saw me they flashed surprise and perhaps a little fear, but the look was not entirely without pleasure either. I tried to read more of what was in it, but she quickly averted her eyes as her companion stood aside for her to enter the row. She sat down one seat away from me. The empty seat between us corresponded to the spare ticket in my pocket, so I knew it wouldn't be occupied.

I leaned over and said to her, "You've developed a sudden taste for cruelty, señorita?"

She flushed beneath her olive skin and looked at me almost imploringly. I said, "It's okay, I won't make a scene," but it was too late because her companion was looking at us curiously.

With more aplomb than I expected of her, she turned to the

large man in the blue-tinted glasses and said, "Rafael, I met this gentleman last night at Pajarito. May I introduce Rafael Iglesias, Señor. . . ?"

"Saxon," I supplied.

There was a sudden lull, as if a dead bird had dropped into the adjacent empty seat. Her irises opened wide, and I sensed a change in the man's eyes behind his tinted lenses as well. The moment of silence was just that, a moment, and then he leaned forward and reached across her and gave my hand a firm shake, and when I felt his soft, lotioned, manicured hand in mine I knew I had been right, that it had been a long time since this Rafael Iglesias had done a day's hard labor.

"Welcome to Tijuana, Señor Saxon," he said. "Is this your first visit?"

"No," I said. "I've been here a few times before."

"You have come for the corrida?"

I knew there was no point in lying. "This is my first bullfight," I said. "Actually, I came to town to see a man named Martin Swanner."

The girl's chest swelled as she sucked in a breath, and Iglesias nodded gravely. "And did you?" he asked, carefully offhand. "See him?"

"About ten minutes too late."

There were some other people filling in the row behind us in the box, and I glanced back to see who they were. Looking back at me with equal parts malevolence and puzzlement were the angry eyes of Jesus Delgado. Since I'd seen him in Los Angeles two days ago, he was the last person I had expected to share a box at the bullfights with in Tijuana. I felt a flutter of fear. I was a long way from my own turf. I had no safe harbor, no nearby friends, and could make no phone calls for a backup if I needed one. I began feeling the way the bull might have had he known why he'd been invited to the party. I turned back to Iglesias. "Did you know Mr. Swanner?"

"He was a business associate," Iglesias said. "And a good friend as well. We are all shocked and saddened."

My discomfort at being in Swanner's bullfight seats heightened. Iglesias and his party obviously knew I didn't belong there.

Jesus Delgado leaned forward and whispered something in Iglesias's ear on the side away from me. He was no doubt filling Iglesias in on who I was and recounting some of the high and low points of our prior dealings in Los Angeles a few years ago. But whatever he said didn't seem to worry Iglesias, who waved him away as one might brush a spiderweb from his face.

"I don't remember Martin ever having mentioned you," Iglesias said to me.

"We never met," I said, and I could see his dark eyebrows arching in surprise above his glasses. "My only interest in him was in finding a girl who might have been with him."

Iglesias smiled tightly. "With Martin there was always a girl."

"Perhaps you might have seen her, Senor Iglesias." I took the photograph from my jacket and handed it to him. "Her name is Merissa Evering."

He peered at the photo through the smoky blue glasses, then lifted them away from his face and studied the picture some more. Shaking his head, he gave the photograph to the woman. "You ever see this one, Carmen?"

Carmen. I'd been wondering since the night before what she might be called, so I could put a name to the fantasy. Now I had one. Carmen. The cigarette girl in the opera. The temptress. And from the look of her companion, Iglesias, she could be nothing but trouble for a smitten Don José.

She glanced at the picture without really looking at it. "I do not think I ever saw her," she said, and passed it back to me.

"Poor Martin," Iglesias clucked. "There were so many. All the faces, all the bodies ran together. I don't remember this one. I do know she's not in Tijuana now."

"And how can you know that?"

He removed his dark glasses and his eyes drilled through me like a death ray. I'm sure that's why he wore tinted glasses in the first place; so that when he took them off and gave someone a glare the effect would be just that much more startling. I admit it worked. I felt like a butterfly on a pin. Finally he said, "Because I know everything that goes on in Tijuana, Mr. Saxon."

I believed him. I wasn't quite as ready to believe he didn't know where Merissa was. I mistrusted him instinctively, because he had some connection to Martin Swanner and an obvious association with Jesus Delgado, neither of whom seemed kosher for Passover either. Then he put his glasses back on and turned to watch what was happening in the arena below, and Carmen was looking at me with her own brand of high voltage that made the heat and intensity of the midday Mexican sun seem like a sixty-watt bulb. I didn't know where she fit in with Iglesias, and the way she was looking at me I couldn't have cared less. Iglesias was speaking again. Requiring an amount of effort that surprised me, I turned my attention back to him.

He was saying, "I love the corrida. In a country that has many traditions, I think it is my favorite. You *norteamericanos* think it barbaric, I know, but you must admit there is something elemental about it. A man armed only with a sword facing a huge beast with horns that hook and slash, and twenty thousand people fall hushed to watch their meeting. Many of your writers have recognized the beauty of it, but a few of your ordinary fellow citizens seem to appreciate it."

I nodded grimly. "What are the odds on the bull?"

"True, the matador usually wins. But there is always that little bit of uncertainty." He took off his glasses again and once more I felt like a lab specimen. "Because the matador is challenging where he has no right to challenge, in the animal's kingdom. So often when we rush in on alien soil, we get gored. All matadors bear the mark of the horns, no matter how skilled they may be with the cape, with the muleta." He chuckled, and back on his nose went the glasses. "That is why we revere them above all other heroes in our country—and why so few of us become toreros. It is a dangerous job."

He settled back in his seat. I couldn't see past Carmen to take note of his expression, but that was all right, because I didn't want to see past Carmen. She looked at me pointedly to make sure I had received the message Iglesias had fired at me, but there was something else there, too, an interest, a wanting that mirrored my own, and the two of us were only mildly diverted by the start of the *paseo,* the little parade of matadors, picadores, and banderilleros that began the strictly executed ritual to unfold in the arena that afternoon.

One of the toreros stopped almost directly in front of our box, looked up and smiled. He saluted Iglesias, but his smile was for Carmen and everyone within a hundred-mile radius knew it, so naked was his longing for her. She inclined her head in a noncommittal fashion. The boy's eyes sparkled. He was almost criminally handsome, with the kind of arrogant beauty that was bound to make every other man distrust him. I was no exception. He was slim, sinewy, of medium height, and his face was dark and unlined. He wore the pigtail that befitted his rank, and his *traje de luces,* his suit of lights, was a dark, blackish shade of green trimmed with gold. His *capote* was the traditional flaming magenta with a golden yellow lining. I wondered if he bore the horn scars Iglesias had mentioned. He looked to be about twenty years old.

As though he could read my thoughts, Iglesias leaned forward across Carmen to speak to me. "Pepe Morales," he told me. "He is young. He will be one of the greats some day. I am his *patrón*, his manager. Martin Swanner and I sponsored his career. It is as it is in your country with racing drivers and bowlers."

I flashed back to the gruesome sight in the El Portal Hotel the night before, and then back another night to Sharon sitting naked on the edge of her bed in her little apartment, telling me about Martin Swanner and some gorgeous bullfighter. I glanced down at Morales with even more interest.

And then, incredibly, Morales blew Carmen a kiss, and Iglesias either didn't notice or pretended not to, and Carmen flushed and turned her head away, ill-at-ease with the overt display. Indeed, the matador was a brave man.

The preliminaries continued, a lot of marching around and saluting and playing of "La Virgen de la Macarena," and the crowd screamed and cheered for no apparent reason. Then everything got quiet all at once, and at a point far across the arena the *toril*, the "gate of fear," opened and the first bull came out.

I'll never forget the feeling in my stomach and chest when I first saw this animal. He was about four and a half feet high at the shoulder and weighed somewhere around a thousand pounds. He was black, which was not unexpected, and wide between the ribs, with a heavy, rounded neck. His head was lowered, his thick, dirty white horns jutting out almost perpendicular to the skull, and he was by far the most fearsome creature I'd ever seen. Even the killer cats at the zoo, the lions and tigers, were nowhere near as awesome, because most of the time they comport themselves like oversize house cats and even in the wild, if left alone they pose no threat to man. But I could not imagine this bull in repose. He was there to inflict bodily harm if at all possible; he had been born for it. I instantly developed a respect for Morales. Whatever else he might be, he was braver than I, because no power on earth could have gotten me down there to face that enormous, snorting beast armed with only a cape and an *espada*. I don't think I would have done it with a machine gun.

As aware as I was of the proximity of Carmen, as nervous as I was about Iglesias and the dead Martin Swanner, and as uneasy as Jesus Delgado made me, staring burnt-edged holes in the back of my head, as anxious as I was to find Merissa Evering and get the hell out of Mexico, and despite my belief that bull-fighting is cruelty incarnate, I couldn't deny my fascination and elemental fear as young Morales stepped out onto the sunlit sand and looked into the eyes of the bull. I suddenly understood what this ancient tradition was all about and why it had survived and prospered in respectability, when cockfights and bear-baiting had either disappeared or gone underground, surviving for the pleasure and profit of gamblers and unscrupulous entrepreneurs.

I won't bore you with the details of the fight itself. Ernest Hemingway and Barnaby Conrad have done it better than I ever could. Suffice to say that Pepe Morales killed his first bull and was awarded both ears but not the tail, because his sword thrust did not kill immediately and a specialized sword known as a *descabello* had to be employed to cut the animal's vertebrae. It was as nauseating a spectacle as I'd ever seen, and it was not only because of the way Morales had smiled at Carmen that I found myself rooting for the bull. The crowd seemed pleased, though, shouting its olés all over the place, and Iglesias kept up a running commentary on the action like a Mexican Howard Cosell, pointing out Morales's superb cape manipulation, his footwork, and his courage in performing maneuvers that put him in even more jeopardy.

I felt that somehow Iglesias held the key to Merissa Evering's whereabouts, so I decided to stay, through the killing of five more magnificent animals. Although I didn't dare, what I really wanted to do was cry. Until you have seen the blood running into the eyes of a beautiful and noble creature, until you have seen the life fade from those eyes, until what two minutes before was standing proud and brave facing its tormentor becomes no more than a large lump of bloodied meat and gristle and bone being dragged through the sand by horses while the crowd whoops and drinks beer, you don't understand what cruelty is.

Then it was finally over and I was thankful, because I had begun to ache all over as though the banderillas and pics and *rejones* had been sticking in my neck and shoulders instead of the bull's. I have a problem with sadism of any sort, and abuse of animals is particularly loathsome to me. Once as a child I'd come home from school to discover that in the family's absence the dog, a sunny-tempered little boxer bitch, had eaten my pet turtle. When I'd found the mangled remains of the cracked shell I'd become enraged, and through blinding tears had swung from the heels and hit the dog with my small fist, powered by all the strength that senseless loss had imbued me with. She'd looked up at me not in fright but in extreme sorrow, and I realized she'd hadn't the faintest idea why she'd been punished. I had felt lousy about it, and some thirty years later I still felt lousy about it, and I was reminded of the incident by the puzzled, sad look on the bull's face when he realized he was about to be hacked to pieces alive and couldn't figure out what he'd done to deserve it.

Somehow I doubted Pepe Morales was going to be guilt-ridden thirty years later. I guess my machismo is not up to Latin standards. Or a lot of other standards, either. I wear no mustache, chains, or tattoos; football bores me; I'll walk across the street to avoid a fistfight, and I don't enjoy baiting homosexuals. Call it another character flaw of mine.

When the last bull had been slaughtered and the stink rising from the sand was almost overpowering, Rafael Iglesias stood up—expanded out of his seat, really, working the muscles of his shoulders while he patted his stomach. He'd apparently had a pretty good afternoon. "So, my friend," he said to me. "A good corrida today, you agree?"

"Fascinating," I said, and the irony wasn't lost on him. But they are gracious down there, and I was a visitor. So he said, "There is to be a victory celebration in honor of the matador at the Hotel El Conquistador. You know it?"

"I passed it on the way here," I said.

"Carmen and I, and *el matador* would be honored if you would come as our guest. There will be food and drink and music, and I am sure many of your countrymen will be there as well. Many have come down, especially from Los Angeles." He gave it the Spanish pronunciation: *Ahn*-hey-leyz.

I felt crappy and dusty, and there were sweat stains on my new pink shirt, but I did have a jacket that I'd kept folded in my lap all afternoon, and I was intrigued with the prospect of meeting the matador. Also, I had no intention of allowing Carmen to disappear again, now that I'd found her a second time. Even Jesus Delgado's intense glower didn't put a damper on my enthusiasm for that woman. It was visceral, from the first time I saw those chocolate eyes and the fullness of that peasant mouth and the cool angle of her neck. So I said, "The honor will be mine, Señor Iglesias. With thanks."

Why the rooster was inviting the fox into the henhouse for margaritas, I had no idea, but the looks that had passed and were passing between Carmen and me led me to believe I was not alone in feeling smitten.

I dislike mixing business with pleasure, and Carmen was certainly in the pleasure category. The beds into which some of my cases had led me were no more than that. After all, a man must sleep somewhere. Even Sharon had been a means to an end: she had given me enough information on Martin Swanner to lead me to Tijuana and this bullfight in the first place. I had hardly given the lady a thought beyond that, though common sense told me she probably hadn't been pining away either since I'd walked out of her apartment in the predawn hours. I wouldn't have been surprised to hear someone else had taken my place on her pillow the next night.

But Carmen was different, drawing me, obsessing me. I would have to be careful about Carmen. There was Merissa to attend to, to be returned to the fouled but elegant nest from whence she had flown, and I sensed that she needed to be found. I was torn between the job at hand and my feelings for a woman I hardly knew. I hoped it wouldn't come to a shootout between integrity and lust.

And if it did, I hoped like hell integrity would win.

Hotel El Conquistador is one of Tijuana's nicest, built in the old hacienda style around a central patio. The Iglesias-Morales party was being held in the Don Quixote dining room. The music in the background was live, courtesy of a not very good strolling mariachi band dressed in maroon velveteen suits with waist-length jackets and wearing sombreros with those little black balls dangling all around the brims.

The party was in full swing when I arrived, and probably had been since before the last bull was butchered. Iglesias, the host, was seated at the head of a long table, or more precisely several tables put together and overloaded with wine, sangria, pitchers of frosty margaritas, fresh fruit, tortilla chips, beef ribs, *puerco en salsa chipotle,* and several varieties of red, green, and yellow salsas guaranteed to destroy the roof of the mouth of the uninitiated. Of course, I was inured to Szechuan and Thai cooking, which often makes Spanish food seem mild as mother's milk.

It was not difficult to pick the VIPs out of the mob, as they were all seated at the head table, while everyone else milled around and took their refreshments buffet style. Carmen was on Iglesias's left, fresh and crisp as if she hadn't spent several hours in the heat of the plaza.

Directly across from her was the bullfighter, looking at her with calf eyes, tearing his gaze away only long enough to graciously accept the homage of the many fans and admirers who came up to assure him that his capework that afternoon had been of a daring and magnificence unknown since the great Belmonte. Surrounded by adulation, his entire demeanor changed, and he metamorphosed from lovesick adolescent to the aristocrat of aristocrats, the superstar graciously allowing the peasants to kiss his ring or touch the hem of his garments. I wondered how aristocratic he'd look with a horn in his crotch. My ungenerous thoughts of him came in part from his obvious enchantment with Carmen and partly from my innate distaste for anyone who cruelly butchers dumb animals in the name of sport. It was going to be difficult being pleasant to this arrogant son of a bitch, especially since, on top of all the other reasons I had for disliking him, he'd had the bad judgment to be born looking like a pre-Raphaelite angel.

I wended my way towards the head table, rubbing elbows as I did so with the crowd of freeloaders, many of whom indeed seemed to be from Los *Ahn*-hey-leyz. There were a few TV starlets and studlets who had come down to Tijuana for the weekend on a studio-financed publicity junket, their press agents watchfully standing guard to see that the merchandise didn't get damaged, drunk, or stoned. A few furloughed Marines, with their ramrod backs, looked as out of place at this gala as Palestinian terrorists at a B'nai B'rith fund-raiser. And there was a large contingent of gays who were standing close to each other buzzing about Morales's beauty. There were also a lot of well-dressed and obviously well-heeled locals, speaking the kind of high-class Spanish not often heard in the barrios of the United States.

Iglesias had caught sight of me and was waving, and when I reached the table he told the man who was sitting next to Carmen to get up and move so I could sit down. The man didn't like the idea very much, but he complied with a show of obeisance. He went down to the other end of the table, where Jesus Delgado and some others were sitting, one of those was Sergeant Ochoa of the Tijuana Metropolitan Police, who looked as startled to see me there as I was to see him. But it wasn't hard to guess how Ochoa figured in this little nest of brigands. Whatever it was they did to make their living probably required the cooperation of the police, which they undoubtedly bought not only with money but with invitations to special social functions like these, to which a poor hardworking cop would otherwise have been denied entry. It was strange, to say the least, seeing a policeman breaking bread with the likes of Jesus Delgado, even though they were both seated below the salt, but then I remembered *la mordida,* loosely translated as "the bite," the slang word that described the police corruption that was more prevalent here in Mexico than almost anywhere else in the world.

Delgado was still looking at me with more hate than our previous relationship should have inspired. He must get tired of wearing his face in a perpetual frown. It didn't bother me. I've never had this searing need to be loved that some people harbor, especially by dope pushers and whoremasters and exploiters of their own people, like Delgado. It's a good thing Christ rose from his tomb that first Easter Sunday; otherwise he'd be spinning in it, knowing a scumbag like Jesus Delgado was bearing his name.

"My friend the *norteamericano,*" Iglesias was saying. "You are welcome here." He looked genuinely glad to see me. "I want you to meet our guest of honor, the star of this afternoon and a rising star of the corrida, our matador, Pepe Morales."

I shook hands with the bullfighter. As slim and young as he was, his hand was as hard and rough and callused as a laborer's, and his gaze was fierce, as if he were face to face with one of his bulls. He seemed to be waiting for the kind of compliment everyone else was paying him, but I was not about to part with one. I suppose it was a monster breach of etiquette. Finally he said in a tone of bored contempt, "You are not an aficionado?"

I shook my head and said I was not.

"You disapprove, perhaps, like so many of your fellow countrymen? The corrida is cruel, barbaric, medieval?"

I was surprised he was so literate and well spoken, although I don't know what I'd been expecting. "Something like that."

"And yet," he went on, "you pay five hundred dollars or more to watch two Negro men hit each other in the face with their fists. There is no tradition there, no beauty."

"You obviously never saw Sugar Ray Robinson," I said.

From the blank look on the matador's face I gathered he'd never even heard of Sugar Ray Robinson. But he was being damn big about it. "It does not matter. You are welcome here," he said.

I sat down at the place so recently vacated for me, and chose some wine from the variety on the table. "*Muchas gracias,* matador," I said, bowing my head slightly, surprised that I was somehow caught up in the business of actually conversing with a national hero. "What I have heard of your hospitality south of the border is true." I took a big sip of wine to stop my mouth. I was starting to sound like a character out of Hemingway. Next I'd be telling him I obscenity in the milk of thy mother.

It was here that Iglesias chose to speak in a loud voice, "To us, Señor Saxon, a guest is a king. It is the least we can do for a stranger to our country—especially one who has possession of the late Martin Swanner's tickets to the *plaza de toros.*"

Ochoa's head snapped around and he looked at me with renewed and not very friendly interest. Okay, good, it was out in the open, although I wouldn't have chosen this as the time or place to expose it. I'd have to deal with Ochoa later, but at least Iglesias had made it clear not only to me why I'd been asked to the party. I wanted to check him out; that's why I'd chosen to come. He wanted to do the same with me; that's why I was invited. He had flung down the gauntlet, and I decided to accept it. The backs of my hands prickled; I was on his turf and in imminent danger not only of blowing things apart but of getting myself into some pretty torrid water at the same time.

"Of what use are tickets to a dead man?" I said callously. "Life is for the living. But I am honored to be here at the celebration." I raised my glass in a mock toast, feeling the exhilaration of a guy going off a high ski jump for the first time. "And I gratefully accept the hospitality of a man who is so wise he knows everything that goes on in Tijuana. Except, of course, the whereabouts of his dead partner's girlfriend. *Salud!*"

I drank, and the clarity with which I heard the sound of my own swallowing told me it had suddenly become very quiet in the room.

At the mention of the late Martin Swanner's girlfriend, Pepe Morales bounced in his seat as if he'd just received a hot salsa enema. Iglesias, a bit stunned by my hard return of serve, took off his glasses and then put them on again very quickly. Jesus Delgado half rose in his chair, looking at his boss. Carmen put her head down and studied her dandelion yellow lap. Even the Hollywood contingent and the tourists and the gays and the marines fell silent. It seems I had taken everyone by surprise, and that's the way I like it. I had snatched back the advantage.

I figured I had a better chance of rattling Morales then anyone else, hoping his coolness in the ring did not extend to matters not involving an enraged bull. I took Merissa's picture from my pocket and passed it across the table to him. "You know her, perhaps, matador? A gringa. Her name is Merissa."

Morales shook his head and avoided the picture, as though it were something unclean. "I do not know her."

"You haven't even looked."

He glanced down reluctantly, just long enough to establish that it was a photo of a woman, not a postcard of the Grand Canyon. "I do not know her," he said again.

"Are you sure?" I pressed.

"I have said so."

"But she was very close to Martin Swanner, and Señor Iglesias here tells me that Swanner was your friend, your *patrón*."

A little mustache of sweat beads appeared under Morales's nose. "That is true, but . . ."

I smiled, knowing I had him on the ropes. "Isn't it also true that you shared many things with your good friend?"

The muscles in his cheek jumped as though there was a small gerbil in the corner of his mouth.

"I have it on good authority that you shared certain private pastimes with your friend, other than those in the *plaza de toros* on Sundays. Wasn't this girl, this Merissa, ever involved in those private little pastimes?"

Of course I knew I was taunting a cult figure, a hero, and pricking the pride of a national symbol of the bravery and nobility of *la raza,* and that I had committed a grave, unforgivable faux pas. Try to imagine, if such a thing is possible, sitting in a crowd of American sports enthusiasts and loudly accusing Magic Johnson of exposing himself in public, or John Elway of being a chicken hawk. That was the effect I had on our little minifiesta at the El Conquistador, and the reactions to it around the room were varied, ranging from dismay to shock to outrage. No one seemed terribly amused.

It certainly made a dent in the icy cool of Pepe Morales. He leapt to his feet, the blue veins in his temples standing out like the river on a three-dimensional map of Colorado. I stood up, too, ready for anything, believing that if he was going to hit me I stood a better chance on my feet. If he did take a swing, I was more than willing to admit I had it coming. What I'd said was unforgivable, even if it was the truth. When it became apparent he wasn't going to hit me after all, I relaxed, but I wasn't so sure about some of the other people at the table.

Several of the Mexican men, Delgado included, were on their feet. I noticed with my peripheral vision than Sergeant Ochoa had taken the napkin out from under his chin and had casually wandered over to the door of the restaurant. I didn't think I liked that very much. But at the moment I had to maintain eye contact with Morales. It was a matter of honor. The only way I was going to get answers about Merissa was to shake these people up and perhaps force them into doing something indiscreet or saying something unintentionally revealing, as people are wont to do in the heat of anger. I was definitely scatter-shooting, but apparently my shot in the dark about Morales and Swanner and their kinky sex games had struck a nerve. The trick here was to keep stirring the shit without stepping so far over the line as to wind up as dog food in the Tijuana barrio.

By this time Morales had regained a sliver of his composure, and when he spoke it was Gary Cooper–like, through gritted teeth. He looked ready to cry. "If you were not a visitor in our country and a guest at the table of my friend, I would kill you for what you have said here."

"You might try," I said with more bravura than I was feeling, "but unlike your bulls, I am not stupid enough to charge a flapping cape."

Iglesias stood up slowly, brushing his hands on his napkin. "I am confused," he said. "Has anyone here offended you, Señor, to cause you to speak to us in this manner?"

"Someone," I said, "everyone, in fact, is lying to me about this woman," and I waved the picture of Merissa at them. "That does indeed offend me."

"Then go to the police with your charges. We have asked you here to share our bread, to share our joy. At the risk of being less than gracious, I suggest it would be more . . . comfortable if you were to leave us now."

I sensed Delgado and three of his companions moving toward my end of the table, and I knew that however polite his words might be, Rafael Iglesias was not used to making mere "suggestions." I had become a pretty unpopular fellow by insulting everyone's favorite torero, and it was no comfort knowing that the few friends I had in this world were at least a hundred fifty miles up the freeway in another country, and that I was alone down here with my ass waving in the breeze.

Carmen's eyes were glittering, and all sorts of things were playing across her expressive face. But my first priority seemed to be getting the hell out of there while I still could.

Morales's olive skin, meanwhile, had turned almost purple from anger and humiliation and hyperventilation, and Iglesias was hiding behind his shades again, his face turned toward me thoughtfully. He had underestimated me, and I had not done so with him. Score one for me. The rest of the people in the room, I was sure, were having unkind thoughts about me, and I tried to think of a good exit line, but came there none. If there was ever a time not to be a smartass, this was it.

Doing my damnedest to leave as though it was my own idea, I was well aware that Delgado and a few of his amigos were following behind me at a discreet distance, and I was almost expecting an ice pick in the neck as soon as I got outside. A backward glance told me that already a stream of people were heading for the matador to express their sympathy and renew their loyalty, and that said matador was still badly shaken up and not doing his noblesse oblige act nearly as well as was his wont. But I had accomplished my mission in any case. I had gotten their attention.

Sergeant Ochoa was standing to the left of the door that led from the dining room to the street, against the wall with his hands in his pockets. As I came abreast he leaned in close to me. "Saxon," he said without rancor, "you are getting to be a pain in the ass, man."

"Where's your partner, Sergeant Ochoa?" I said. "A hot day like this, he makes good shade."

He shook his head and sighed. "Señor Saxon, these are not kids to fool around with," he said. "You come down here, you don't know the culture, you don't know the language, and you start saying bad things to people. We try to be good hosts, but you don't try to be a good guest."

"Etiquette lessons now?"

"You're better off learning it from me than some of these people. Saxon, you are one stupid gringo motherfucker." As do most Chicanos who use that expression, Ochoa put the emphasis on the last two syllables.

"So stupid that you're just going to stand and let Delgado carve me up the minute I walk out the door?"

"I don't know what you are talking about," he said. "I am going back to finish my meal; there is nothing worse than cold Mexican food, you know. If there is a disturbance outside, I will certainly investigate it—when it happens."

"You can keep it from happening," I said. "You've got a badge."

He smiled with the triumph of a man who didn't often get the last word. "We don't need no stinking badges," he said, and went back to his place at the table on the far side of the room.

When I hit the open air my first impulse was to break into a run, but that would have earned me disdain, and for reasons I couldn't fathom at the time, it was important to me not to do that. Perhaps it had something to do with Carmen, or maybe it was my stubborn pride. In any case I was in no position for detailed self-analysis at that moment. I headed for my car, moving briskly without actually giving the appearance of haste, hoping the presence of several people in the crowded hotel parking lot would dictate discretion to the Delgado crowd. As I fumbled for my car keys, Jesus came up beside me, and I turned casually to face him, noting with relief that the other three muscle boys had stayed in the doorway of the restaurant.

"Get out of Tijuana, Saxon," Delgado said in a voice like a viper's rattle. "There is nothing for you here."

"I wanted to get my picture taken riding a zebra-striped burro," I said. He was standing very close to me, and I was not pleased with his breath. His hand was in his jacket pocket, holding a gun or a knife or a sap. I didn't think it was a rosary.

Whore's son!" he snarled.

"It was nice seeing you again, too."

"You have insulted Señor Iglesias and dishonored the matador. It will be bad for you to stay in Tijuana."

"I have some things to do."

"The girl is gone."

"I think you're a liar." I watched the color rise up past his ears as though he'd taken too large a bite of jalapeño pepper. I noticed he wore his hair too long for current Los Angeles fashion, and that he used grease on it. His hairstyle had gone out of vogue with the demise of Bill Haley and the Comets. I continued on my roll. "And a thief and a pimp. And a *maricón*."

Ah, that one did it. I knew it would. Call a Hispanic man anything you want, any foul name, or accuse him of any crime, and he won't like it but he might be judicious about retaliation. But cast aspersion or doubt on his manhood and you have one angry Latino on your hands.

Whatever Delgado had in his jacket pocket, he started to bring it into view, the better to use it on me. It was probably a knife, since he could have used a pistol without taking it out of his pocket and would only have had to worry about re-weaving a cheap jacket. I never found out. I never wanted to. I brought my knee up hard between his legs and felt his testicles squish at the impact.

"Aiyeee!" he said. I used to read that word in comic books when I was a kid. The bad guy always said "Aiyeee!" when he got zapped by Captain America. It was a great revelation to me, at my advanced age, to find that the comic books on which I had nurtured my imagination and literary tastes had some basis in reality.

Delgado was holding his nuts with one hand, the other still in his pocket, and he was sinking slowly to one knee in front of me the way Errol Flynn used to when talking to Queen Elizabeth. He was humming a strange high-pitched hum, which I realized was the final syllable of "Aiyeee!" being stretched to its ultimate. At the hotel entrance the backup squad was moving into action. I got into my car very quickly, dignity notwithstanding, revved it up, and backed out, leaving Delgado kneeling beside my parking place. The three muchachos were trotting right at me, spread out across the parking lot in a flying wedge, so I simply aimed my car at the middle of them and got an unreasonable kick out of seeing them scatter like chickens in a dirt driveway. One of them even went flying over the hood of a nearby car, just like on "Miami Vice." I chuckled about it until I was safely out of the lot and driving down Boulevard Agua Caliente, and then I stopped chuckling. Delgado and his boys would no doubt be raging for revenge, and if I stayed much longer in Tijuana they were likely to get it. But Sergeant Ochoa had told me not to leave town, and even if he weren't a friend of Iglesias's and Morales's, as he seemed to be, he still had me under suspicion for doing Martin Swanner.

It all boiled down to my outmoded sense of chivalry. It isn't much, but it's mine, and it wouldn't let me leave until I had managed to rescue the fair maiden Merissa—if I could ever find her. And if that isn't straddling the horns of a dilemma, I'd sure like to know your definition.

5

After I had more or less assured myself that I hadn't been followed out of the hotel parking lot and could breathe a sigh of relative relief, I decided I didn't know enough about my new-found friends and their activities. Some research was in order. If I were back in Los Angeles I'd have a score of sources to go to— people like Joe DiMattia, a cop who hates my guts because I used to go out with his wife before he married her. I believe he always helps me out because it gives him a chance to tell me what he thinks of me. Friends in the various city offices are willing to part with a few nuggets of confidential information for a good steak lunch at the Pacific Dining Car. The various bookies, hookers, low-lifes and snitches I've gotten to know so well during my career as a private investigator always keep their eyes open for reasons of survival, and they are always willing to accept a small contribution for sharing what they've learned. In the business world they call that sort of thing networking, one of those verbs that three-piece-suit types have so resolutely been making out of nouns the past few years. But here in Tijuana I was a man without a network. And even had I known which people knew what needed to be known, I didn't even speak the language. So I drove back downtown to the Avenida de la Revolución, the main shopping and tourist area of the city, parked the car in a dirt parking lot that charged me three dollars for the privilege, and headed for the editorial offices of Tijuana's English-language newspaper.

Downtown Tijuana comes up a bit short in the charm department. Looking around I couldn't see any discernible reason for anyone from north of the border to drive down, unless it was for the women, and there seemed to be precious few of them around. On the corner near the parking lot was a rather picturesque old Catholic church, and over the entry, towering some thirty feet above the sidewalk, was a mosaic of the Blessed Virgin done in garishly colored tile and lit by two harsh spotlights. Directly beneath this stood three young prostitutes. The streetwalkers in Tijuana were not as aggressive as their sisters on Western Avenue in L.A., but they were quick to return a look and a smile. They were not dressed tackily, either, and anywhere else in the world might be mistaken for high school girls out on the town on a Sunday evening, save for their come-hither smiles. Much more forward were the merchants, who would step out from their open shop doorways, take my arm and say, "Hey, amigo, nice leather jackets?" The pushy sidewalk vendors just wandered up and down the streets, detaining the tourists, pitching their blankets and serapes, gum, cigarettes, or little toy mice on a string, the last scaring hell out of the gringas by scooting up to their feet and squeaking plaintively.

The newspaper office was small, as dingy as everything else in town, and poorly lit. The young woman who had obviously been left there this Sunday night to hold down the fort was somewhat hostile, even after I turned on the old charm and in the very nicest way I knew asked to look at some old files. It was not so much my winning ways but the accompanying ten dollars that melted her cold heart, but finally I was in the morgue of the Tijuana paper, looking up clips on Rafael Iglesias, Pepe Morales, and Martin Swanner.

The Swanner file was slim, made up mostly of society notes: Mr. Martin Swanner and party down for the corrida, Mr. Martin Swanner hosting a dinner for Sr. Rafael Iglesias at Boccaccio's Nueva Marina, Martin Swanner dining with Rafael Iglesias at Reno's. None of it told me anything except that Swanner was recognized in Tijuana as a social lion. I already knew that he was famous among desk clerks and bartenders. Not very helpful.

The file on Pepe Morales was of course more complete, since he was a public figure on the way to becoming a legend. He was twenty years old, I gleaned from the clips, a native of the state of Sinaloa in northwest Mexico. He had taken a horn in the thigh during a bullfight in Tijuana about a year ago, and had sustained a few busted ribs about six months after that. Morales had yet to perform his art in Mexico City, which was the Big Apple for matadors. For the time being he was content to be a big torero in a little pond here on the border. Much was made in many of the articles of his devout Catholicism, but I knew from reading Barnaby Conrad that that was also SOP for bullfighters. If I had to go out and face half a ton of angry bull three times each Sunday, I'd probably be a regular churchgoer too.

Most of the material on Morales didn't differ from the standard puffery we read in American newspapers about our own athletes, except, of course, for its decidedly Mexican slant. Quarterbacks and left-handed screwball pitchers and seven-foot-one NBA centers are lionized in the United States, but in Mexico a first-rate matador is practically an icon. To me, being a celebrity would not be worth the risk of fighting those bulls one on one. Being emperor wouldn't have been worth it.

There was one item in the Morales file, however, that stood apart from the rest of the sports and personality pieces, a story that had made the front page. It seemed that some fifteen months earlier a truckload of illegal immigrants, mostly from the state of Sinaloa, had paid an unnamed agent from six to twelve hundred dollars per head to be smuggled over the border into the United States. This was not unusual. What made the story noteworthy is that the entire truckload, some fifty-three men, women, and children, had been driven into the desert on the U.S. side of the border and there dumped unceremoniously out of the truck to fend for themselves. All but four had perished from thirst and exposure. It was a grim tale, one I remembered from the TV news, and at the time it had stirred up a lot of do-gooders and knee-jerk liberals to "do something" about the problems of illegals from Mexico and Central America.

What the newscasts had not reported, or maybe I'd had no reason to take particular note of it at the time, was that among the dead was a fifteen-year-old girl named Guadalupe Morales, the sister of Tijuana's up-and-coming young matador. The story in the paper recounted that she, along with three other teenage girls, had been raped.

I shook my head. It was no wonder Morales was such a terror in the ring. He had a great deal of anger to expend on the bulls. It probably explained why he had been careless enough to take a horn in the thigh three months after the date of the story. It must be tough keeping your mind on your work when you think of your young sister badly used by unknown and evil men and then left to die of thirst in 115-degree heat.

I felt great empathy for Morales after reading the story. I still didn't like him much, mind you. It's hard for me to like a man that physically beautiful to begin with—like the late Mr. Swanner, I'm not much for competition. Add to that the fact that he was in a profession of which I heartily disapprove, garnished with his obvious infatuation for a woman with whom I was also enchanted, and it was just about a foregone conclusion that Morales and I were never going to be best friends. But an emotional burden like that is tough to lug around with you every day. Every time you took a drink of water you'd think of that poor child out there under the relentless sun.

The rest of the Morales file was pretty dull stuff, so I put it aside and started reading up on Rafael Iglesias. He was in real estate, the paper said. He was also into the exporting of Mexican food specialties, and he owned leather manufacturing companies in Sonora and Sinaloa. One article mentioned that he had a Chevy dealership in Mazatlán, and you have to figure anyone who sold Chevrolets in Mexico must be big rich. According to what I was able to piece together, he had various small investments in businesses all up and down Baja California. And of course, I already knew that he was the sponsor of Pepe Morales. That wasn't in any of the clippings, but he'd told me that himself. Iglesias had quite a lot going for him, lots of irons in lots of fires, and probably a lot more that nobody knew about. He was obviously not one of Mexico's impoverished millions that we read about. No one was ever going to dump him out of a truck to die in the desert, that was for sure. There was no biography on Iglesias, as there was on Morales; I couldn't find out how old he was or where he was born. But I had the feeling he had not been born to money. He hadn't inherited a seat on the stock exchange or taken over his father's mills or been given a partnership in grandpappy's blue-chip law firm. He had too many different scams going for him not to have scrabbled for every peso.

I went through the stack of clippings methodically. Then I spied one that hit me right under the ribs: it was the announcement, dated four months earlier, of the wedding of Rafael Iglesias to Señorita Carmen Guitierrez. A photo showed the happy couple at their wedding supper at the Pajarito Beach Hotel, partly owned by Iglesias and partly by a U.S.-based company called The Allegiance Corporation, along with their honored guests, including Mr. Martin Swanner of Los Angeles and Laguna Beach and the popular matador Pepe Morales. In the picture, Morales, off to one side, was looking at Carmen with his love eyes, which somehow didn't surprise me. Carmen was dressed completely in white, which was also no great surprise. She didn't look particularly happy in the photograph—rather grave, as a matter of fact—but she did look gorgeous, as usual. To me she'd look radiant with intestinal flu at four o'clock in the morning.

I put the folders down and dry-scrubbed my face, trying to digest the information, to accept it, and to put it in its proper perspective. I had assumed when I saw her at the corrida that she was Iglesias's mistress. How did I feel now, knowing she was his wife? Did that make a difference somehow? Did that make her even more inaccessible to me, even more of a fantasy that could and would never be flesh, and therefore even more desirable? I shook my head, trying to rattle my brain back into the logic mode and figure out how all this would help me find Merissa Evering. The clippings in the newspaper files hadn't advanced that cause very much, other than to give me an idea of the kind of people with whom I was dealing. I neatly stored the scraps of knowledge I'd gleaned in my own built-in computer bank for possible future reference, thanked the hostile lady in the front office, and headed back onto the now dark street toward the lot where I had parked the car.

I didn't get there directly.

Milliseconds before it happened I sensed there was someone behind me, someone coming from out of the darkened doorway of a shop, and I turned and took the first blow on the top of my shoulder instead of on my head, where it had been aimed. It numbed my right arm and stunned me. A forearm snaked around my neck and started squeezing my throat, and I felt a wave of blackness covering me up, like an old-fashioned bottle of ink that spills and slowly works its way across the top of a Formica table. Half conscious, there was very little I could do to keep from being dragged down a small alley and thrown face first against a brick wall.

There were three of them. All were considerably shorter and lighter than I, but the combination of surprise and their superior numbers made it not much of a chore for them to beat and kick me to my knees. Then they beat me some more. It was a curious sensation, like being overrun by sixth graders with a grudge. I didn't know which one of my enemies in Tijuana instigated this, but I didn't imagine for a moment that it was a garden-variety mugging. For one thing, they kept hitting me longer than necessary if all they wanted was my wallet. Secondly, each one seemed anxious to get his own licks in. I tried to catch a look at them, but it was dark as death in that alley, and my main concern was to try to protect my eyes. I got the impression, though, of stolid Indian faces, men in their early twenties, whom I didn't recognize. I just shut my eyes tight to keep them from being put out by a flying fist or finger, but also as a basic reaction, instinctive since childhood—close your eyes until something scary or unpleasant goes away.

I wasn't exactly frightened. I had taken beatings before, and I figured if my life were in danger I would have already been dead. But it was well within the parameters of unpleasant. I was lying down in the fetal position to protect my groin, my arms over my ears, so all they had to work on was my back and kidneys. Finally they were satisfied, or else they just got tired, so by the time they stopped I had passed through the pain barrier and was only feeling impact. My ears rang with the tintinnabulation of the bells going off inside my head. They were speaking Spanish to each other, which I understand little of, but I did manage to pick up the word *matador* from one of them just before a final kick slammed into my back and I heard their retreating footsteps. I was bleeding into the pile of garbage on which I was lying, which I didn't like at all, and I realized they had torn my brand new pink shirt. It occurred to me that my nose might be broken, and I worked it around with my fingers, the pain making me giddy; later I discovered they had just managed to bloody it badly.

I stood up slowly, my cuts and bruises singing an aria of protest. If this was south-of-the-border hospitality I was spending my next vacation in Oregon, thank you very much. After checking to see that all my various body parts were still attached and functional, I staggered out of the alley and onto the street. There was a fair amount of traffic that hadn't yet headed back to the U.S., but my appearance didn't cause nearly the stir it might have. Somehow all the policemen I had seen on the day of my arrival were absent from view, occupied elsewhere; a bloody and limping gringo was of a lower priority than keeping the cars moving at a brisk pace on the Avenida de la Revolución on a Sunday evening.

The parking lot attendant charged me three dollars and seventy cents, which he collected without commenting on my rotten condition. When I got back to the hotel, Nacio at the desk reacted instantly, looking startled, and then he avoided my face as one looks away from an accident victim, his mouth settled into a rigid serves-you-right line. No one else was in the lobby save a fat lady from Glendale in a polyester pants suit bitching at her husband that she was not about to eat any of the native food down here and spend the rest of her vacation with the trots, so I was able to slink to the elevator without attracting any more attention. I was a properly whipped dog, and all I wanted to do was to lie down and lick my wounds and perhaps fall asleep with a whimper.

Alas, it was not to be.

Someone had visited me while I was out and in lieu of a calling card or a short note had left the place a shambles. Every drawer in the room was opened, every pocket in my clothing hanging in the closet had been turned inside out, and my suitcase had been dumped onto the bed upside down, leaving colored Jockey shorts and socks rampant on a field of chenille. I had no idea what they were looking for.

Maybe it was my gun, because that was the only thing I could tell was missing. And I couldn't very well report its theft to the police because I had brought it into Mexico in violation of several different regulations of both countries, and I had a sneaking suspicion the person or persons who had taken it knew that. I was pretty angry. I'd spent three hundred dollars for it. It was a good gun.

I felt all the things you're supposed to feel when your digs are burglarized: used, violated, sullied, etc. But I also was mad as hell that, hurting and bruised as I was, I would have to set right that room and its contents before I could sleep. I undressed wearily, tossing the torn shirt into the wastebasket, and climbed into the shower.

The hot water hurt like hell but it boiled out a few of the fearsome aches in my back and neck. After all the blood had washed away I looked in the mirror to take a damage inventory. There was a healthy—or unhealthy, I suppose—gash behind my left ear. My face was discolored and puffy and my nose resembled Bozo the Clown's. I was well on the way toward a black eye. My ribs, back, and abdomen bore blossoming red bruises that would turn purple in a day or so, but I fingered my rib cage and couldn't find any breakage, and for that I was thankful.

But puzzled. One doesn't toss a hotel room and then take nothing but a gun no one knew about in the first place. And to what end was the beating? I gazed at my out-of-shape face in the mirror and was ready to blame it all on Delgado, but thinking it over I realized he would have sent the goons I'd seen with him at the hotel and would probably have come along in person to watch the festivities and laugh. But the three who had attacked me in the alley were not professional bullyboys, that was for sure. For one thing, they were too small, and for another they were too emotional, not nearly methodical enough. They could have inflicted a lot more damage if they had known what they were doing, but the fact was they didn't give very good beating. Neither were they ordinary street hoods, as no effort had been made to rob me. They hadn't even bothered checking my pockets.

The questions before the house, then, were who? and why?

I set to repairing the wreckage of the room and my scattered clothing, grunting each time I bent down and strained the muscles that had been thumped on. I can be very compulsive sometimes, like never leaving the dishes until morning after a dinner party. After I finished, I lay down on top of the covers and closed my eyes. There was no position in which I could get comfortable, but I figured the pain would lessen eventually and exhaustion would take over from nerve endings and I would drop off to sleep. When I did so the reality of the past few days kept sticking its nose into my dreams, so that when I heard a tapping on my hotel room door I was glad for the opportunity to wake up. I wished I still had my gun. I pulled on my dusty pants and went to the door, listening. Again the tapping, soft and discreet. I yanked the door open quickly, hoping to startle whoever was knocking. It worked. Carmen almost dropped the paper bag she was carrying. Still, it was a toss-up as to which of us was more surprised.

"Oh!" we both said.

Then Carmen said "Oh!" again and put her hand up to her face in genuine dismay. "What happened to you?"

She looked at my battered face and reached out and put her hand on my cheek the same way she had done the night before at Pajarito, and it was only the second time in the incredibly long twenty-four hours we'd known of one another's existence on the planet that she had touched me, and where her fingers touched felt well again. Some of our TV faith healers could have learned a few things from Carmen about the laying on of hands.

I stood aside and she walked past me into the room. My efforts at tidying up had not been completely successful; it still looked as if the place had been tossed. When Carmen glanced at me, frightened, I said, "Two separate incidents. Probably happened at about the same time."

She sat on the edge of the bed, the grocery sack on her lap. *"Pobrecito,"* she said, which I knew from my high school Spanish meant "poor little thing." I was touched and flattered by her concern for me and hoped it was genuine.

"You take too many foolish chances, Saxon," she said. I loved the way she said my name. "You are fortunate to be alive."

"We're all kind of lucky that way," I said, "except Martin Swanner."

She shook her head. "Foolish," she said. "Rash. The things you said to Rafael this afternoon! He is too powerful a man to be spoken to this way. And Pepe—he is a hero in Mexico. No one insults him like this."

"He's in love with you. It's obvious."

"He is a boy," she said, discarding Pepe's cult idol status in four words. "But Rafael is his *patrón*. And Rafael can be a dangerous man."

"I guess you would know best about that—señora."

She looked up at me, those brown eyes impossibly wide, and I felt my heart beating in the vicinity of my Adam's apple, an almost painful constriction in my throat that made me forget about the aches and pains all over the rest of me.

"You never told me you were his wife."

"You never asked me. We've hardly spoken. Is it so important?"

"Not for the moment." I suddenly realized I was standing there barefoot and shirtless, and she let her gaze drop to the bruises on my chest. I shifted uncomfortably. I don't have a lot of hair on my chest. Some. Enough, I suppose. But not a lot. I said, "What's in the bag?"

She blushed and fluttered her hand over the opening of the grocery sack, and then she said, "Sometimes I take foolish chances, too." She took an iced bottle of expensive champagne and two glasses out of the bag. She'd obviously just bought them at a liquor store. I went and sat down next to her and took the bottle and glasses from her and put them down on the bed, and she put her hand out again and touched an angry red welt on my rib cage. We locked eyes for a moment, and then we touched our lips together very slowly, no tongues, just lips, and hers were soft, like a young child's. It was a special kiss, this first kiss, tender and tentative and frightened, and nearly sexless except that the sexual tension between us, that had always been between us, was now almost a palpable thing hanging in the heavy and hot air of the hotel room, and when I opened my mouth slightly she pulled away, not prudishly or with haste but as if she simply didn't care to deal with an openmouthed kiss just then, and I respected her wishes and took my lips from hers. Neither one of us said anything, so I began working at the champagne cork. To my delight she held her hands up to her ears, cringing in anticipation of the pop, and when it came she gave a little jump. Then she held out the glasses so I could fill them. It tasted the way only good champagne can taste, and we both smiled at the sinful sensuality of it. I tried hard and almost successfully to forget it had been purchased with Rafael Iglesias's money.

There was a quiet time while we sipped, each with our own thoughts. Then I said, "Why did you marry him?" and could have bitten off my tongue for asking.

She looked away. "You still dig too deep."

"Maybe so," I said, "but unless I'm wrong you feel the way I feel, and I don't know what that is. I do know you're married to somebody else and that's usually a no-no for me. But you're here and I want you. I just like to know what the rules are first."

"Why must there be rules? I am here, and I want you too. That's all you need to know, isn't it?"

"Is it? I suppose it should be enough."

"I didn't ask you any questions. You might have a wife too."

I shook my head.

"You might be in love with someone else."

That I could neither confirm nor deny, because when you're in love with a memory it doesn't count, except that it does. Memories have a way of sticking to the heart. That's why they call them memories.

She went on, "None of that matters to me. What matters is that we are here, we are together, now, tonight. All right?"

I murmured that it was all right and I raised my glass to her and we toasted the night, and then I kissed her again, at first the same way as before and then all at once not the same, because her mouth opened under mine and our tongues touched and fenced. What had been warm became hot, and her clothes, all color-coordinated blue tonight, were raised and then pulled aside, and then pulled off.

Maybe the bullfight and the Hemingway associations were getting to me again, but I'm willing to swear the earth moved. Truly.

We slept for a time. We had to. After we'd made love and were both gasping on the bed like beached whales, there was nothing further to distract me, and I remembered the pain. It came back to me like the insistent sound of a parade on the next block that somehow intrudes into your consciousness even after you've closed all the doors and windows to shut out the thud of the bass drum. It wasn't a restful sleep for me. I never got past the shallowest end of the dark sleep pool. When I finally opened my eyes her mane of hair was on my shoulder and against my face, and she turned in her sleep and it tickled me and brought me wide awake. I rolled toward her and she moved closer against me, and then I touched her round flank, stroking gently with my fingertips, and she made a soft little noise, half awake, and I moved my hand around and down so that it was between her legs and touching her again there, tentatively, almost shyly.

To no one's surprise desire stirred and we made love again. It was slower this time, less frantic, better than the first time. Her cries were loud enough to be heard in the next room of the hotel, but neither of us cared. Carmen was especially abandoned at the moment of her climax, stopping just short of the scratching and bruising and fingernail-raking that I don't find particularly erotic. I had been bruised enough this night. She was not as technically skillful or as practiced as Sharon, but she was less mechanical, more spontaneous, as though she were making things up as we went along.

When we were finally done with each other's bodies again and had lain motionless together for a long while with every possible area of bare skin touching, she finally sat up and told me she had to go away.

It was as if someone had taken back all my Christmas gifts on the morning of December 26th after I had played with them and grown attached to them. I felt a keen sense of loss that I was unused to, had grown unused to during a long period in my life of not really caring whether or not there *were* toys to play with. But she was still a stranger to me, and someone else's wife, someone rich and ruthless. And she was linked somehow to a particularly savage and grisly murder. I pleaded with her not to go. I was afraid somehow she'd disappear and I'd find she had only been a hallucination brought on by the hot sun or the beating—that she had never really existed at all nor would again, except to haunt my already overburdened memories. But she protested that she had to leave, and that I must understand.

"I'll see you again," I said. I wasn't asking but telling her, and hoping that by the saying of it, it would be. I watched her dress, and she leaned over and kissed my mouth and then she was gone, a light blue shadow-figure in the dark blue shadows of predawn, and I heard the *tick-tick* of her high heels against the terrazzo floor in the corridor. The scent of her, feral and strong, lingered in the bed and on my hands and face and loins, and I fell finally into a sleep of surfeit on the damp, tangled sheets where we had repeatedly taken each other.

6

In the morning I was feeling many things, the hangover pain from the beating being the least of them. Happiness, euphoria, and fear were all ricocheting around in my head like a handball gone wild. And guilt, too, that I had come no closer to finding Merissa Evering. I had planned to go back to Iglesias and pump him to try to confuse him into saying something that might lead me to Merissa, but that was before I'd spent the night making love to his wife, with her touch and taste and the insistent coolness of her hands on my warm body, the fire in her eyes and the turn of her mouth as she sat astride me in triumphant climax. No, it would not be easy dealing with Iglesias today. Perhaps I'd tackle Morales again, if I could figure out how to get near enough to talk to him without him killing me.

The other feeling I had was ravenous hunger. It had been a long time between meals, twenty-four hours, because I hadn't eaten at the post-corrida party. Sex always gives me a hearty appetite, and on this morning my appetite was as healthy as I could remember. I surveyed my battered face in the mirror and decided I was not terminal. I took another long, hot shower, although I was loath to wash the traces of Carmen away, and then I put on the cleaner of my two dirty shirts and went out to breakfast.

There was a bright little café I hadn't noticed before not too far from the hotel, and I went in and ordered and devoured a plate of scrambled eggs and chorizo, that wonderful hot Mexican sausage that tastes so good you try not to think about what might be in it, and with my coffee I drank a Corona beer to help cool off the chorizo's fire. Quite a breakfast. I even polished off an extra order of corn tortillas dripping with butter, and it still didn't fill me up, but I made do because I have to think about my waistline. I'm not eighteen anymore, and meals like that tend to settle around my midsection and make it tough for me to wear the kind of tailored shirts I like so much, and that reminded me that if I was going to stay in Tijuana much longer I would need some more shirts. I bought three of them on the way back to the hotel, not expensive ones this time, but good, serviceable oxford cloth dress shirts, one blue, one yellow and one white. I couldn't find a pink one in my size.

I strolled back to the hotel. Now that the weekending crowds of *norteamericanos* had gone back home, Tijuana was a sleepy little border town again, the traffic had thinned to its normal brisk pace, and once more the language heard most often on the streets was Spanish.

When I got to the hotel lobby there were three men sitting on the cheap, uncomfortable furniture, looking at me. As I walked through the door they conferred briefly, stood up, and walked toward me. I sighed, shifting the bag with the shirts to under my left elbow. I put my right hand in my pocket and wrapped my fist around my key ring with the point of my car key protruding out between my knuckles. If I were to take another beating, I vowed I would count coup on my enemies before I went down.

But these men were different. They were middle-aged, for one thing, and their eyes showed no animosity. In fact, their demeanor was almost obsequious, and that made me more uncomfortable than hostility would have. I don't enjoy being bowed and scraped to.

"Pardon, señor," said the oldest and shortest of the three. "Your name is Señor Saxon?"

"It is."

"Is it permitted we might speak to you?"

"Go ahead."

"Is there somewhere we can speak alone?"

"I'm a little busy," I said.

"It is a matter of some importance." His eyes beseeched me.

Nacio was glaring at me from his post. It seemed he was on duty twenty-four hours a day, as I had yet to see anyone else back there behind the desk. I think it was more to jerk his chain than for any other reason that I invited the three men to come upstairs with me. I hoped the maid had been in to clean while I was out having breakfast, because between the burglars doing their thing and Carmen and I doing ours, the room had been in no shape for company when I left.

In the elevator the shortest of the three, obviously the group spokesman, introduced himself with a string of seven names, ending up with Mendez. He told me who the other two were and we all shook hands—hard, horny, work-worn hands they all had—but I forgot their names at once because neither of them spoke a word all the time we were together. I knew they spoke English, because from time to time they would react with nods or smiles or looks of apprehension to my conversation with Mendez, but they remained silent partners in this little game we were about to play. We got off the elevator and went to my room, which to my relief had been pretty well restored to its original condition by the maid, cleaned and dusted with the bed neatly made up. A smell of Lysol lingered in the air.

The three men stood with their hats in their hands until I invited them to sit. There was only one chair, and none of them were about to seat themselves on my bed, so they remained standing. I still wasn't feeling that terrific, so I sat on the edge of the bed, looking at Mendez and waiting for him to speak. After all, this party was his idea.

He stayed a respectful distance away from me and cleared the frog from his throat like a fourth grader at show-and-tell. He was obviously a poor man, but he had worn his good clothes to come and see me. The suit was a kind of greenish-blue or bluish-green, I couldn't decide, and the stains and strains of a hundred wearings had not been completely washed or dry-cleaned away, but it was clean, as was the white shirt with the fraying collar, and the necktie so cheap it hung straight and cardboard stiff. He was ill-at-ease to the point of fright, as were his companions, and I tried to lighten things up and make them more sociable by offering to order up some coffee or breakfast from room service, which was a pretty iffy proposition at best in a Tijuana hotel. They declined with effusive thanks, and I remembered vaguely my high school Spanish teacher at Saint Aloysius back in Chicago, Sister Gabriel, explaining that in Spanish-speaking countries it was considered impolite to offer anything to a guest less than three times, a point she had illustrated by pantomiming peeling her fountain pen like a banana and vouchsafing it to the class thrice. Earnestly I made the coffee tender twice more, and dutifully they refused, each time with a more sincere outpouring of gratitude. I didn't think, in my current condition, that I could get through too many more cultural amenities.

"Is there something I can help you gentlemen with?" I said. Such abruptness might not have been according to the Mexican Amy Vanderbilt, but I was tired of playing charades.

"Señor Saxon," Mendez said, "I have three children. Two fine sons are fifteen and eighteen, and a beautiful daughter who is seventeen."

He stopped. I said, "Congratulations."

"These men also have children. We would wish for our children to have a decent life. To have a better life than we have had." He stopped again.

I said, "Well, that's a good thing to wish for."

"We wish for them that they may live and work up north in your wonderful country, the United States." He pronounced the final word as though it had an *e* at the beginning. He was looking at me almost eagerly. The next move was obviously mine—I just didn't know what it was.

"Yes?" I finally said.

"Yes," Mendez said.

Silencio. A long *silencio.*

Mendez said at last, "We have some money." He took an envelope from his breast pocket and proffered it to me. It was not sealed. Inside there were twenty U.S. one-hundred-dollar bills. The other two men also removed envelopes from their suit pockets and extended them. I handed the money back to Mendez. I didn't know what he was talking about, and I told him so.

"No comprendo," I said. It's amazing how much high school Spanish comes back to you.

"We wish," Mendez said, and then faltered. He took a big bite of air to compose himself and began again. "We wish that the señor be kind enough to help us."

"How can I help?"

"To get our children across the border."

I said, "You mean, illegally?" Sometimes I think I'm not very bright at all.

Mendez looked down at his scuffed old shoes as though he'd proposed something shameful.

"I can't get anybody across the border. I can't even get out of this town myself."

"*Por favor,* señor. As you see, we can pay."

"I can see that," I said. "But I'm just a tourist. I can't smuggle—help anyone leave Mexico."

Mendez only nodded sadly at me. He didn't believe a word of what I was saying, but he was either too polite or too frightened to insinuate that I was not being truthful.

"Really," I assured them. "I'd like to help you out, but I don't know how. I can't."

They all just kept smiling their sad, accepting smiles. They sure weren't giving me much information, or many conversational strokes, for that matter. I felt like a stand-up comic who had run out of saves when his act was bombing. And I still didn't know what the hell they were doing there. Perhaps this was some new scam the locals pulled with well-dressed tourists who came through the border checkpoint in search of bullfighting, bargains, jai alai, whores, or dope.

I said, "Why do you come to me, Señor Mendez?"

He shrugged politely. He did everything politely, and it was beginning to unnerve me. It was the way non-Catholics often act in the presence of a nun.

"You are a friend of the *patrón,* Don Rafael?" he said.

"Iglesias?"

"You were at his box at the corrida. You were a friend of the *abogado,* Swanner?"

I flashed back to the previous Friday morning—was that a hundred years ago or more?—in Martin Swanner's office in Los Angeles, to the desperate and downtrodden and beaten faces in his reception area, to the old lady in black with eyes like burn holes cut in a brown blanket, to perky little Debbie with the overweight upper arms telling me that Swanner's legal specialty was mostly immigration law—"You know, green cards and stuff." The precious green card gave an alien an identity in the United States, automatically changed him from a hunted fugitive who lived in the dark and moved from one address to another each week to keep one step ahead of the immigration cops to a respected member of the community with every legal right to be there, to work and enjoy the benefits of a prosperous and free society, although in actuality it didn't often turn out that way.

I remembered, too, Rafael Iglesias sitting in the hot afternoon light at El Toreo de Tijuana telling me that Martin Swanner was a business associate as well as a friend, and the scope of their association began to come clear to me. The Mexicans would pay

Iglesias to smuggle them across the border illegally, and when they arrived in Los Angeles they were funneled into Martin Swanner's tender care. He would either hit them up for more money and allow them to stay and get a green card, or he would turn them over to Jesus Delgado, who would use them for whatever his needs were at any given moment: burglary, prostitution, drug running. It was a neat little hustle, all right, and these three poor bastards thought I was part of the program simply because their jungle drums had told them I was sitting talking to Iglesias at the bullfights. Apparently in a city as small as Tijuana Iglesias couldn't scratch his behind without everyone in town knowing about it, discussing it, and analyzing the meaning of it.

"Why don't you approach Don Rafael directly?" I said.

Mendez shook his head sadly, staring at his shoe tops again. "We are afraid."

"Of what?"

"Don Rafael is a rich and powerful man. He wants much money. He wants twelve hundred dollars for each person in our families to go north. We are poor men, señor; we cannot pay such a sum. We thought perhaps if we came and spoke to you directly . . . We have heard people of your country are kind and compassionate. We thought that the money we have saved would be . . . *suficiente*." He indicated his two friends. "We each have two thousand of your dollars," he said. "That is much money for you."

It was much money for me, but it was a king's ransom to them. I said, "I'm sorry, Señor Mendez. I hardly know Don Rafael and the others. I am down here looking for someone, a young American girl. I hoped that Señor Iglesias could help me find her."

Mendez waggled his arms like a marionette.

"I still don't see why you are afraid to go direct to Iglesias."

"We have heard things," he said. "I do not wish to repeat

them because I can not say if they are truly so. But we have heard some things. We have daughters, señor." He ducked his head, and I felt his shame too.

"If we go to Don Rafael, and these things we hear are true, then we must kill him. For the honor of our families. And we are afraid of him, señor. He has protection. He has people everywhere in this city. It would cost us our lives and perhaps the lives of our families as well. So we thought that you, being of another culture, would perhaps be more *simpático* and would help us. Without shaming us. Without taking our honor."

I looked at the other two men, who nodded, corroborating Mendez's words and sharing his humiliation as well. "Gentlemen," I said awkwardly, "I'm sorry to disappoint you. But I only met Don Rafael yesterday. I'm not . . . in the same business. I have no resources to help you."

Mendez's shoulders slumped, and with profound resignation he put the envelope full of his life's savings back into his inside pocket. For a wild, brief moment I was ready to spirit his entire family into the United States in the trunk of my Le Baron. For free. But I was in enough trouble with the Mexican police already and was not about to add alien running to the list of my real and imagined offenses. The three men were filing from my room as if I'd just examined their X rays and pronounced them positive. I watched them go with frustration and regret. I was feeling low about the whole business and wished with all my heart there were something, anything, I could do to help them. I was imagining how long and hard they had all labored to sock away two thousand dollars or so each. My God, I knew how long it would take *me* to put aside two thousand dollars.

Which reminded me I was down here to earn some money of my own, considerably more than two thousand dollars, although by the time I paid off some debts, took care of Marvel's tuition for the next school year, and gave Jo the raise I'd been promising her there wouldn't be much more than that left of Mark Evering's fee. I began riffling the pages of the phone book to locate Pepe Morales. There were only about ten million people named Morales in the Tijuana directory, but I hoped there would be some sort of guild or association that dealt with bullfighters and the like. If not, perhaps I could go back to my friend at the newspaper office and pay another ten dollars for some more information.

I decided to call Jo in Los Angeles. She had no doubt been expecting me back that morning and would be fussing and worrying and raising hell if I didn't call and let her know I was alive and reasonably healthy.

"I've been worried sick," she said predictably. Having Jo in my life was a lot like having a wife without any of the fun. "Why didn't you call me?"

"I am calling you," I reminded her.

"I called Marvel at the house, I had Marsh drive by. I was starting to check the hospitals."

"And the jails?"

"You aren't funny. Where are you?"

I told her.

"Tijuana? What are you doing in Tijuana?"

"I just had this overwhelming urge to see a stage show with three girls and a donkey," I said. "Any calls?"

I heard papers rustling. Jo's desk was always a total disaster area, unlike mine, which was compulsively neat. "Mark Evering called for a progress report."

"Did you tell him where I was?"

"I didn't *know* where you were, remember? And if I had I wouldn't have told him. That's against the rules."

"Anyone else call?"

"Somebody from Mastercard, this morning. They aren't very happy with you."

"I'm not very happy with them. Tell them that when they call back."

"Anything I can do?"

"Run down to the hall of public records and see who the principals are in a firm called The Allegiance Corporation. I'll check back with you tomorrow. If you can, look in on Marvel, see if he needs anything, maybe give him a few bucks to tide him over. That would be great."

"Do you want me to stay over there with him tonight?"

"If you can stand to be away from that big stud hunk of a husband for one night, I'd really appreciate it. Otherwise you could take Marvel somewhere for dinner."

"Okay," she said. "We were going to eat deli tonight anyway. We'll just stop by and get him first. He loves deli."

I sighed. My young charge was going to be the only black kid in Los Angeles with a twenty-dollar-a-day matzoh ball habit.

"Okay," I said, "but no halvah afterward unless he eats all his knishes."

"When are you coming home?"

"Miss me?"

"Get serious, will you?"

"If I ever get serious, look out Marshall Zeidler."

"Well, when *are* you?"

"Getting serious?"

Sigh. "Coming home."

I debated telling her I'd been asked not to leave Tijuana, but I thought better of it. I also eliminated any mention of the murder or my getting beaten up. And I didn't mention Carmen. Jo might be married to Marsh, the Writing Waiter or, as I called him, the Waiting Writer, but she was as blue-nosed about my erotic adventures as if she were *my* wife. She thought I was overdue for settling down with a nice girl some place with a picket fence and honeysuckle vines and had once even gone so far as to introduce me to the sister of a friend of hers, who was a dental assistant with thighs like Walter Payton's.

"I don't know when I'll be back," I told Jo. "This may take a bit longer than I thought."

"What shall I tell Mark Evering if he calls again?"

"Tell him that you loved his last picture and saw it four times. That should keep him happy for days." We hung up laughing. I loved Jo very much, and I knew it was she that kept Saxon Investigations afloat, juggling the books, dunning the slow-pays, acting as Marvel's surrogate mother, and occasionally pulling off a neat bit of detective work. Loyal and good friends like Jo are an endangered species and should be protected and treasured.

I was continuing my perusal of the Tijuana phone book when I heard a heavy tread out in the corridor and a knock on the door like the first swing of the wrecking ball. I wasn't surprised to find Sergeant Ochoa and Officer Cruz on the other side of the door. They came in without waiting for an invitation, and Cruz slammed the door much harder than necessary. I just heaved a tired sigh, because I'd been slapped around enough since crossing the border and I wasn't in the mood for any more of it.

Ochoa asked me, "What happened to your face?"

"I cut myself shaving."

"You always shave behind your ear?"

"Sergeant Ochoa, is there something in particular you want? Because if not, I have things to do."

"Listen, Saxon," he said evenly, "I don't like you much, so don't give me no shit." He pronounced it "chit," which afforded me a great deal of merriment. I had the wisdom to keep it to myself.

"Where were you yesterday?" he asked abruptly. While we were talking Cruz was poking through my things, fingering my dirty clothing. It angered me. It was one violation too many.

I called out, "You have a warrant for that?"

"Stupid!" Ochoa said. "Where do you think you are? Don't come to my country and quote your laws! Now, where were you yesterday?"

"I went to the bullfights," I said, glowering at Cruz, who had opened the closet door and was going through my pockets. "Then I had a drink with one of the matadors, which you well know because you were there, Sergeant. Then I kicked someone in the balls in a parking lot, which you probably also know. After that I went to the newspaper office and did some research. You can check that very easily with the woman who was on duty there. I gave her some *mordida* for her cooperation. On my way back to the hotel I was mugged, which is why my face looks like the inside of a burrito, and then I came back to the room here to find that I'd had visitors who did a much better job of searching the place than Officer Cruz is doing now."

"What were they looking for?"

"I haven't any idea."

"Was anything missing?"

I debated mentioning my stolen gun and decided against it. "Nothing."

Cruz's huge bulk disappeared into the closet.

"You were alone?"

"Look, what's the point of all this?"

"I'll ask the questions," Ochoa said.

Cruz came out of the closet with my bloody shirt from the night before, held it up, then went back inside. Ochoa looked at me.

I was annoyed, and when I snapped, "I told you I got mugged," I guess it showed.

Ochoa bellied up to me. "You watch your fucking tone of voice when you talk to me," he roared in my face. Right about then I knew I was in trouble, although I didn't yet realize why.

Ochoa took out a cigarette and stuck it in the corner of his mouth. He didn't light it, but just seeing it there made me want one. We seemed to be having a staring contest, and for some reason it was important for me to win. I might have, too, had not Officer Cruz lumbered out of the closet again like a bear from its den at the end of hibernation season. In one hand was my tweed jacket, which he offered to Ochoa to look at.

Ochoa examined the jacket carefully. I didn't know what he found so interesting, but I somehow didn't think he was into labels. Then he said, "You have a button missing, Saxon."

He showed me. The bottom button was indeed not there.

"The curse of bachelorhood."

"Where'd you lose the button?"

"If I knew where I lost it, it wouldn't be lost."

Ochoa glanced at Cruz, and one of those big hands came crashing into the side of my head. Cruz was into openhanded slaps. Of course, when you have a hand the size of a walrus's flipper there's no real need to make a fist. The slap lifted me off my feet and threw me halfway across the bed. This time I bounced back upright, ready on instinct to defend myself until I realized I didn't have a chance, that I was all out of chances. I glowered at Ochoa.

"I'm going to ask you one more time," he said. "Where did you lose the button? And watch your smart mouth before you answer."

"I told you someone broke in here and searched the room while I was gone. They also searched my clothes. I guess the button probably came off then. Look on the closet floor, you might find it."

"I've already found it," Ochoa said, reaching into his pocket and taking out what looked to me like a Ziploc sandwich bag containing a button. He compared it to the one still on my jacket, and I had to admit it was a match.

"Where'd you get that?"

Ochoa nodded to Cruz once more and all of a sudden I was face down on a bed again with the big Mexican cop kneeling on the small of my back, except this time he twisted both my hands up behind me and was snapping a pair of handcuffs on my wrists, tight enough to seriously impair the circulation in my fingers.

"You are under arrest, Señor Saxon," Ochoa said.

I worked my head around so that my face wasn't buried in the bedcovers. "On what charge?"

He said "For the murder of Rafael Iglesias."

7

They didn't throw me into a miserable, rat-infested cell. Not right away. Instead they left me in a locked room for most of the day, furnished with nothing but a straight-backed chair and a rickety table, with nothing to do, no one to talk to, and nothing to read except a two-year-old copy of the San Diego classified telephone directory. They took away my cigarettes and matches, and they took away my belt in imitation of American television cop shows. I wasn't likely to try to hang myself from the light fixture, because the only one in the room was a 60-watt bulb swinging from a frayed cord, and I didn't think it would have held my weight. I always wear loafers, or I'm sure they would have taken my shoelaces as well. I do know it was several hours that they left me in splendid isolation to think about things, and I can't be any more specific than that because they also took my watch. No phone calls and nothing to eat or drink, which of course saved them the bother of having someone take me to the bathroom. The chorizo I had for breakfast that morning was beginning to solidify in my stomach like a hot stone, and I didn't feel very well. It was a long day. Solitude is a wonderful way to soften up a prisoner, as I'm sure they discovered on page 243A of the jailer's manual. I began reading the yellow pages but couldn't seem to get hooked on the plot. I had worked my way through Furniture, Unfinished and was just about to get into Garbage when Ochoa and Cruz came to get me. I'd been alone so many hours I was even glad to see them. One of my many mistakes.

Ochoa took the one chair in the room, which left me standing almost at attention and Cruz lounging against the wall as if he were holding up the building. He probably could have. Ochoa put a cigarette in the corner of his mouth but didn't light it. Again it made me want one very much.

"How about," Ochoa said, "you tell me what you're really doing down here in Tijuana?"

"I already explained that the first time we met. I'm a private investigator from Los Angeles. I'm looking for a young girl, and my information was that she was probably with Martin Swanner. Since he's dead, I've been talking with his associates to see if I can get a line on where she is."

"And now one of his associates is dead as well, no?"

I shrugged. "I had nothing to do with that."

"Didn't you?"

"I think you know I didn't."

"I don't know nothing. I'm just a dumb cop." He took the directory from me and thumbed through it for a moment, then pushed it away. "You are *muy interesante,* Saxon. You come to Tijuana and ask every bartender and hotel clerk in town about Martin Swanner. Ten minutes after he's killed you show up in the room where he died. Then you go skulking around the hotel room where he is registered at Pajarito." I started to say something but he put up a hand to stop me. "Sure, the officer saw you there and made a report. I knew right away it was you. The description: tall, good-looking gringo with gray hair, look like a movie star. You think we're just stupid beaners or something?"

"No way," I admitted.

"Next thing is you show up at the corrida with Swanner's tickets. You make polite conversation with Don Rafael, you get invited to his party, and then you insult him publicly. You insult Pepe Morales as well. I know, I was there."

"I remember," I said. "You have rich friends."

His eyes narrowed. "Then you try to run down some of Señor Iglesias's friends in the parking lot with your car. A few hours later, Iglesias is murdered in a vacant lot near your hotel, killed the same way like Swanner, with his stomach cut open and his insides on the ground. We find a button in his hand that belongs on your jacket. And when we come to ask you about it, your face is all smashed to shit."

Damn it, he said "chit" again, and I had this totally irrational urge to laugh. Once more I opted for self-control.

"Now, if you were me, wouldn't you think that you had something to do with both these killings? I can't believe you are so *estúpido* that you think you could get away with it."

"I'm not trying to get away with anything. I never met Swanner and I hardly knew Iglesias."

"Why did you pick a fight with him at the party, then?"

"I wanted some answers about Merissa, this girl I'm looking for. I thought Iglesias and Morales were lying about not knowing her, and I was trying to shake them up."

"You say."

"That's right, I say. Look, I'm entitled to one phone call."

"You're entitled to shit," he said, doing it again. "Now I want some answers. In one fucking hell of a hurry."

"I'd like a few myself," I said. "But I'm afraid I don't have any of yours, because I don't know anything about Swanner and Iglesias. All I know is I've been set up. Whoever tossed my room took that button and planted it where you'd find it. And I want to talk to the U.S. consulate. Right now!"

Ochoa made some sort of sign to Cruz. The big dumb son of a bitch must have been trained to respond to hand signals, like a killer whale at Sea World. Yes, very like a whale, I thought a moment later on my hands and knees, looking at my half digested breakfast on the floor, the imprint of Cruz's fist still making a crimp in my stomach.

About two seconds before I might have caught my breath, Cruz hauled me to my feet by the hair and slammed me against the stucco wall hard enough for me to bounce. I watched, almost detached from the proceedings, like a casual observer, as Cruz picked up the San Diego phone directory and with his huge, strong hands folded it lengthwise as easily as if it had been a campaign pamphlet, and I knew this was going to be different from those three angry men in the alley. These guys knew what they were doing, and how to do it in such a way that it would last a long while.

Cruz swung the phone book at me, catching me in the middle of the forehead, and all the bombs bursting in air that we sing about in our national anthem went off inside my head, and I went down to my knees, not falling so much as crumpling, sinking into a sickly yellowish quicksand of semiconsciousness where the only part that wasn't numb was the nauseating agony behind my eyes.

The first thing to penetrate my awareness in any real way was the smell. Even before I opened my eyes, even before I became fully cognizant that I was in an inordinate amount of pain, I was accosted by the odor: human waste and stale sweat and disinfectant in almost equal parts. The stench was almost worse than the torture rack that had hold of my head and neck and abdomen and ribs and back. When at last the yellow light bulb swam into fuzzy view, when I was finally able to wrestle my aching brain into a thinking mode so that I was aware that the smallest inhalation of breath brought agony to me all over my body, my surroundings took shape like the image on exposed photographic paper when it is sloshed around in the development fluids. I was in a stinking cell in the main jail of Tijuana, Baja California, Mexico, under suspicion for two particularly brutal murders, and I had spent a few hours being bashed around with a telephone directory to get me to confess to them, and the stink was emanating from an open toilet that probably had not been cleaned out since the days of Emiliano Zapata, and from my cellmates—winos, bums, petty thieves, pickpockets, and for all I knew, hatchet murderers, child rapists, and international terrorists. Whether they had been in jail for a day or a year, they all looked the same: gray, haggard, lifeless, and squashed. And I was one of them, the newest pledge to their fraternity of hopelessness.

I was lying on the filthy floor in the corner, and one of the prisoners, a scrawny, elderly Mexican with the sallow skin and dead eyes of a longtime rum-pot, gray hair lank and thin against his scalp, was looming over me, going through the pockets of my jacket, which had evidently been thrown on top of me when the authorities had dumped me in here like a sack of week-old garbage. He held the photo of Merissa in his hand.

I sat up as quickly as I could, my damaged stomach muscles shrieking a protest. I grabbed the front of the man's cheap, dirty shirt with one hand and snatched my jacket from him with the other. My head felt as if it were the size of a large pumpkin, and every centimeter of me throbbed with malaise as I pulled myself to my feet, the room doing loop-the-loops and Immelmann turns all around me. I stalked the cringing little man across the cell, not sure if my upraised fist or my face was frightening him more. I must have resembled the second runner-up in the Notre Dame gargoyle look-alike contest. The last thing I felt like doing was fighting, but I knew enough about jails to figure if I didn't assert myself my other cellmates would steal the undershorts right off my body and then do all sorts of things to me I'd just as soon not imagine.

The little man put up his hands to ward off a blow, all the while babbling, *"No, señor, por favor, por favor,"* and I really didn't have the stomach to hit him anyway, and then he said in heavily accented English, "The girl. I know the girl."

That stopped my fist. "What?" I said stupidly. My brain still wasn't functioning at full capacity. "What girl?"

The other unfortunates in the cell were watchful, wary, ready for anything, as the little man waved Merissa Evering's picture under my bloodied nose. "I know the girl," he said again. I was dizzy, and when I shook my head to clear it, whatever was loose inside it went clang-a-lang-a-lang and I thought for a minute I would pass out again, but then the room stopped bucking and pitching and I said, "This girl?"

He nodded, his head bobbing up and down like one of those fuzz-covered plastic boxer dogs in the rear windows of vintage Chevrolets, and he said, "Sí, sí," and I wondered if he always said everything twice.

"Where is she?"

He lowered his eyes the way Mendez had, and shook his head to indicate he wasn't going to tell me. I gathered his shirtfront in my hand again and raised my fist, and now I became aware of a collective intake of breath, straightening of backs, edging forward on the balls of feet. I was probably going to have to fight the whole bunch of them, and in my current condition I doubted if I'd last twenty seconds. But the little man cringed away from me, more frightened than I was.

And then he told me, in his broken English, that the girl in the picture was a *puta*—a whore—working out of a sleazy hookshop in downtown Tijuana, just a block off the Avenida de la Revolución.

8

Have you ever been to jail? I don't mean visiting, or on a civic-minded tour to observe conditions, I mean as a resident guest. Most people haven't ever seen the inside of a jail, unless it's for driving under the influence or getting caught with a pocket full of grass, or maybe getting nailed for that forgotten parking ticket from 1983. So they have no concept of what it's really like. It's pretty frightening. And degrading. And dehumanizing and intimidating and demoralizing and all those other adjectives they use to complain about prisons in the liberal press. But when you get arrested in the U.S.A., scared as you might be at the time, you know you can call your lawyer or your lover or your mom or your best friend and somehow get bailed out. But now I was hunkered down on the floor of a filthy, bug-crawly Mexican jail cell with twenty criminals who didn't speak English and wanted to steal my clothes. I was suspected of committing two murders and had every expectation that I would be beaten regularly until I confessed to those murders. And there was no one to call. The only one who even knew I'd gone to Tijuana was Jo, and by the time she figured out I was missing, checked the jails, called the consulate and got the ponderous wheels of Mexican justice rolling, there might not be enough left of me to sweep into a paper bag. I've bitched about it in the past, but here in this border town hoosegow I began to have a great deal of respect for the American system of justice. I was as frightened as a little kid on the first day of kindergarten who thought his mother was dumping him in a strange place and going away for good.

I've been scared before. I just barely got out of the way of a hammerhead shark once while skin-diving alone in the

Bahamas, which taught me that the buddy system is more than the title of a flop Richard Dreyfuss movie. I was in a compact car that was hit broadside and rolled over three times on a Georgia highway. I've even been shot at on several occasions. But this was the first instance in which I'd had the luxury of time to think about my predicament. I had the leisure hours to wonder when my next drink of Scotch might be, my next decent meal, my next hot bath, my next woman, my next breath of clean air. I didn't even know when, or if, I would ever see the sky again, or whether I'd survive the next beating, or the one after that.

Realities and fevered fantasies and some pretty bizarre scenarios tumbled around in my abused head like lacy underthings in a Laundromat dryer, always changing shape and position but yet remaining essentially the same. I wanted to yell for help, but none would be forthcoming. I wanted to cry. I wanted my mother! But she had lain these many years under a gray sky and a white marble stone in the churchyard behind the rectory of Saint Aloysius Roman Catholic Church on the North Side of Chicago and could no longer comfort me and reassure me and kiss me where it hurt. And it hurt bad.

There seemed to be nowhere to turn for assistance. I gravely doubted Mark Evering had the same kind of clout with the Mexican police as he did when it came to getting a good table at L'Ermitage. Besides, I was half convinced he was the guy who had put me here in the first place with a clever and well-orchestrated frame. I knew someone was setting me up to fall for murder, and Evering, who had started this whole thing with his missing daughter, was as likely a candidate as any.

Unless I was experiencing blackouts during which I committed strange and unspeakable acts I could not remember, I hadn't killed anyone. I had no reason to. Yet the evidence against me seemed pretty compelling, and I understood Ochoa's suspicions. Someone was obviously setting me up, and Mark

Evering and his lovely wife Brandy were the first names that came to mind. It was more than possible that Evering might have wanted Martin Swanner dead because of his involvement with Merissa, or maybe for plain old business reasons, and had put me on his trail so that I'd be conveniently present when the lawyer checked out. I was a ready-made suspect who would keep the police from looking any further. That was a strong possibility. I certainly didn't know anyone in Tijuana or its environs, or at least I hadn't up until the time that Martin Swanner had been murdered and I had received that mysterious note summoning me to the place of his death in time to walk into the arms of Ochoa and Cruz.

That still didn't explain the killing of Don Rafael Iglesias, or why I had been nailed for that one as well.

Of the acquaintances I'd made or renewed since crossing the border, I could put Jesus Delgado on the top of my suspect list. From what I knew of him, murder wasn't one of his specialties—he usually concentrated on extortion, blackmail, intimidation, drug dealing, and whore mongering—but we all grow a little every day, even the scum, and maybe Delgado was expanding his horizons. Right behind him came the handsome bullfighter, Pepe Morales, who played Swanner's kinky sex games with him by night, prayed to his patron saint by day, and served as idol and role model for the youth of Mexico on sunny Sunday afternoons at El Toreo de Tijuana. Señor Mendez and his friends, who seemingly didn't have the nerve to squash a cockroach, were also contenders, despite their appearance of subservience—I've been across the street enough times to know that appearances can be deceiving. I could hardly forget Sergeant Ochoa sitting there at Iglesias's table with the likes of a cheap crook like Jesus Delgado, or the way he watched while his Neanderthal buddy Cruz spent half the night smashing me in the head and kidneys with a rolled-up telephone directory. Nor had I ruled out my unknown assailants from the alley, who seemed to have their own agenda, which was all mixed up with Swanner and his crowd.

There was Sharon, too, of course, she of the round heels and the bitter memories of Martin Swanner and his kinks and perfidies and perversions. But she didn't fit the role of framer and murderer. And she'd had no idea I was going to Mexico when I put on my pants and left her little apartment over a garage in Laguna Beach. I'd have to call Sharon a long shot.

And what of Carmen? I couldn't allow my feeling for her to obscure the possibility that her involvement in this whole affair might be more than a simple case of mutual hot pants. She was the wife, now the widow, of one of Tijuana's heaviest hitters. How much she might know about the death of her husband and his partner, or the damning evidence that seemed to drop a snug noose around my stuck-out neck, was a matter to be considered.

Apart from wondering who was trying to have me shot at sunrise for murder, I was extremely frustrated about Merissa Evering, the girl I'd been sent to find, the girl I'd never met. I now knew where she was, if the old guy was telling the truth, but I couldn't do anything about it. I wanted to find out why a beautiful woman whose father was one of the richest and most influential producers in the movie industry was turning tricks for nickels in a Tijuana whorehouse, if only I could get out of jail and ask her. But I didn't see much chance of that.

In my delirium I fantasized a prison break, complete with Pat O'Brien as the tough, street-smart priest telling me to throw down my gun, Rocky, because I didn't have a chance. It must have been fever-induced, because I had no gun to throw down and I was pretty sure the local priest would not have had a lilting Killarney brogue and a face like the map of Ireland. Besides, in the movies jailbreaks always start in the laundry or the library, and from what I could see the jail I was in had neither.

Also, if I were to break out of the building I didn't imagine I'd last more than ten minutes on the streets before I was spotted and rearrested. A bloody and battered Anglo with a thick shock of gray hair and a face that had been used for heavy-bag practice had to be a noteworthy sight on Tijuana's busy boulevards. And I didn't even want to think of what Cruz might do to me after my recapture.

Almost more frightening than anything else was the fact that I had no plan. I always map things out carefully ahead of time to avoid surprises, but being arrested had not occurred to me, and I just couldn't seem to figure a logical way out of my present pickle. I tried to ignore the problem by going to sleep, but the sights and sounds and smells of my environment mingled with troubled dreams about San Diego phone books and disemboweled corpses, so I was better off staying awake and dealing with the throbbing in my head and back.

When a guard came and got me out of the drunk tank I assumed it was for another round of heavy interrogation. I flirted briefly with the idea of taking Officer Cruz out with one well-placed karate blow to the carotid artery and then letting them kill me quickly and mercifully, a fate preferable to languishing in a filthy cell and letting them beat me to death slowly over a period of weeks. But to my immense relief and astonishment I was led to the front desk, where I was given back belt, wristwatch, cigarettes, and other personal effects. I counted the money and it was all there. Then I was taken to Ochoa's private office, which was a scant improvement over the interrogation room, in that it had several chairs in it and a window overlooking the street. It also did not have Officer Cruz, nor a phone directory.

It did have Sergeant Ochoa, grim and tight-faced. It also had Carmen Iglesias. Today she was a vision in several shades of beige silk and chiffon, looking as out of place in this grubby station house as a zit on the nose of Miss America.

"You are free to go, Saxon," Ochoa said. He didn't want to say it. It cost him dearly. His voice fairly dripped with dislike and distaste as he nodded his head toward Carmen. "The señora has given you an alibi."

I looked at her. Her chocolate eyes were huge. She had been crying.

"She said she was with you in your hotel room at the time of her husband's death." His words had honed edges like Gillette Blue Blades. "Somewhere around midnight."

She had saved me, and I knew what it must have cost her in the way of pride and reputation. She had come here to tell this hard, mean Mexican cop that she'd spent the night in the bed of a foreigner while her husband was lying dead in an alley nearby. In Ochoa's eyes, and in the eyes of the community as well, she would now be no better than a whore. Hispanics take their infidelity pretty seriously, especially when it is the wife who has sinned. For me, a man whose bed she had shared but whom she hardly knew, she had brought the scorn of her countrymen down upon her head, only fortunate that public stonings of adulteresses were a thing of the past. I wanted to enfold her in my arms and kiss those eyes and thank her, to tell her I understood her sacrifice and appreciated it all the more, but we were both acutely aware of Ochoa's unwelcome presence in the room.

I wheeled on the policeman, my relief clouding my better judgment. "I've been falsely arrested and imprisoned here," I snarled, "and I've been tortured. I intend to contact the U.S. consulate the second I walk out of here. This is an outrage. And if you plan on hauling me in here a third time and letting your pet ape beat on me some more, you'd better think twice about it and kill me on the street, because I'll take him down with me, and you, too, if I get the chance! Paybacks are rough, Sergeant."

Ochoa raised his hands to let me know he was all too human and that everyone makes mistakes. I didn't have much self-control left, and I was itching to bust him in the nose, but I knew if I did I'd be back in the cell, this time guilty as charged.

Ochoa smiled at Carmen with his mouth, while his eyes were lumps of coal without depth or warmth. "*Por favor,* señora, may I have a moment alone with Mr. Saxon?"

"I'll wait for you outside," she said to me, giving him a dubious glance, and left the small office.

Ochoa turned back to me, and I wondered if this might be the preliminary to a little private Marquis of Queensberry right there in the police station. If he'd be willing to make it unofficial, I'd go for it. Gladly. But he only said, "Saxon, I don't like pulling the wrong guy in here. It don't make me look good with my superiors, you know. But if I had to bring in an innocent man and give him a hard time, then you'd have been my first choice. You have a big smart mouth, you think you're so much better than everyone else, and you talk tough. But you are dumb, amigo. You are one dumb gringo *maricón*."

"You've said that before, Ochoa. Is that your best shot?"

"You want some advice?"

"No," I said.

"You come to Mexico, where you don't even know the language, flashing pictures of some American girl, and you get up to your ass in murder. Instead of getting out while you can and cutting your losses, you jump in with both feet and splash some more shit around"—God, I wished he'd learn to say that word correctly!—"and get all tangled up in a second murder, and wind up fucking the wife of the victim. You have no friends down here, Saxon. No backup. No Los Angeles police pals, no informers. You're all alone on the streets, like a stalking wolf who's been separated from the pack. You're gonna wind up taking the fall for this, amigo, one way or the other. You're playing with some pretty heavy people down here."

I rubbed my eyes with thumb and forefinger, trying to quiet the timpani that was working overtime in my skull. "*Muchas gracias* for the advice, sergeant. But while you're looking for someone to take the rap for a double murder, where were *you* when your pals Swanner and Iglesias were taken out?"

His mouth closed tight like a bear trap snapping shut, and I could tell by the way he was flexing his fingers that he wanted some more of me. But I had been cleared of charges, and he didn't dare put his hands on me again. He didn't say anything more. He turned his back on me and went behind his desk and sat down, making a big show of opening the file in front of him and busying himself studying it. He figured if he ignored me long enough I'd go away. He was right.

I went out of his office, past the front desk where the gargantuan Cruz was chatting up the pretty policewoman on duty there. Carmen was at the curb waiting for me, the motor of her big Cadillac purring softly.

How do you articulate gratitude to someone who has just awakened you from the worst nightmare of your life? I thought of several ways and then settled for cupping her face in my hands and looking at those big brown eyes shining in the light of the streetlamp. That's all it took.

She drove me back to my hotel, and we didn't speak to each other in the car, nor even when we were back in my room. I climbed out of my filthy, stained clothes and showered, standing under the spray for so long that finally the hot water gave out. I shaved with difficulty. I was trembling and my arms ached almost too much to lift them as high as my head. My face was more than sore. Afterward I felt less like a hobo, but I could do nothing to alter my Grand Guignol appearance. My forehead was swollen up so I looked like Karloff as Frankenstein, and it was a funny blue color. My eyes were puffed half shut. I put a towel around my waist and went back out into the bedroom. I felt bad.

She had turned down the covers of the bed and was sitting on the edge waiting for me, and I lay down next to her with a loud, involuntary groan. She smiled a pitying smile at me, and put her hand on my bare chest. I took it and held it close to me, first to my chest and then to my face. It smelled good, of soap and perfume and that special smell that was Carmen's alone.

"I'm sorry," I said. "About your husband, I mean."

She shook her head, not looking at me. "No," she said. "He was a pig. But—" She shuddered. "They cut him open. It was awful. I had to identify the . . . him." It's tough to get out a phrase like *the body* when it's someone you know.

I put two fingers on her lips and she stopped talking, and I felt the sobs she was attempting to stifle. She put her head down on my shoulder, and the feel of her hair against my skin, of her cheek, was so wonderful I made a conscious note to remember it, the sensory illusions of touch and smell and taste all comingling in my mind, making me almost giddy.

She put her arms around me and held me tight, and said softly, "I could not let them keep you there to rot and die. I know how that is, to be a prisoner."

"How do you know?"

She didn't answer me. We were quite for a while, and I concentrated on just the feel of her, while she was careful not to touch any of the more severely bruised portions of my face and body. For a moment I thought she had fallen asleep. Then she buried her head against my neck and whispered, "I love you."

It was surreal, coming from nowhere. We had known each other so briefly, yet so intensely, because the electricity had been there from the very first look, as when you look at someone and know they are going to be significant in your life. It goes way beyond lust and physical attraction, and you both know it, so that when you finally do get around to making love it is as if it were preordained, written into your life script a long time before, so that you know exactly what to do and how to do it. I was afraid to move—moving might break the spell and wake me up and I'd be alone.

Her lips brushed a sensitive spot in the hollow of my neck, causing waves of sensation to gallop all over me, and then she was moving downward, running her tongue across the skin of my chest, over my nipples, my side, her lips nipping painlessly, her tongue darting in and out in an irregular rhythm, teasing and tantalizing and soothing the sore places. I writhed, playing havoc with my bruised ribs, but I didn't care, especially when her mouth reached the towel, and she undid it from around my waist and the electric tongue tip caressed my navel and then below. The mixed messages of pleasure and pain were giving me adrenaline rushes. All I could do in my weakened condition was lie there and let her do all the work and the giving.

Afterward, when she had moved back up and put her face next to mine and her arms around me, warming me, I just dozed, my sleep filled with a combination of some very good dreams and some very bad ones.

Somewhere in the middle of that doze I was dimly aware of her lush, full mouth on mine, softly, just brushing my lips, and she whispered in my ear that she had to go back to Pajarito and would see me later. Only partly waking up, I kissed her again. I didn't want her to go away and take with her the warmth and the sweetness and the soft muzzy smell of her. She covered me with a spare blanket before I heard the door open and click quietly shut and the tap of her heels down the tiled corridor outside.

I was awakened hours later by my own violent myoclonic

spasm, a malady I have suffered since childhood, a convulsive jerk that shook the entire bed and was absolutely guaranteed to awaken anyone who might be sharing it with me. I was disoriented for a moment when I opened my eyes, and then when I realized where I was I became frightened again. I had been through a harrowing few days both physically and emotionally, and waking up in a place with which I was not yet familiar gave me a start, bringing back echoes of those past days and hours I didn't wish to think about anymore.

Nagging at me, too, of course, was Merissa. The reason for all the pain and terror, the motivating factor for my being here in the first place, and now I knew where she was and what she was doing, and I felt duty-bound to find her. I sensed she was a little girl in a lot of trouble, and if my lance was bent and my shield dented after the last few days, I still had my white horse, and I figured I'd better get on it pretty quickly. I almost looked forward to telling her father where I'd found her, him with his cocaine and his nymphets and his Filipino eunuchs—I didn't know that for sure but it was my fantasy from the moment I'd entered his house and I was enjoying it too much to abandon it—and his touchy-feely wife and his two top-twenty biggest-grossing pictures.

I'm not sure why I felt such animosity toward Mark Evering. Perhaps it was because he was so busy being a mogul that he left fatherhood up to his associate producer and wound up with his only daughter being anybody's girl in a Mexican cathouse. Maybe it was everything I had already gone through in the course of my job for him. And I was still half convinced he had killed Swanner out of revenge for despoiling his daughter and then had set me up to go down for it. In truth, it was a combination of all these factors that had me thinking thoughts about my employer that were less than charitable. I've always been a combination man. I find several reasons to dislike someone and then combine them to get a really good hate going. It works out better for my mind-set. Even if one of the factors changes, enough of the others usually stay constant, so that I can keep my hatred on the front burner.

I checked my watch, which said seven forty-two. That's all it said, no A.M. or P.M. or Tuesday or September the eleventh or what time it was in Hong Kong. It was a Timex with a big hand and a little hand and a sweep second hand, the kind you hardly ever see anymore, so that kids grow up not knowing how to tell time without a digital readout. I had no real idea of what day it was, and only the orange cast of the sunlight on the blinds indicated that it might be evening and not morning. I staggered off the bed, rewrapping my middle with the towel, and it took me about ten minutes to put through a call from Tijuana to my house in Venice, California.

"Marvel?"

"Hey."

"Hey."

"Wha's up?"

"I'm still in Tijuana."

"Tha's cool. You missed the baseball game."

"I know. I'm sorry, I couldn't get away."

"Tha's cool. I went on Sunday. Hershiser pitched a four-hitter. Gibson wen' three for four. It was a good game."

"I'm glad you got to see it," I said. "Who'd you go with?"

"Paula. She come by, we wen' to the game, then she took me for pizza. With everything."

"Everything?"

"Yeah. 'Cept anchovies. They's gross. Even Paula don' like no anchovies."

Paula. I hadn't given Paula a single thought since I'd seen Carmen at the Pajarito Beach Hotel on Saturday night. If she had known what was going on in my life she would have been frantic. And shattered. And angry.

"Are you staying out of trouble, Marvel?"

"How I gonna get in trouble, you don't leave me with no money? I just sittin' here watching TV."

"You're turning into a couch potato."

"Tha's okay. Ol' Jo an' whassisname comin' over again tonight."

"You know damn well his name is Marshall."

"Yeah. Well, I forgot."

I could understand that. Jo's husband Marsh was one of the world's more forgettable people. It wasn't unusual to completely forget he was in the room. I said, "Listen, Marvel. Tell Jo to give you some money and I'll pay her back."

"When you comin' home?"

"In a day or so," I said. Then I said, "I spent yesterday in jail."

His manner brightened noticeably, his voice going up almost an entire octave. "Naw!" he said. "Fer real?" I knew he'd like that. Marvel had probably spent a few nights of his own in the slammer. "Wha' fer?"

"Suspected murder," I said.

"Shee-it! If they nail you, could I have your big-screen color TV?"

I laughed. Marvel had my number as far as getting me to laugh was concerned. It came in handy for him when I got pissed off at his cavalier attitude about homework or leaving his room looking like the ruins of Pompeii. "They won't, Marvel," I said. "I'm innocent."

"That makes a diff'rence then, man. I mean, don't nobody ever go to jail when they innocent. Any foo' knows that."

The sarcasm in his voice made me a little sad. He was very young to be so hard and cynical, but then Marvel had not had an idyllic childhood. When you're fifteen years old and have to survive on the streets of Los Angeles you come by your cynicism honestly.

When we'd finished our conversation and I'd put down the receiver, I realized I was ravenous. I hadn't eaten for so long I was out of the habit. The breakfast of *chorizo con huevos* had been some thirty three hours earlier. Jail and torture are wonderful for the waistline. Well, Merissa Evering was going to have to wait until I got something to eat, because I was light-headed from lack of food, and that wasn't a particularly desirable trait in one off to rescue a damsel in distress.

I dressed slowly. I didn't look particularly spiffy, since I had only brought two sport jackets with me to Tijuana and one of them was missing the button that had shown up in Iglesias's dead hand, and the other had gone through a mugging in an alley, a police interrogation, and a night in jail. I chose the one with the missing button. At least it was clean, and I could just leave it open and be Southern California supercasual and hope no one would notice. When I went into the bathroom to brush my hair I wondered who the eighty-year-old man in the mirror was, the one with the battered, pulpy-looking face. I realized his identity soon enough. My hair had started to go gray while I was still in my early twenties and had stabilized somewhere around thirty at a kind of pleasant smoky silver, but I could have sworn, looking at it now in the mirror, that it had turned several shades whiter during my day and night in prison.

After the initial shock of becoming a candidate for the Gray Panthers almost before my teenage complexion problems cleared up, I had always liked having gray hair. It was very thick, and the gray that framed my youthful features had always made a terrific conversation opener. People always asked me if I were prematurely gray. Lately I had taken to answering "Not anymore." But on this night I wished it were the medium-brown of my adolescence, because coupled with the attrition the past few days had made on my face, it made me look like the kind of man young women addressed as "sir" when they ask for directions to the nearest boutique. I splashed cold water on my face, knowing even as I did so that it wouldn't make a damn bit of improvement in my looks. It didn't even make me feel better.

I drove downtown through much lighter traffic than I had experienced on the weekend and parked in a cavernous concrete structure that had been built as a parking garage but more resembled, in both look and aroma, the sewers of Paris. I couldn't find a space until I'd driven almost to the top of the five-story building, and after locking my car I had a moment of disorientation when I couldn't seem to find any way out except down the winding ramp I had just driven up. At length I discovered an elevator, but after punching the down button several times and not hearing the whir of machinery or the grinding of gears inside, I gave up and started down the ramp, walking with that peculiar gait people use when descending a steep incline, half run and half pigeon-walk.

I strolled down the Avenida de la Revolución, a street with which I was becoming more familiar than I'd ever cared to. I was heading towards the jai alai fronton and the large restaurant on the corner that catered to the American tourists, for although it's against my principles not to eat the native cuisine whenever I'm away from home, I didn't think my stomach could handle anything like *machaca* on this particular evening. All I wanted was a steak and a cold beer.

It being a Tuesday night, the pedestrians on the street were mostly locals, so I became a magnet for every beggar, peddler, and street hustler in town. One of the scams commonly practiced in Tijuana is for sad-eyed young women to stand in doorways with their tiny infants in arms, begging handouts from *turistas* who just can't bear the thought of a child going hungry. One of these daughters of sorrow kept holding out her baby to me as if she wanted me to buy it, or at least take it off her hands so she wouldn't have to feed it anymore. It was pretty depressing, but not nearly as much as when a little girl not more than three years old came toddling up to me, palms outstretched for alms, and when I shook my head no she took a mighty swing at my crotch with her tiny balled-up fist. I turned just in time and caught the punch on my thigh. It was a pretty good punch for a three-year-old kid. I just kept walking, and it was about thirty seconds later, too late to do anything about it, that I realized the poor little thing probably had a nightly quota and that she'd be punished or beaten if she didn't fill it. I couldn't turn around and retrace my steps to give her some money, so I tried to put the incident out of my head as I went along my way. I didn't succeed, and I knew it was one of those moments that was going to haunt me for a long while to come.

A man, a sidewalk peddler, came up to me with several bright-colored blankets and serapes over his shoulder, and several more draped over his arm. He wore a big straw sombrero and a white cotton shirt and pants bisected by a gay red sash, dressed strictly to impress the tourists. "Look, amigo, beautiful blankets, no? Only eighteen dollars."

I shook my head and kept walking, but he dogged my steps. On the quiet street tonight I was one of the few fish in the sea, and he wasn't about to let me swim away that easily. "Okay, how much you give me for it, then? Fifteen? Here, I give you this one for fifteen dollars." He pulled out a drab, ugly blanket from the bottom of the pile. "Fifteen dollars, okay?"

My eyes strayed from the blanket to the face beneath the wide sombrero, and for a second or two I struggled to place it. When you see someone you've met before in a different context it sometimes takes a while to sort things out in the card catalogue of your mind. I finally did so, and nodded. His demeanor here on the street, in his own element, was very different than it had been in my hotel room, but the sad eyes above the wide nose and bushy mustache were unmistakable.

"*Buenos noches,* Señor Mendez," I said.

For a moment he had trouble recognizing me, too, but that was perhaps because my face had a somewhat different configuration after my night in the police station. I suppose at first he just saw another gringo, a tourist, and had approached me to make his sales pitch without ever really looking at me. When he finally tumbled to who I was he seemed startled.

"Señor Saxon!" he said. "Forgive me, I didn't—"

"That's all right," I said. "I was hoping I would see you again anyway."

His face lit up. "You have decided to help us, then?"

"No, I can't. I told you the truth about that. But I did want to ask you a few questions. About what we spoke of in my hotel yesterday."

"I don't understand."

"You told me you didn't want to go to Don Rafael directly about your family. You said you had 'heard things' about him."

"He was a mean man."

"Then you know he was killed?"

He raised his hands helplessly as if apologizing for his knowledge. "It was in the newspapers."

"Are you sure that's the only reason you didn't want to go see him? Maybe you had a more personal one?"

I could tell he was getting uncomfortable, and the soft sadness in his brown eyes turned darker and steelier. I began to think the subservience I'd seen in him when we'd first met was just an act. "I have told you the reason, señor," he said.

"Señor Mendez, have you done business with Iglesias before?"

The eyes flashed. In my business you learn to read eyes. They have a language all their own, and his made a spoken answer unnecessary.

"Isn't it possible that at some time you paid him money to send someone else over the border? Another daughter? A sister? Your wife, perhaps?"

His eyes spoke profanity, hatred, shame, and I knew once again I was flirting with the possibility of treading on a Latino's pride. And that is like stepping on the tail of a scorpion.

"You have no right to speak to me this way," he rasped, and for the first time there was a little beef in his voice and manner. "You have no right." He spewed out a string of rapid-fire curses in Spanish, and then he spit on the sidewalk between my feet. I don't know whether his aim was perfect or if he had simply missed my shoe. He moved away from me, head held high, down the street and into the rabbit-warren complex of shops and stands, and I lost him again. But he made me realize there were more people in this town with wonderful motives for killing Iglesias and Swanner than there were fans of the bullfights. It was no wonder every hotel clerk and bartender jumped when their names were mentioned. If I had guessed right, and from his behavior I figured I had, Mendez had paid Iglesias for some female relative to be taken across the border; she had wound up going to Martin Swanner for help with her legal status, and he in turn had given her over to Jesus Delgado, who just might have her working the streets of the Los Angeles barrio to pay for her green card. And if that were so Señor Mendez, and many others like him, might have every reason to wish Swanner and Iglesias horribly dead.

The restaurant was not doing a booming business, but there were a few tables full of noisy Californians and a couple of single males, American, who sat over their drinks at the bar in that peculiar hunchbacked posture of those who spend all their leisure time in saloons. This particular restaurant, with the bar running along one side of the wall of the dining room, was brightly lit, almost garishly so, and reminded me of a certain chop house of old and nostalgic acquaintance on Wabash Avenue in Chicago under the shadow of the "El," except that the Chicago chop house had white linen and flowers on the table and not Formica tabletops and truck-stop sugar pourers and plastic creamers in the shape of a cow. I sat at a table near the window and ordered a medium rare steak, french fries, and a beer. I managed to finish the beer, and then another one, and so of course I had to order a third to wash down the rather indifferent steak, which came medium well.

I didn't bother asking whether they had Armagnac, or my favorite Scotch, Laphroaig. It was too much to hope for. I settled for a plain old brandy to go with my lousy coffee, and I suppose I lingered over it longer than necessary. I wasn't too anxious to venture into a Tijuana whorehouse for any reason whatever, and an attempt to remove one of their star performers was not going to be smiled upon by the proprietors, I was sure. I missed the gun that had been stolen from my room. Tucked under my left arm, it would have given me a sense of security and comfort.

I finished my coffee and paid the waiter, who was sullen about something—perhaps getting stuck with such a lousy shift. Then I went out onto the street again. During the week, when the day-trippers from Los Angeles are gone and the tourists from Iowa have retreated back to their hotels over the border in San Diego, Tijuana takes on more of an exotic ambience, as though you are truly in a strange foreign culture and not just down the road a bit from the nearest Burger King or video rental store. I went back down the avenida to the address I'd been given by the little man in my jail cell, thinking despite the hurt places on my body, which served as remembrances of that overnight stay, that the whole episode seemed a long-ago bad dream, almost forgotten.

I turned off the Avenida de la Revolución and went down a side street, and I use the word *down* advisedly; at that particular point in the city the avenida runs up along the crest of a hill, and the streets that intersect it lead downward over broken and uneven cement steps, leveling off about a block and a half away, where the commercial area gives way to some squalid homes and eyesore auto body shops. And then I reached the place my cellmate had described, a really scummy bar called the Shot o' Gold.

9

From inside I heard badly amplified American rock and roll playing. Two young Mexican men stood outside the door, both wearing blue windbreakers and holding flashlights. "Cho-time, cho-time!" they sang out to me, and seemed pleased and surprised when I nodded to them and walked through the doorway, which was covered only with a dirty white muslin sheet. One of them went in with me and aimed a flashlight beam at an empty seat against the wall, which I took gingerly, as the chair didn't look as though it would hold my weight. I looked up to see if the man expected a tip, but he simply walked away from me, back through the sheet and out onto the street again.

A word about the Shot o' Gold: it was a large, cavelike room with a dark bar running along one side. In the center of the room was a raised stage, maybe twenty feet square and elevated about three feet. Around this stage were tables and chairs, all of them occupied by men except for one, where two American couples, looking very much as though they were from the San Fernando Valley, tried to seem as if they were having a good time. The recorded music was so loud it was impossible to think of it as music; it was simply a rhythmic noise. On the stage was a Mexican girl with dyed red hair who was not very good-looking, although she wasn't altogether unattractive, either. She was topless, showing her large breasts, and wore only high-heeled shoes and a kind of G-string which was pulled down low enough to reveal about half an inch of black pubic ringlets that had not received the benefits of the red hair dye. She was not really dancing, nor did she have any sense of the rhythm of the sounds that engulfed us; she just sort of chugged around the stage, breasts bouncing and swaying, her fleshy thighs quivering with each move. Whenever she danced near the edge of the stage, whatever customer was within reach would stand up and run his hands up between her legs or across her ass, some attempting to pull the G-string down further, but each time she would dance back out of their reach. Several of the men, most of whom were Mexican, would run their tongues out over their lips suggestively and make rude kissing noises whenever she came their way or even looked at them.

One ringside table was occupied by four young American Marines in self-conscious civilian clothes, their crew cuts neatly trimmed to about a half inch in length, and all pretty hammered, judging from their bleary eyes, slurred speech, and the number of plastic beer cups on the table in front of them. They were very vocal in their admiration of the dancer. One of them, whose large glasses and acne covered about equal portions of his face, looked absolutely love-struck. At one point, when the girl danced over near their command post, he stood up and opened his arms as though greeting a long-lost love, then clasped her around the hips, his hands on the ample globes of her buttocks, and buried his face in her pubic area for a few seconds until she moved away uninterestedly. He sat back down to the cheers and applause of his buddies, his expression dreamlike, as one who'd experienced an epiphany. I nearly gagged.

The waiter, a man not over five feet tall, arrived and took my order for a beer. When he brought it, along with a cup made of soft, thin, pliable plastic, I found it to be six ounces of a brand I'd never heard of, and he charged me two seventy-five. I was obviously supposed to tip him the quarter change, so I did. Sipping beer from the plastic cup made me feel as though I were watching a ball game at Wrigley Field, an illusion dispelled by the dancer sticking her nearly bare behind in my face and waggling it from time to time. She had a fiery red pimple on her left buttock.

I looked around the room, at the hookers ranged along the wall, at the hard-core drunks who hunched at the bar and concentrated on their tequila while they ignored the women, at the tourists, at the young men making obscene suggestions and catcalls to the dancer, and at the large, mean-looking guys who were obviously the bouncers standing at one end of the bar. I didn't see Merissa Evering among the crowd, even though I knew she probably would no longer much resemble her high school graduation picture.

My inquiring glance around was misconstrued, and I was soon joined by a chubby Mexican girl with a discolored front tooth. She was wearing a pink hip-length togalike affair with pink panties that didn't quite match, and she sat down with me and put her hand on my inner thigh.

"You buy me a drink?" she said.

I said yes and she signaled to the diminutive waiter, who quickly brought her something that was supposed to be tequila and was probably a shot of water with a water chaser. When I paid him he handed her a slip of paper, which she would redeem at the end of the evening for her cut. She downed the contents of the shot glass in one gulp and then proceeded to drink the rest of my beer, which further reinforced my suspicion that she had been served water.

"You know all the girls who work here?" I asked her.

She squeezed my thigh for an answer. She had quite a grip for a little girl. When I turned and looked at her she moved her hand up higher and squeezed my crotch. Hard. It certainly got my attention. "You like to fuck me?" she asked. "Come on, we go upstairs."

"No," I said.

"Come on," she said. "I fuck you, suck you, everything." Then she elaborated further as to which of her bodily orifices would be made available to me. I don't think she left any of them out.

"Not right now," I said.

"You a queer?"

"No."

She looked crestfallen, rejected, cast aside. Then her expression brightened as a new idea crept into her head. She pulled aside the loose pink tunic to show me one of her breasts. "Nice?" she said.

I told her it was. It wasn't—it was too sagging for someone of her tender years—but I sensed the question had been rhetorical anyway.

"Touch it," she ordered.

The dancer on stage retired after the song ended and her replacements were two overweight women of a certain age who were clothed simply in their underwear. One had a black bra and white underpants—not the sexy bikini type but the cotton ones that came up higher than the waistline and were usually favored by elderly ladies. The other wore a bra that had once been white, and flowered panties. They were both smoking unfiltered cigarettes, and they walked around the stage looking every bit as bored as they must have been. They made no effort to move to the music, or against it. Obviously the much touted Latin sense of rhythm had somehow eluded the dancers in the Shot o' Gold.

The muff-diving Marine had subsided into a sullen slump now that his favorite had left the stage, and his buddies were trying to talk him into going somewhere else, but he seemed disinclined to move at all, a condition probably brought on by his taking that one sip, one swallow, that exceeded his capacity for drinking and remaining concurrently functional. In the meantime, the couples from Los Angeles were putting on elaborate pantomimes for each other, the men trying hard not to get their wives angry by showing too much interest in the half dressed women on stage, and the wives making a great effort to be good sports and not to express their disgust with where they were and what they were doing. This was not going to be a trip to be cherished in their book of vacation memories, with slide shows to bore the neighbors.

"You come upstairs with me now?" the little whore was entreating, as though thirty seconds might have changed my mind.

"No, not now," I said.

"I'm clean. I don't fuck nobody for four months already."

I tried not to laugh, but my expression seemed to require further amplification on her part. "I just started working here yesterday," she explained.

"And you didn't fuck anybody yesterday?"

"Oh, no," she said, shaking her head gravely and giving my testicles another squeeze. I wasn't sure how I was going to get out of this.

I said, "I'm sorry. But I like really young girls."

"Young," she said, puzzled. She couldn't have been more than eighteen. Her brows knitted in thought for almost a minute. Then she had a suggestion. "You give me fi' dollars, I come back in ten minutes with a really young girl. Nine years old, ten—young."

I drank the little beer she'd left in the glass to cover the horrified expression on my face. I said, "Tell you what. I give you *ten* dollars, you take me to Merissa."

"Merissa?"

"You know Merissa? Blond, gringa, about twenty? I know she works here," I said. "Where is she? Upstairs?"

"Ai, you can have plenty girls like that where you come from. How 'bout a nice Mexican girl?" She took my hand and rubbed it against her bare nipple.

I pulled my hand away, put it in my pocket, and came up with a ten-dollar bill. "Merissa," I said. She reached for it and I held it away from her as Mark Evering had done to me with his check. "First you take me to her."

The little hooker looked miffed, and then her shoulders slumped as she acknowledged defeat. She raised a finger, admonishing me to wait, and went over to talk to the bartender in rapid-fire Spanish. He glowered over at me during the confab. Obviously blond gringa prostitutes were much in demand down here, as they were in many Third World countries, and the bartender couldn't quite reason why I had left wherever I had come from and driven all the way down to Mexico to pay to have sex with a blond California girl. Finally she returned to my table. "You got fi' dollars for the bartender?"

I gave her the five. It was all Mark Evering's money anyway. She took it over to the bar and there was more protracted discussion. Then she came and got me.

"Come on," she said, "we going upstairs."

We went out the back door of the club, past a malodorous coed latrine, and into an alley, where there was a rickety flight of wooden steps leading up to the second floor. I followed the girl up, watching her shiny pink bottom bobbing in front of me, and wondered exactly what I was in for. I didn't know if this place was a legitimate hookshop, which I suppose is a contradiction in terms, or if I was heading up the stairs to be mugged, rolled, or possibly worse. After what I'd been through in the past few days I was in no mood to be roughed up, and if that was what awaited me at the top of the stairs I was going to kick a lot of ass before I was through.

We entered a rank hallway, illuminated by the sad strivings of a single small bulb, and reeking of stale cigarette smoke, old perspiration, cheap perfume, and Vaseline. I wished it had smelled a bit more of disinfectant, but that didn't seem to be the way my luck was running these days. I followed my hooker—

that's how I thought of her by this time, as my own personal hooker, and I was becoming rather fond of her—until we reached a doorway near the end of the corridor. She knocked, and when the male voice inside made an inquiry she answered with her name, which I think was Linda, and the door was opened into a grubby suite of two tiny rooms. In the front room was a Formica table with aluminum-tube legs and a few mismatched chairs and a man in a short-sleeved beige polo shirt with a counterfeit alligator on the pocket. He looked me over and informed me it would be fifty dollars American, payable in advance. I dutifully gave him a twenty and three tens, and he counted it twice before stuffing it into the pocket with the sewed-on alligator and disappearing into the back room.

Linda looked at me wistfully, her feelings obviously hurt. "I show you a good time," she pleaded, gamely hanging in there until the last. "Better than her. You come to my room?"

I smiled as warmly as I could and shook my head. "That's okay, Linda," I said. "Thanks for your help." I gave her the promised ten bucks, and another ten just for the hell of it.

But she regarded the money almost sadly. "Okay, baby," she said, disappointment etched on her used young face. She went out into the hallway, casting one sorrowful glance over her shoulder before disappearing into the shadows. Feeling guilty, I had to remember where I was, and who and what she was.

I fidgeted alone in the awful room for a few moments, the adrenaline racing through me. I'd gone through a lot to get here, and now I was within seconds of finding my quarry and completing the first phase of my commission. Of course the second phase—getting her out of there—was going to be something more than a cakewalk. I would figure that out when I had to, however. There was always the possibility that Merissa might not want to go home, but as grotesque and screwed up as Mark

Evering might be, his overpriced Beverly Hills zoo was one giant step up from a whorehouse in Tijuana.

The man came back from the inner room holding a blond girl by the wrist, and I almost recoiled in shock. She wore a cheap maroon dress that hugged every curve of her body, and high-heeled red shoes. Her hair was in a pony tail that had been tucked under itself, giving the effect of a kind of bun, and her skin was sallow and pasty-looking, and even the thick layer of pale makeup she wore couldn't cover up the terrible condition of her skin. Her eyes weren't really focusing on anything in the room, they were looking inward someplace where neither I nor her keeper had ever been. I couldn't testify that the man was exactly dragging her, or that she was even reluctant to come, but on the other hand she didn't seem to be nearly as eager as Linda. I had to look carefully to match the puffy, lifeless face in front of me to the apple-pie bounciness of the high school grad whose picture was in my jacket pocket.

"Merissa?" I said tentatively.

"Yah," the man said by way of confirmation, "this here is Merissa. Real hot stuff. She's real blonde, too." And he reached down and pulled the girl's dress up around her hips to show me she was indeed a real blonde. "She'll show you a good time," he continued. "You got half an hour from right now. Any more costs extra." He flipped me a wave and walked out the door, shutting it behind him, leaving Merissa standing there with her dress up around her hips. She didn't seem to mind. She didn't even seem to *be* there.

"Merissa," I said softly, "I'm a friend."

She looked around, finally found my face, and tried to adjust her eyes to me. Her pupils were dilated and she kept blinking stupidly, and I realized she was completely looney-tunes on drugs. That was something of a mixed blessing. She probably was too far gone to give me any trouble about leaving, but she was too zonked to be of much assistance either. I went to her and gently pulled down her dress. "I'm going to take you home, Merissa. Okay?"

She shook her head as if that would clear up her thought processes. "Where's Marty?" she said in a whiny little-girl voice. "I want Marty."

I walked past her into the back room, where there was a badly soiled cheap blanket on a sagging mattress on the floor and a lamp with an absurd pink ruffly shade. I looked out the window and saw there was a sheer drop of eighteen feet to the alley. In a place like this, a fire escape would have been too much to hope for. I went back to the doorway between the two rooms and met Merissa coming in. She had evidently neither heard nor understood me when I told her I was her rescuer.

"So whattaya wanna do?" she said. She moved to the mattress and flopped down on it heavily, pulling up her dress again, spreading her legs, and looking up at the ceiling with her dull eyes, waiting for me to decide in which manner I wished to use her body. Hot stuff indeed, I thought. She didn't even know where she was. I went and stood over her but she didn't bother looking at me, and I leaned over and pulled her dress down once more, and took her by the hand.

"Upsy-daisy," I said, tugging at her hand. "Come on, Merissa, get up on your feet."

She took my wrist with her other hand and tried to pull herself up, but she had little strength and succeeded only in lifting the upper half of her body from the mattress, her hips still firmly anchored where they were. I backed away a step or two to get some leverage but managed only to drag her lower half off the mattress and onto the dirty linoleum. Her eyes rolled back in her head. She was barely conscious. "Come on, Merissa. Come on, honey, stand up." I grabbed her under the arms and hauled her to a more or less upright position, having to hold her there so she wouldn't slip down again like a boneless vaudeville drunk. Most of her weight was on me, and she swayed on her high heels as if her ankles were weak. She smelled of the same cheap perfume I had noticed in the hallway; perhaps the wearing of it was a condition of employment at the Shot o' Gold.

Merissa said something then, but it came out an indistinct moan, and I bent my head down close to her mouth to hear her better. "Marty," was what she said. She was not mistaking me for her deceased lover. She was just calling for him the way a scared child calls for its mother. I began wondering where Merissa's own mother might be. Probably middle-aged and matronly, living with her second husband, a nice orthopedic surgeon in Cheviot Hills, collecting interest on the huge settlement she must have received from Mark Evering when he divorced her to marry the hot-eyed Brandy. If so, it just might shake up her well-ordered life if she could see her daughter now. I didn't know what kind of crap Merissa had snorted, swallowed, or shot into her arm, and I had no idea how to snap her out of it. For a guy who lived in the middle of the entertainment community in Los Angeles I am amazingly unfamiliar with the narcotics subculture. Perhaps I was born too soon to have become a card-carrying head, but my idea of hard drugs is Extra-Strength Tylenol. I've smoked a couple of joints in my day, usually when they were wordlessly handed to me at parties, and some of them had been laced with other things that made me feel like the Wicked Witch of the West when Dorothy threw water on her, but mostly I preferred getting my highs from a beautiful woman, a sunset at Trancas Beach, a 1966 Chateau Palmer with a perfectly seasoned and expertly cooked leg of lamb, or a Charlie Parker solo. Looking at Merissa's red, drug-dimmed eyes and her puffy, flaccid cheeks, watching her pathetic and Sisyphean efforts to stand up straight made me wonder why so many people built their whole lives around the consumption of controlled chemical substances.

"Come on," I said again, and guided her into the front room and to the door. I opened it and stuck my head out into the corridor to see if anyone was watching. The little man with the beige polo shirt was down at the end of the hallway near the exit sign, smoking a cigarette that smelled like Bandini fertilizer. He looked up and frowned.

He hitched up his trousers with his wrists the way Jimmy Cagney used to do. "You got a problem?" he said.

I complained, "This fucking broad's giving me some shit. You either handle it for me or I want my dough back."

He cursed bilingually under his breath and started down the hallway to where we were standing, his fists clenched. I stepped back into the room and let him walk by me. His cursing escalated when he caught sight of the girl, and he started to remove his thick belt, I suppose to help him convince her of the error of her ways. I caught him with the edge of my hand just below the ear, and the sound he made when he hit the floor was like when you accidentally drop the turkey out of the roasting pan on the way to the oven.

For a second I thought I might have hit him too hard and he'd never get up again. I don't like to hit people. It looks easy, looks like fun when you see it in the movies. But think about the damage that can be inflicted by the impact of a fist or a karate chop and it isn't quite so casual anymore. I checked quickly to make sure he was still breathing, and when I was satisfied that I hadn't murdered anyone I took the semiconscious Merissa by the elbow and steered her out of the room and into the hallway.

As we headed for the door that opened out onto the alley stairway I was glad I had made such careful mental notes on the way up. It certainly beat scattering bread crumbs. The building was situated in the middle of the block, and I knew that if I turned right when we reached the alleyway we would be headed in the direction of the parking garage where I had left my car. Merissa stumbled almost every other step as she walked. I anticipated a long trip. I couldn't know just how long.

I opened the door and guided Merissa out onto the landing at the top of the wooden stairs, and for a moment she swayed so badly I thought she was going to pitch right over the railing. Foul as it was, the Tijuana air was a big improvement over the stink in that hallway. But I didn't have much time to savor it. Jesus Delgado and his three musclebound friends were waiting for me at the bottom of the stairway, and I wondered if I had my little whore Linda to thank for letting him know where I was. More likely it was the bartender, who had taken my five bucks, who had betrayed me. I'll say this for Delgado, though: he was smiling.

I smiled back. It seemed the only friendly thing to do.

10

I truly think Delgado was happy to see me. Not that he enjoyed my company all that much, but he had probably been singing soprano ever since I kneed him in the *cojones,* and doubtless his days and nights had been filled with fantasies of revenge. How often does one get to actualize one's fantasies? No wonder he was smiling.

"Saxon," he said, rolling the two syllables over his tongue as though to speak my name aloud was to bring revenge from the fifth dimension of daydream into reality. Then he began cursing me, methodically and quietly, and I must admit to being impressed with his creativity. I've been vilified by the best, especially by my nemesis from the Los Angeles Police Department, Lieutenant Joe DiMattia, the cop whose wife I had dated when she was still single. But this put DiMattia to shame.

During Delgado's obscene fusillade I had come partway down the steps, my hand firmly supporting the weaving Merissa by the elbow, and when I was approximately seven risers from ground level Delgado took out a gun and pointed it at my navel. My recognition of the gun as my own, the one that had been stolen from my hotel room, was cold comfort. A handgun, unlike a dog, is only loyal to the person who happens to possess it at a given moment.

"Where you think you're going?" Delgado said. The five words strung together without any scatological connectives gave me a bit of a start. I hadn't imagined him capable of it.

"Put the piece away," I said, one of my more hollow tries at bravado, "or else give it back to me. Either way, stand aside."

"You dumb fuck," he said. It was somehow reassuring that he had begun swearing again. It put me on more familiar ground.

I don't like it when people point guns at me. It makes me uneasy to think I might have only one one hundredth of a second of my life remaining. That is only a rough estimate of the time it would take a bullet to travel the distance between Delgado's gun, or rather my gun, and my person, but it's close enough for conversational purposes.

"Let the girl go," I said. "You don't want her."

His glance flicked to Merissa and then back to me, and his lip actually curled in profound contempt. "Want her? I've had her. We all have." He cackled a lewd, nasty laugh. "You both stay." He waved the gun. "Get upstairs."

It's bad enough having a gun pointed at you. It can put a damper on the entire day. But when the gun-pointer begins waving his hand, the hand holding the gun, around in the air like an Italian telling a joke, it becomes almost intolerable. So I decided to do something about it. I didn't think the situation out as thoroughly as I might have liked, but then I didn't have a lot of lead time. More often than not, finding yourself at gunpoint is a spur-of-the-moment thing. I decided to take it step by step, and I surmised that step one would probably entail getting down off the wooden stairs and onto solid ground, or solid alley. I couldn't do that while Delgado pointed my own gun at my middle, and I knew I had to distract him. The best way of doing that was to throw something at him, so I threw the only thing I had at hand.

I threw Merissa.

As limp as she was, she offered no resistance, but sailed down at Delgado and fell into him. I was gambling that he wouldn't shoot her, and it turned out to be a successful bet. He stumbled a few steps backward, which gave me just enough time to vault over the handrail and down onto the rough cobblestones of the alley, a six-foot drop. I landed hard, jarring the fillings in my teeth and causing a sharp shooting pain in my ankle. Nothing serious. I was now in a position to make a clear run down the alley toward the street, where my garage was located, but unfortunately if I ran now I would be leaving Merissa literally in Delgado's hands, and since the very purpose of the exercise was to get her *out* of his hands, running was an unacceptable course of action.

There was one goon standing between me and Merissa, looking not at me but at his boss, who was trying to push Merissa away from himself in order to free his eye and gun hand for a clear shot at me. I took the goon out with a short, hard punch under the heart. That slowed him down and let me grab Merissa's arm and yank her away from Delgado, using her almost as a counterweight so I could swing a hard right at Delgado and send him tumbling backward into the two goons still on their feet. By the time they had all regained their composure and equilibrium I was fairly flying down the alley, dragging the girl along with me.

Normally I would have run down the center of the alley, even though the light at the end would silhouette me and make me an easier target. It was a lot safer than risking the ricochet of a bullet off the bricks. But in this case, by moving to my right and hugging the wall as I went, I would force Delgado to take about five extra steps getting around the stairway before he could squeeze off a round. This rapid calculation probably saved my life and Merissa's, because when the first shot came it hit behind us by about four feet. The second one was closer.

The bullet bit into the wall and did indeed ricochet, but I don't know where it went. Tiny bits of pulverized brick flew all around me, stinging my face as I ran, and I squeezed my eyes shut to protect them. I crouched and tried to pull Merissa lower as well, but I was afraid she'd simply fall on her face, so I just kept moving as best I could. The third shot obviously came from next to the wall, as it didn't hit the bricks at all but whizzed by my ear, sounding for all the world as if a DC-10 was landing on my left shoulder. Now was the time to move into the center of the alley and run a serpentine pattern and hope Merissa could keep up without losing her footing. She was almost a dead weight behind me.

The end of the alley was just a few agonizing yards away, but it seemed as if I were running in slow motion, like the Bionic Man churning through deep soft sand, and the monster of my childhood nightmares was gaining on me. Another jumbo jetliner roared past my head. Delgado had two bullets left. Of course, I wasn't sure the goons were unarmed, and I calculated that the odds of both Merissa and me dodging twenty-four bullets was slim indeed. It was best to simply get out into the open. Fast. And yet the end of the alley looked like the end of a long tunnel viewed through binoculars the wrong way, still a country mile away.

Finally I reached the street, bursting into the brighter lights like a sprinter breaking the tape with his chest, and the fact that I was running like a maniac dragging a spaced-out hooker who wore nothing but a skimpy maroon dress caused little stir among the few strollers on the sidewalks. In Tijuana it takes more than that to make people look twice, so accustomed are they to public uproars. Maybe it was because the police considered the horrendous auto traffic a priority over two gringos silly enough to get themselves shot at by local mobsters.

I slowed down a step and took a great gulp of air, once again gambling with my own life and the girl's, this time betting Delgado would not come out of the alleyway onto a fairly well-traveled street with pistol blazing. But their footsteps still thudded on the cobbles behind me, so I wasted no time congratulating myself for getting out of the alley. I turned left, heading down the hill away from the Avenida de la Revolución and toward the parking structure, pounding right on past it, knowing that if I went in there with my pursuers right behind me I'd be trapped. I had to lose them first, or at least some of them.

Merissa picked this precise moment to fall all the way to her knees on the downhill slope of the sidewalk. Of course, with her wrist firmly in my grasp she acted as an anchor, and I almost lost my own footing as I swung around and tried to drag her to her feet. Once more she hung there limply, her top half vertical and her bottom half horizontal, the whites of her eyes showing whenever she opened them at all, and I cursed her father, and Delgado, and Martin Swanner, and the nameless Beverly Hills drug pusher who mooched around her high school hooking kids on heroin and cocaine and various and sundry illegal substances.

I looked up. Thundering down the hill toward us, almost in tandem and looking like a four-legged toboggan, were the two biggest goons. The third one, the one I had punched under the heart, was lagging behind a bit, and Delgado was riding drag. I was pleased to see that the front-runners were apparently unarmed. I think we surprised them by stopping; they were coming far too fast and with too much momentum to be able to break stride, so I crouched down low, at about the same level as Merissa, and when the first one arrived I simply employed an old judo principle and used his own speed to toss him past me through the air about four uneven steps downward. He landed on both knees, hard, and I knew from the sickening popping sound, similar to the one you hear when you stomp on a paper cup in the ballpark after the beer has been drunk, that he had broken a kneecap. His scream was another clue. If he wasn't carrying a concealed weapon that he could shoot even in his crippled condition, I wouldn't have to worry about him anymore.

I was then free to turn all my attention to Goon Number Two. Not that I had a lot of choices. Before I could get my head turned to face him he was on top of me and had fetched me a sound cuff on the left ear—the same ear that had been gashed open during the Sunday night mugging in an alley not three blocks from where we stood. It sounded in my head as if that huge gong they once used to announce J. Arthur Rank movies had been relocated to somewhere in the vicinity of my left mastoid bone. But I lashed out instinctively and felt my fist crunch into something soft; in my kneeling position I was exactly level with his crotch and my fist had found his testicles. He made a louder and higher noise than Delgado had, and I wondered how many more Mexican gangsters I was going to have to unman before Merissa was back in the warmth and safety of her father's palatial Beverly Hills manse. As Goon Two doubled up, knees buckling in agony, I shoved him backward into Goon Three, who tripped over him and fell down, giving me just enough time to haul Merissa back up on her feet and start running again, nimbly sidestepping the one with the shattered kneecap, who was yelling imprecations at me in Spanish and clawing at the air.

I managed to get to the corner and turn right before Merissa, for reasons known only to her, began screaming at full volume. It didn't matter, though, because this particular street was almost deserted, and the few pedestrians in view were probably engaged in pursuits of dubious merit anyway and didn't want to get too involved with a bloody-eared Anglo running down the street at ramming speed, dragging a yowling blond prostitute behind him.

I'm not sure just how far we ran. I wasn't doing much sightseeing along the way. We cut across the street several times and turned a couple of corners, propelled more by fear than logic, until finally I couldn't hear footsteps behind me anymore, and when I got to the middle of the block on a particularly dark street and had a clear view of what might be coming at me from any direction, I stopped for the first time, leaning against the wall and gasping for breath, pain knifing into my side. I also became cognizant of just how badly I had injured my ankle by jumping off those steps behind the Shot o' Gold. It was swelling ominously. As for my ear, I felt the blood that had run down my neck and into my collar coagulating. There is nothing more disgusting than your own blood drying on you. What felt like a honeydew melon was growing on the side of my head, and it crossed my mind that I couldn't hear footsteps anymore because I couldn't hear *anything* out of my left ear.

Merissa had skinned both her knees when she fell, and although her screaming had finally stopped, she was now babbling in that peculiar singsong way that stone druggies have. Try as I might, I couldn't pick up any intelligible words at all except an occasional "Marty" in there amongst all the gibberish. I tried to imagine what our flight through the streets would seem like to me if I were drugged to the teeth and decided it might resemble the last ten minutes of *2001: A Space Odyssey*. Merissa was too zonked to be frightened, or to feel the pain of her skinned knees. My ear pounded and my ankle throbbed and I envied her. No one had warned me when I took this case that I was signing up for the Tijuana 10K Run.

When my breathing finally was coming a bit more easily, I managed to pant, "Are you all right?" to Merissa, and immediately felt like an idiot. She was so far gone that had she not been all right, someone would have had to tell her. She wasn't much of a companion for escaping from killers in the night, and I decided not to talk to her at all anymore until she came down from whatever astral plane the drugs had taken her to. When I was ready to move I didn't say anything, not even a cursory "Let's go!" but just took her arm again and pulled her along beside me.

We walked past a few more streets, coming finally to a kind of block-long plaza replete with dry and dead-looking fountains and lots of tilework, stucco archways, and stone benches. The plaza was lined with shops, which were all closed, and from what I could see they were not the tourist traps I'd become so familiar with on the more populated streets of the city, but seemed to cater more to the locals.

Lots of things were going on in that block, including a political rally with a loudspeaker truck plumping for some candidate or another down at one end of the plaza. Mostly, though, there were just people hanging out. Old people, young ones, winos, weirdos, courting couples, ragged kids, and an awful lot of short Mexican men needing shaves. Well-populated benches, colorfully tiled, were built in a square shape around pathetic-looking trees and shrubs that were striving to stay alive despite the trash, cigarette butts, and urine deposited at their roots.

I felt all eyes were on us, since Merissa and I were the only Anglos in sight, and somewhat special-looking Anglos at that. At one place a vendor stood behind a portable hot plate on which he displayed some of the most awful-looking stuff I'd ever seen, at first glance great chunks of marinated meat. But as we passed his little rolling cart and drew downwind I realized they were hunks of reddish-brown candy, jagged and irregular in shape and about the size of baseballs. The sickening sweet smell hung in the air and made little prickles in my sinus passages. It was one of those odors that was so unpleasant it made you want to smell more of it, and I inhaled deeply through my nose.

Merissa and I went through the large archway at one end of the block and crossed the thoroughfare to find ourselves on a very crowded avenue with a narrow sidewalk. The street seemed to consist of decrepit hotels and seedy bars whose neon signs turned the pavement and everyone on it a surreal red-orange hue. Music blared from the saloons, loud salsa music with lots of conga drums and strident brass horns, forcing its way through the muslin sheets or canvas flaps that seemed to cover the doorway of every lower-class drinking establishment in Tijuana, all coming together in the heavy air on the street to create an ear-shattering dissonance. The last thing I wanted right then was a drink, but I wouldn't have gone into one of those places if I were dying of thirst. I never would have made it back out intact. Call it an attack of tourist paranoia.

All the looks we were getting now were hostile, most of them coming from eyes bloodshot and squinting and pink-rimmed, or so it seemed in the neon glow. Hands reached out from doorways to paw at Merissa's breasts and buttocks and crotch, but I was in no shape or mood to play knight errant and defend her virtue, such as it was. I just walked that much faster, pulling her along beside me, and tried not to make eye contact with anyone, thus avoiding a possible confrontation, which would slow us down, make us conspicuous, draw a crowd, and perhaps cost us our lives.

A quick glimpse of one of Delgado's bullyboys down near the end of the block made me do an abrupt to-the-rear-march, heading back the way we had come, swinging Merissa around with me. I didn't think he'd seen us, but I couldn't be sure.

As we walked along I realized I had been lumping Merissa and me together in my thoughts. The fact was, no one wanted to kill her. They'd had plenty of chances to take care of that long before I showed up, but they had kept her alive. It was me they were shooting at, me they were trying to stop, although I had no idea why. My astonishing lack of popularity here below the border and the vast number of enemies I seemed to have accrued were way out of proportion to any actions of mine since my arrival the previous Saturday morning. Yet for some odd reason, two people had died in a hideous fashion, including one I had come to Mexico to talk to. And now Jesus Delgado and his gangsters, one of whom, at least, was neutralized with a shattered kneecap and one of whom was slowed down to a stately walk with a pair of very sore testicles, were ranging the streets and alleyways of their home territory, hunting for me. From what I could tell, I was next on the schedule to wake up in purgatory and have to try to talk my way past the Pearly Gates.

I don't know why purgatory had come to mind all of a sudden. I hadn't thought of it in many years. I guess all the things the nuns and priests had tried to beat into my head, knuckles, and ass back in parochial school died hard. There is nothing like a Catholic education.

But now I wanted to thank Sister Concepta for all the whacks with the metal ruler. Her efforts were finally, after almost thirty years, about to pay off, because they had given me an idea. It wasn't a solution—I didn't have one of those. It was kind of a Band-Aid to buy me some time. And as I hobbled across the street, my face battered, my ankle swollen and pulsing with pain, my ear bleeding, and a half-conscious stoned hooker hanging onto my arm as though it was a life preserver, I saw myself all at once as the misshapen Quasimodo after he had snatched the unconscious gypsy girl Esmerelda from the gibbet and, murmuring "Sanctuary! Sanctuary!" lurched his way up the steps to the great doors of the Cathedral of Notre Dame. I guided Merissa up three risers and through the splintered wooden door with its flaking green paint, into a small and obviously impoverished Catholic mission church there on a Tijuana back street. It was a far cry from Notre Dame and Paris, I admit, but it was the very best I could come up with on the spur of the moment.

11

The inside of the tiny church was dark, not in the way of those Old World churches of Europe, steeped in atmosphere and mystery, but in the fashion of a tenement apartment one in the ghetto of a large city, dark because no ray of hope had ever really shined there, or if one had, it had been so long ago that there is no longer any residual glow, no illumination of the human heart or soul. Sure, it was a church, a house of worship, where God supposedly lives, but I had a feeling that if God had indeed ever been in residence here He had long ago moved out because no one fixed the leaks in the roof or the cracks in the plaster or the hot water pipes that belied their name and issued no hot water.

I had always found precious little comfort in the religion of my mother, anyway. This was the first time I'd even been inside a Catholic church since shortly after my sixteenth birthday, save for one wedding and a couple of relatives' funeral services. This particular church was not likely to give me back my faith. The smell of hot wax and incense assaulted the senses, and the little place on top of my head where my occasional severe headaches took seed started to hurt just the slightest bit. It was typical of my readiness to blame everything on Rome that I attributed the headache to the smell of the church and the memories I associated with a repressed Catholic childhood instead of the ordeal I'd just been through: dragging a practically comatose Merissa several miles through the streets at top speed while dodging bullets. It was, however, stuffy at best in the church, and that was neither imagination nor parochial school guilt. Merissa was too far gone to know or care where she was, but even had she been able to react at all to her whereabouts she probably would have mistaken them for the foyer of a trendy little Andalusian restaurant in Brentwood.

I made a quick reconnaissance around the church and found there was a doorway to the left of the tiny altar, which led into a wretched dark hallway in which another small door opened onto an alleyway. I was considering writing a guidebook on the alleys of Tijuana, since I was acquiring expert status in the field. I also reflected that each time I found myself in one of those alleyways something disagreeable happened to me. I went back into the church, where I had left Merissa leaning stupidly against the wall near the front door, and guided her down the center aisle to one of the pews, onto which she sank, grateful to finally be off her feet. There were two black-clad old women up front near the altar, murmuring their prayers to a Blessed Mother badly in need of a paint job. From the wall the crucified Christ looked down at us, and in this shabby setting even he seemed more impoverished and hopeless than agonized, as though to him and his parishioners here, crucifixion was just one more bum trip in a life that included squalor, hunger, futility, and the loss of human dignity. I could hear hushed whispers from inside one of the two confessional booths to the right of the altar. The flicker of many votive candles could not dispel the coldness and gloom.

I sat next to Merissa and leaned back against the hard pew, closing my eyes for as long as I dared. Memories again, of squirming on the bench, my bare legs in their short pants sticking to the hard polished wood, and my mother leaning over and giving my thigh a savage pinch so I'd stop wiggling, be still, and show the proper reverence. I relaxed for ever so brief a time, not even feeling guilty that I had failed to make the sign of the cross before sitting down. I was weary in mind and bone, tired of this whole Mexican adventure, of my body hurting in more places than I'd ever known it possessed, and eager to get out of town, back to Los Angeles, and start putting the pieces of my life back together, if indeed my life was salvageable. I tried again to communicate with my companion-in-flight. "Merissa," I whispered, "it's all right. You're safe here. I'm going to take you home."

Her head moved in a circular motion, counterclockwise, bobbing around as if it were attached to her shoulders by a rubber band. I can't imagine what she must have thought when she opened her eyes to all the fading religious statuary and the flickering candles, but when she finally focused on my face she seemed to know me, or at least have some vague remembrance of what had transpired. She licked her lips and made her first verbal utterance, except for calling for her lost Marty, since we had fled the Shot o' Gold. "Oh, shit!" she said, and so far removed am I from my Catholic roots that the obscenity, uttered in the church before the altar and under the unwavering gaze of the plaster Saviour, didn't even bother me. I have no idea what prompted her to say it, or to what specific aspect of our mutual situation she was alluding, but that was her big speech for the moment, and it was an improvement over mumbling Martin Swanner's name over and over. Apparently the old women saying their rosaries up near the front did not hear her obscenity, or they didn't comprehend it, although I've always thought it was one of those words, like its French counterpart, *merde,* that was understood all over the world.

I bowed my head, less from reverence than exhaustion, and waited. All the emotions engendered by being in a church again after so many years caromed crazily around in my head. I still didn't know why they were trying to stop me from taking Merissa back across the border. It couldn't be that she was such a valuable property at the Shot o' Gold. From her actions when we'd first met, as a hooker she was obviously a washout. Though there were faint traces of the pretty high school grad whose picture I carried in my pocket, too many men and too many black beauties and too much crack had made the girl middle-aged at twenty, and the listless posture and lifeless eyes couldn't have turned too many of her customers on.

The door to the confessional opened and another old woman all in black came out and went to the railing to do her penance. Whatever sins she had just owned up to probably weren't terribly interesting. However, the minor disruption made me realize we had been sitting there for almost ten minutes, and I started getting nervous. It was time to make some sort of a move, unless we planned to stay in the church all night, and that might prove as dangerous as the streets.

I whispered to Merissa to stay put, though I doubt she understood me, and went back to the front of the church. I opened the door just a crack, and peeked out. Scanning the street I noticed one of Delgado's *pistoleros* wandering around out there, opening any door that wasn't locked to check inside the buildings. They were apparently deadly serious about finding us, and it was only a matter of minutes before they got around to checking out the church. I wondered if the goon's upbringing had been as Catholic as mine, and if he would hesitate to come into a house of worship to search out and kill another human being.

I went back to Merissa. She had placed both her hands on the back of the pew in front of her and her head was dangling dead-chicken style between them. If I hadn't known better I would have thought she was in deep and pious prayer, instead of simply stoned out of her gourd. I lifted her upright and steered her over to the two confessionals. I threw her into the far one and went into the near one myself.

The flood of associations that engulfed me on my entry into that little box startled me even more than I had imagined they would. The confessional smelled of incense and sweat and the mustiness of many years of sins great and small. My childhood came rushing back to me in one claustrophobic moment. Here came Father Kaveny, he of the lion's roar and the twinkle in his eye, which was brought about by a great fondness for things Irish, especially Irish whiskey. The father was intoning mass with the Gaelic lilt that we kids found funny enough to make us stay awake and listen to the Latin words. Sister Concepta, of the hawk's eye and the starched habit that sounded like crinkling parchment as she walked. Sister Bernadette, née Mary Frances Healy, from the neighborhood, who was subject to unexpected attacks of the giggles at most inappropriate times, after which she would cross herself as soon as she regained control of her laugh muscles. The boys' playground at St. Aloysius, where the Irish had the east end and the Italians staked out the west, and the few Poles in the parish with their odd patterns of speech—"Oh, Lee-o-oh, I seen from Foster Avenue Stashy Kula down by the car tracks you!"—which was not so much Warsaw as the West Side of Chicago. The rituals of the church, the catechism, the communions, the receiving of the Host and how I could never understand why they couldn't use chocolate Necco wafers instead, thus making it at least palatable to receive the body of Christ. The endless speculation among the high school boys as to whether the priests and nuns had ever "done it"; the terrors of the confessional—"Aw, Jeez, don't get no Fadda O'Gara, he's murder! He give Pat O'Malley twenny Hail Marys and twenny Our Faddas!" . . . "Do you sincerely believe you will not sin like that again?" And me cursed with a low mellow baritone voice from the age of thirteen, so that the priests behind the screen could always tell who it was: Saxon, confessing (like a damn fool) the time we found that place in the boys' john where there was a little space between the plaster and the toilet pipes, which allowed us to look directly into a stall in the girls' bathroom next door, and I knelt down and peeked while Annie Connolly lifted her blue uniform skirt and pulled down her little white underpants to sit on the throne. The first time I smoked out behind the rectory. The first time I drank alcohol. The first time I thought impure thoughts and touched myself in a sinful place. The first time . . .

I heard the wooden panel slide open and could sense the priest behind the screen, knew he was waiting. Was he bored? Half asleep? Half crocked? Understanding and forgiving? Righteous and unbending? I knew I wasn't there to confess, that I hadn't believed all that Catholic voodoo jazz since I was sixteen years old, and yet, and yet . . . That old feeling was getting to me, pushing aside even my fear of the men who were looking for me. I cracked open the door of the confessional. Yes, Delgado's hood was there, standing near the apse, and I realized I had no choice but to recite my sins. I hoped there was only the one priest, that no one would go into the next booth and expect Merissa to take part in a religious ritual she'd probably never even heard of. I took a deep breath and spoke to the screen in front of me.

"Comprende inglés?"

There was a rustling. "Yes, my son." He spoke with a heavy accent. That disembodied voice from the other side of the screen had always seemed so scary, so mystical when I was a kid. It didn't anymore. Now it just sounded tired.

"Bless me, father," I began quietly, "for I have sinned. It has been . . . eight months since my last confession." That, of course, was a lie. It had been twenty-two years since my last confession, but I didn't want to complicate things. Besides, we even lied about that when we were kids. We never told the priest how long it had been since the last time, not even when it had been only a week. It didn't dawn on me until many years later that by starting out the confession with a lie we were defeating the whole purpose.

And now for the sins, I thought. What was I going to confess? Which of the five thousand sins I had committed in the last twenty-two years was I going to share with this priest? Lust was always a good start, I figured, and it would give him something to keep him awake after listening to all those elderly women. It was certainly more fascinating, I hoped, than all the silly stuff about pride and not going to communion and taking the Lord's name in vain. I began.

"I have committed sins of the flesh," I said. "I have fornicated." I sneaked another quick peek out through the door to see how many sins I was going to have to own up to. The goon was still there. I was in for some heavy penance.

"How many times?" the priest said. His voice sounded tentative, young. That was a new one on me; priests were not supposed to be younger than you were. Wasn't that why you called them father and they responded with "My son?"

"I don't remember," I answered, and that, at least, was the truth.

Many sins later I stepped slowly and carefully out of the confessional. I had kept adding sins until I was certain Delgado's goon had left the church, and for a while after that as well, to give him enough time to direct his attention elsewhere. I'd confessed a lot of things that I had done, and I'd made up a few. I guess I got pretty inventive there at the end, and I don't think the young padre will forget me for a while. I was drenched with flop-sweat and shaken to my very bones, and more than a little bit convinced I was going to roast over a slow mesquite fire throughout eternity for what I had just done. But I had no time to recite the Hail Marys and Our Fathers I had been assigned, not with people out there trying to kill me. I made a mental note that I owed God some penance, opened the door to the adjoining confessional, and yanked Merissa out of there just as I heard the priest sliding open that side of the screen. The girl had been asleep, and by the time she got her eyes opened we were barreling out the front door of the church and onto the street.

My sense of direction has never been very good. I was born and raised in Chicago, but when I went back there after a fifteen-year absence and found a network of new expressways and a skyline completely different from the one I'd grown up with, I couldn't even find the lake, and in Chicago everyone knows where the lake is. Now, in Tijuana, I was trying to remember all the twists and turns we had taken in our flight from the bad guys, and it was difficult indeed. The only good news on the horizon was that Delgado's army seemed to have gone elsewhere to look for us.

We walked for a couple of blocks, and Merissa, somewhat more lucid now, began complaining about her feet. "My fucking feet hurt" is the way she put it, and the message was repeated several times to make sure it had been received. There wasn't much I could offer her in the way of succor, and I certainly wasn't going to carry her. I had problems of my own. My ankle hurt, I had a full-blown headache, and the pain in my ear, at one point in the evening very severe, had subsided into one of those grinding, throbbing hurts that carries its own rhythm section. I was lacking in sympathy for Merissa Evering with her sore tootsies.

About ten minutes later, after several turns that were more instinctive than reasoned out, we found ourselves in an area of small locally patronized shops. The garish displays of multicolored shoes and gaudy shirts and more mundane items such as underwear and blue jeans differed greatly from the merchandise in the downtown tourist traps, and the ghastly fluorescent lighting inside the stores made the tacky goods look even worse. Everyone stared at Merissa and me curiously; in our bedraggled state, we constituted something of a novelty. I think they mistook us for street entertainers, expecting us to go into a comedy musical routine at any moment. But no one really bothered us, because Tijuana is that kind of town. One is always on the safe side when the business one minds is one's own. I finally stopped at a corner and tried to get my bearings, looking so utterly baffled and confused that a kind-hearted Samaritan took pity on us and asked if he might help.

"I'm trying to get to Fifth Street near Avenida de la Revolución," I explained. There was a fleeting second when I wondered whether I could trust him or if he might be one of Delgado's people, although he didn't look like one of the boys. Far from it. He was middle-aged, paunchy, wore glasses, and had an open, pleasant face. I decided to put aside my incipient paranoia and accept the help he offered. He gave me very explicit directions and told me I was about seven blocks away from where I wanted to go. Then he suggested with a completely straight face that perhaps I might want to visit an emergency room to have my injuries looked at, and told me where the nearest one was. I thanked him and even considered offering him money, but I decided not to. He had offered his help out of the goodness of his heart and might well have been offended. In a town where one of the main pastimes was leeching from tourists it was good to remember that there were real people, nice people. I would have to keep that in mind later when I thought back over the whole enchilada—the beatings, shootings, disembowelings, sexual exploitation, egomaniacal bullfighters, power brokers with tinted glasses, and cops who bend the rules to hurt you.

There seemed to be no need for running anymore; it would have only drawn unwanted attention to us. So Merissa and I simply strolled, looking for all the world like lovers out for an evening constitutional, except perhaps for the blood running into my collar, my limp, and Merissa's maroon dress, which was so thin and flimsy that each time we passed a lit shop window the fabric became translucent and it was more than apparent to those who cared to look—and they were legion—that she wore no underwear.

We finally got to Fifth Street, where the parking garage was located, and I felt an ally-oxen-free sense of relief. My plan was to drive down to Pajarito or even to Ensenada, just to keep Merissa out of the way of Delgado and company until I could get her back across the border. Perhaps I could reenter the United States by way of the Mexicali-Calexico crossing point and not even have to drive back through Tijuana. In any case I wanted to get out of town right away.

We started up the concrete ramp to the upper level, where I had left my car. Climbing the Matterhorn would have been easier. My ankle twinged with every step, and Merissa's added weight was no help. The air in the parking structure was stale, even though the building was open on one side, and I doubt its ramps and levels had been hosed down in a year. We got almost to the upper level before the pistol shot shattered the quiet. It did a pretty good job on my nervous system too.

The bullet caromed off the wall with a whine, and the fear, an almost palpable, physical thing, gripped me by the throat so I could barely breathe. I hit the floor, pulling Merissa down with me as the next shot came, and I wondered if Delgado had reloaded since the last time I'd seen him. I crawled between two cars, hauling the girl along with me like a dead body, and then I slithered with her under one of the cars, or rather a pickup truck, which unfortunately had a slight oil leak. I pulled Merissa clear and then, crouched over, began running, dragging her after me. Another shot blew out the side window of the car nearest to us, and somewhere in Merissa's foggy half sleep the reality that live ammunition was being fired at us penetrated. She started to whimper and lost control of her bladder, the stream flowing down the slanted concrete floor, and then she screamed, rattling an echo off the walls. I just ran and kept her running with me. It seemed the shots had come from below us, which meant there was no one between us and my car parked above, or at least, no one with a gun, assuming Delgado was still the only one of his little group carrying a piece, and again I remembered sourly that it was my own revolver he was using to plink shots at me.

I heard his hollow-sounding footsteps, but in this structure of crazily angled concrete walls and floors I couldn't tell where he was, whether he was getting closer or farther away. It didn't matter; all I wanted was to get to my own car, illogically thinking that would mean safety. At least it was first base. We ran upward on that strange tilt, and now Merissa, who seemed to have shocked herself awake with her own scream, was going at a pretty good speed, as fast as she could on those silly Joan Crawford fuck-me shoes she was wearing, and I even let go of her wrist when I saw she was keeping pace with me. It was a little late, but at least I didn't have to drag her along anymore, and that last forty feet of nonencumbrance might have made a difference.

I got to the car and fumbled around in my pocket for the keys, cursing myself for locking it in the first place even as I realized what folly it would have been to leave a new car with California plates unlocked in a downtown Tijuana garage. When I finally got the lock turned I swung the door open, and Merissa dived in over the steering wheel. I went in after her, pulling the door shut behind me and jabbing the key into the ignition almost all in the same motion. The engine kicked over, I released the parking brake and slammed into reverse with a great grinding of gears, and the car shot out of its parking space backward and smashed into the rear of the car parked across the way. I felt sorry for the guy whose car I hit, but I couldn't very well stop and leave an apologetic note under his windshield wiper.

I shifted into first and started down the winding, twisting

ramp. "Get on the floor," I said to Merissa, and she obediently slid down off the seat, her knees tucked up under her chin, a frightened baby in whore's raiment, her makeup smudged, her knees skinned, her dress and shoes wet with her own pee, and her eyes shut tight in hopes the bogeyman would go back into the dark closet where he lurked in her bad dreams. The thunder of the car's engine in the cavernous garage made it sound like a spring Sunday at Indianapolis.

I switched on my headlights and pumped the little lever at the side of the steering column that changed them to high beam, not quite flooring the accelerator but driving entirely too fast for safety, my tires screaming their protest at every turn, and when I rounded the hairpin curve that put me on the middle level I saw Jesus Delgado in a slight crouch off to the right side of the ramp, both hands on my Colt Trooper in TV-cop fashion, and I could swear I saw his finger squeeze off a few rounds. My windshield became two big spiderwebs with ugly little holes in the center, and I flattened myself over the steering wheel to present as small a target for him as possible. Maybe turning on my brights had bothered him enough to screw up his aim. One shot went by my head and through the back window, and the other slammed into the safety headrest just behind me. I twisted the wheel to the right and saw for an instant the whites all around the pupils of his eyes, and then I felt the nauseating impact as the right fender mowed him down like a stalk of wheat under the blades of a combine, hearing the crunch of metal and the snap of bone. After that came the two jarring jolts, bouncing me high enough that my head hit the headliner, as the front and rear wheels passed over him like a speed bump in the parking lot of a shopping mall. I gunned the motor and the roar was magnified tenfold by the cement walls and floor of the garage, and I never heard Delgado yell, if indeed he did yell, and I never looked back at what I had done, but kept driving, wrestling the steering wheel. I careened down the twisty ramp to street level, where a frail plywood gate arm stretched across the exit. It was designed to lift up only after I had deposited my parking fee in the coin slot. I barely slowed down, didn't give it any thought at all, and rammed through it, snapping it like a No. 2 Faber pencil and not even feeling any impact or resistance.

And then like that moment in a Western movie when John Wayne first comes over the rise and sees the vistas of Monument Valley, I was out of the garage, in the fresh air, out on the street, far out of the range of any handgun, and I headed south, out of Tijuana, for the moment at least, safe.

12

There are two roads leading from Tijuana to Ensenada farther to the south. One of them is free and one requires the payment of a toll, and there are few differences between the two, except that the toll road is slightly shorter and much better maintained. I chose the free one, not out of penury but because the front of my car was smashed, there was undoubtedly blood on my right fender, and I didn't want to have to explain to the toll collector the bullet holes that peppered my windows front and back for fear of him notifying the *Federales.* The night was warm and very dark, and in the blackness I could smell the sea off to my right somewhere, the briny fishy odor that characterizes the Pacific. The wind whistled through the broken glass, but it was a hot wind and did little to dry the perspiration that had drenched me, wilted my clothes, and made me feel sticky and sick. I squinted, trying to see the dark ribbon of the road through the network of cracks in the windshield. The effect was kaleidoscopic, and the occasional headlights coming toward me were refracted into a thousand tiny points of light, each separate and distinct and on a slightly different angle, fusing into one giant ragged ball of brightness as the car drew closer to me and then passed.

There was a heaviness in me, in the pit of my stomach, a despair I was sure would stay with me all my life. I was experiencing guilt the likes of which I had never known before. I had killed a man this night, done so deliberately and with malice. Taking a human life was not in my game plan. It never had been. He had attempted to kill me, to be sure, and probably would have done so if I hadn't run him down with the car, but that was a cold fact, an intellectualization on my part to make what I had done okay. Jesus Delgado had been a pimp, a dope dealer, a whoremaster, and probably a killer: in other words, a totally reprehensible human being. There are some that might say he deserved to die. I might even say it myself. But no one had appointed me judge, jury, and executioner, and it was a role I was miserable playing.

At some time during Jesus Delgado's existence on the planet, he must have burbled with delight at the antics of a puppy or the unpredictable bouncings of a rubber ball, or swelled with pride at his first pair of long pants. He'd manfully learned to tie his shoes and tell time, and mastered the mysteries of the first grade primer, and agonized over teenage complexion problems. Some woman had probably loved him at one time, and perhaps he had loved her back, and they had lain together in that postcoital silence that says more than a thousand conversations ever could. He had overtipped a waiter, known disappointment, caught a cold, suffered the runs, cried and exulted and sorrowed and crowed his triumph just like all the rest of us. He had been a terrible man—but a man he had been, and I had snuffed out his life with the slight flick of the wrist it took to turn my car's steering wheel.

And it was eating me alive.

I passed the Pajarito Beach turnoff without even a glance at the town or the hotel, but drove south on El Camino Libre along the coast to a beach that was fairly accessible to the road, where I pulled off onto the shoulder and got out of the car, leaving Merissa asleep on the front seat. She was curled into a fetal ball, her hand at her mouth, and it would be neat and fitting to report she was sucking her thumb, but she was not. I walked through the sea oats past various decomposing body parts of expired gulls and fish and mollusks and beach rats, and onto the sand. The wind here at the ocean was colder and less benevolent, but I took off my jacket and shoes and socks, leaving them on the beach, and walked all the way down to the water's edge. The surf ran up around my ankles, took an icy bite, and then darted back away again, as if it were playing a tag game with me, a game in which I was perennially It.

I rolled my pants legs up around my knees and waded calf deep into the sea. I stooped and gathered water into my cupped hands, holding it as though it were some precious liquid gold, and bathed my head and face and neck with it, and when the salt hit the gash behind my ear a million crawly insects with needle-sharp shoes did a Mexican hat dance in the wound. I washed all the blood off my face and neck, and soaked my hair with sea water, saturated my shirt with it until that awful, sticky, sweaty feeling was gone, to be replaced by the not unpleasant sensation caused when ocean water evaporates and leaves its slightly gummy saline residue gritty on your skin.

There were lots of stars, more than I was used to seeing in the smog-locked Los Angeles sky, and a sliver of a moon that looked fake, as though it had been created by a theatrical spotlight that had been masked on one side, badly, with the shield stage electricians call a "barn door." A fine sea mist hung in the air, cold and peppery on my face, making the stars dance. I looked up at the sky as the tide churned around my feet, foamy like the water in a washing machine's rinse cycle, and I felt the tears come salty and unbidden on my face. I wasn't crying for Delgado, but for myself. I'd never killed anyone before. I hoped I would never have to kill again, and that if I should have to, it wouldn't get any easier. I wouldn't like myself very much if it did.

My feet were numb from the ankles down by the time I walked out of the surf and reclaimed my shoes, socks, and jacket and went back to the car. When I opened the door the light in the dash went on, there being no dome light in a ragtop, and I saw that Merissa Evering was awake and looking at me. She didn't say anything for a while. She was still curled up in a little ball, and I put my jacket over her, since all she wore was the damp maroon dress. She continued to stare at me as I started the car, bounced it through the weeds, and carefully pulled back onto the highway, which was pitted with potholes and dips.

After about two miles she finally said, "Who are you?"

I was shocked, I guess. I'd lugged her around for the better part of two hours, ducked bullets with her, and killed a man on her behalf, and I felt understandably connected to her. But she hadn't the foggiest idea of who I was or what I was doing in her life.

"My name is Saxon," I told her. "I'm working for your father. He hired me to find you. He wants you to come back home."

"Shit," she said, drawing the word out, drizzling it with rattler's venom. We drove in silence for a few more miles until the highway turned inland through some burnt-brown roller-coaster hills that looked barren and lunar in the darkness.

She shifted on the seat, and her eyes glittered in the darkness like an animal's. "Marty won't let you take me back," she said. "He won't let you fuck with me."

Anger rose in my throat, at her and her precious Marty and at all the low-lifes and users and brutes and degenerates I had met since the day I had taken her father's offer out of my own money-lust and because of the vague and distant carrot he had dangled before my nose, the possibility of a part in his next lousy movie. I said, "Marty isn't going to do jackshit about it, Merissa. Marty is dead!"

The words hung there in the warm air, with the murmur of the road beneath us like underlying mood music in an old film. She was staring at me in disbelief. I nodded grimly. I felt lousy for having told her so brutally, but not very. I turned my attention back to my driving. My eyes were getting weary from squinting out through the shattered glass. When I finally looked over at her again the tears were coursing down her cheeks and her nose was running, but she wasn't making a sound, and that was fine with me. I didn't want to discuss it. I had the great grandfather of headaches, I was exhausted, and the free road to Ensenada was no place to make small talk about the dear departed.

I did wish that she would stop looking at me while she cried.

It took us another twenty minutes or so to reach Ensenada, a middle-size Mexican coastal town. It wasn't much of a resort as tourists spots go, but it had Tijuana licked hands down, if for no other reason than the proximity of the ocean to just about anywhere in town you might likely wind up. The shops were not quite the rip-offs to be found forty miles north at the border, and the sleaze was kept to a minimum. The restaurants were fewer in number but a cut above. The biggest attraction was Hussong's Cantina, a smoky, stuffy, rowdy, rollicking place. It attracted the under-twenty-five crowd from Southern California, who flocked there in the summertime, lemming fashion, in buses and vans and overstuffed VW Rabbits to drink beer, carouse, sing loud songs, sometimes fight, frequently get laid, and invariably throw up in the alley or pass out in one of the rest rooms.

I found a small hotel by the waterfront, and an extra five dollars to the gimlet-eyed clerk kept him from asking too many embarrassing questions about the condition Merissa and I were in. I parked my crippled car around back where it wouldn't be visible from the street, sadly remembering its past glory and thinking about how angry the lessees were going to be when I brought back their brand new Le Baron held together with piano wire and Juicy Fruit gum. We went up the outside stairway to the second-floor room we had been assigned, and I was thankful Merissa was finally able to navigate under her own power, because I was weary of pushing, pulling, and shlepping her around. In fact, weary was a pretty good general description of me.

The room was like every roadside motel room everywhere, all Naugahyde and cheap veneer, but it was clean. Merissa had stopped crying, but she was benumbed, sitting on the edge of the bed and staring off into her own reverie. She wasn't very stoned any more, but her grief was a kind of novocaine. I took her by the shoulders and gently eased her back onto the bed, and she looked up at me and screamed "No!" and rolled away from me, her knees pressed tightly together. There couldn't have been very many men to whom Merissa had said no in her short but full postpubescent career, but she had me wrong. The sexual victimization of children in mourning was not one of my kinks.

I said, "Shh, shh. It's all right," and covered her with the wafer-thin blanket, smiling my most avuncular and reassuring and nonthreatening smile, and after a second or two she relaxed and slipped off into uneasy sleep, her regular breathing occasionally broken by a sob.

I showered in the postage-stamp bathroom, put on my shorts again, and came back out. There was one distinctively uncomfortable upholstered chair in the room, plus a straight-backed chair by the table. I had no place to lie down. I suddenly felt silly, like a sappy leading man in a 1930s comedy who has to sleep in the bathtub so as not to compromise Claudette Colbert. I shrugged and crawled into bed next to Merissa, turned chastely away from her on my side, and went immediately to sleep.

My dream had a cast of thousands, all of whom behaved in a completely unrealistic fashion, but the stars were Delgado and Iglesias and Officer Cruz and Carmen.

Carmen was the good news.

In the morning I awoke to shower sounds. I got out of bed and opened the window to let in the ocean. It wasn't visible from our room, but the whisper of the surf and the salty-fishy smell told me it was somewhere close by. I love the ocean. Being near it makes me feel more vital, more alive, and strangely more peaceful, and any peace I could find on this particular morning put me well ahead of the game. I put on my pants and shirt and sat down to wait for Merissa to finish in the bathroom. After a while she emerged, wearing only a towel, her hair wet and tangled and dripping. All the crap had been washed off her face and now she looked about twelve years old—until you caught a glimpse of the depths of her eyes and noticed they had seen way too much for any age.

"Morning," I said.

She nodded at me and went over to the window and started doing things to her hair to dry it.

"How do you feel?"

"Neato-benito," she said dryly. "This morning is one of my high spots."

"Are you hungry?"

"Starving."

"I'll go down and buy us something to wear and then we can go out for breakfast."

She didn't look at me. "Whatever," she said.

I went downstairs. The morning was already hot and humid, the breeze blowing moistly off the water. It only took me five minutes to find a shop, where I bought her a pair of blue jeans and a lacy Mexican blouse in bright yellow. I also bought myself a light blue Mexican shirt with white piping and a pair of white duck pants, and since they would have looked pretty silly with my black dress loafers, I purchased some leather sandals, the kind where the thong goes between your first two toes and cripples you for a week until you either get used to them or they gouge a permanent dent in your foot and become comfortable. My wardrobe expenses were sure to raise Mark Evering's eyebrows a bit, as would the bills for auto repair. I went to a sort of drugstore where they sold toiletries, sundries, and dried stuffed bulge-eyed frogs mounted on little wooden bicycles, and picked out a plastic hairbrush, a lipstick, and an eyebrow pencil for Merissa, and a packet of disposable Gillette razors for me. I also got a Reese's Peanut Butter Cup and a Mounds candy bar just to hold us together until we could get to a restaurant. Then I went back up to the room.

She was still wearing the towel, still standing at the window, looking out at the parking lot but not really seeing it. I dumped all my purchases on the wrinkled coverlet and she came over and looked at the pile as if it were so much cow manure. She poked around and finally took the Reese's. "I hate coconut," she said, and put the whole piece of candy in her mouth at once. I left the Mounds where it was. I hate coconut too.

"I got you something to wear," I said. She held up the blouse and examined it critically, trying to hide her disgust at its lack of a Saks label. Then she gave a sort of shrug which served the dual purpose of signifying her resignation to wearing inferior goods and of divesting herself of the towel, which fell in a damp tumble at her feet. She put on the shirt and stood there thoughtfully, unbuttoned on top, naked below, as though impervious to my presence in the room. I realized then she wasn't unaware; she just didn't give a shit.

She turned with a little half smile, the shirt not doing much to cover her. "Are you straight?" she said. It was inconceivable to her that she could be standing there nearly naked in front of me and yet not be desired. But I knew too much about Merissa and had been through too much with her to feel anything toward her but impatience.

"Put your pants on, Merissa."

The smile grew more insolent. "Whatever you say, pal."

The jeans didn't fit her too well, and they lacked the designer cut she was undoubtedly used to. She zipped up her zipper without even a glance in the mirror. She hadn't taken her eyes off me all the time she was putting the jeans on, nor had she bothered to turn around while dressing. She pulled at the baggy seat of the pants halfheartedly.

"Great fit," she said. "But I don't suppose we'll be going any-place fancy. What did you say your name was?"

I told her again.

"And you work for my father?"

"I'm a private investigator," I said. "I'm currently doing a job for your father."

"And I'm the job?"

"Something like that." I handed her one of my business cards. "In case you ever need a friend," I said.

"I wouldn't know one if he fell on me—which is probably what would happen." She studied the card carefully. Then she said, "What happened to Marty?"

"He's dead."

"Did you kill him?"

"No."

"What happened to him then?"

I certainly wasn't going to go into detail. "Somebody else killed him."

She took a deep breath, as though by inhaling the pain she could make it disappear. Then she handed my card back to me. "I don't have any friends, so I've learned not to need any. Could we eat something now? I'm not going to make it on just a candy bar."

"Sure," I said, "I'll just change." I picked up the new clothes and started into the bathroom.

"Modest little flower, aren't we?" she said. "You don't have to go in there. I've seen a dick before."

I closed the door behind me as though I hadn't heard. If there was one thing in the world I was sure of, it was that Merissa Evering had seen a dick before.

We had breakfast at a little restaurant overlooking the harbor. I ordered a seafood stew and she had ham and eggs. The meal was a quiet one, not strained-quiet but peaceful-quiet, with Merissa deep in her own solitude. We were almost through with our coffees before I decided to intrude upon it.

"Merissa, did you know a man named Rafael Iglesias?"

She looked up at me. "Past tense. Is he dead too?" She was pretty astute for a stone druggie.

I nodded as the waiter came and refilled our cups. She used a lot of sugar, not measuring it with a spoon but cascading it directly into her coffee.

"Yes," she said finally, "I knew him. He and Marty were friends. Partners."

"Merissa, the police think I killed them, but I didn't. It would help me a lot if you could tell me anything at all about them."

"What makes you think I know anything at all, or that I give a fuck?"

"I don't, necessarily. But the one link in all of this seems to be you. Two men have been murdered, and last night the same people, I think, tried to kill me. So I'm naturally looking for some answers. I thought maybe you might have some."

"You certainly manage to get yourself into some pretty deep shit, don't you?"

"That happens sometimes."

"I know the feeling. Look, I don't know anything. I've been stoned for days. I don't even know how many."

"Maybe if we could start at the beginning. Where did you first meet Martin Swanner?"

She gnawed on the inside of her cheek, remembrance bringing back pain, loyalty slowing her answer. "At the house," she said at last. "He was a friend of Daddy's. A business associate, really." She thought about that for a minute and then said, "Oh, fuck it, let's call a spade a spade. He was my father's personal procurer."

I offered nothing. Experience has taught me the less I talk, the more other people will.

"Producing a movie doesn't just start with day one of principal photography," she said, sounding very much like a breakfast meeting at the Polo Lounge. "You have to raise the money, develop the script, sign a deal for distribution, hire the actors and the director, and put all sorts of complicated legal stuff together. You have to know the right people, be able to shmooze the right people, find out what it is you can do for them to get them to do something for you. With a letter of intent from a bankable actor you can raise an unlimited amount of money anywhere. Without one, you're just another asshole running around town with a tattered script and a tin cup."

She tore open the pack of cigarettes I'd bought her, took one out, tamped the end against the matchbook cover like Bette Davis, and fired it up. "Everyone has their own little number, Saxon. Dope, money, power, booze, little girls, little boys. Whatever. Marty had lots of government contacts, and he knew all sorts of ways around and through the immigration laws. He'd supply the young Mexican girls, and I mean young—thirteen, fourteen, like that. When it came time to make the deals or put the packages together or to negotiate with the right actors and directors and their agents, Daddy would give the girls out as gifts, almost the way other businessmen give out bottles of Scotch for Christmas."

"Was one of Marty's immigration contacts Rafael Iglesias, by any chance?"

"You name it, Iglesias is—was—in it. He just about ran things down here."

"What about Delgado?"

She shuddered at the mention of the name. Maybe she was thinking about the sickening lurch as the car ran over his body. Maybe she was remembering other things. "Delgado had a piece of the action, I guess, but as far as I know he was just an employee, a hired hand working for Iglesias."

"But with Marty and Iglesias out of the picture, wouldn't that leave Delgado as the honcho?"

"I suppose," she said. "Why? Are you saying you think Delgado killed them? I thought abusing women was more his speed." Her look turned inward for a second, and what she saw wasn't pretty. She shook her head almost violently.

I lit a cigarette of my own and signaled the waiter for more coffee. After he'd poured it and gone away I said, "I hate to have to ask you this, Merissa—"

"I know, it's breaking your heart."

"Why Martin Swanner? What got you involved in the first place?"

She fairly spit out the smoke. "Mr. Saxon, you are looking at a genuine twenty-four karat JAP. A Jewish-American Princess. You've heard all the jokes? What does a JAP make for dinner? Reservations." She snorted. "From the time I could sit up and say goo I could get anything I wanted from Daddy. He was so busy making money he eased his guilt at being a shitty father with an open checkbook and unlimited charge accounts at every rip-off store on Rodeo Drive. After a while it got boring for me. I mean, what do you give a twelve-year-old girl who has everything? So I started looking for my giggles elsewhere. By the time I was out of junior high school I'd fucked fifty different guys and was a bona fide head. Reds, whites, angel dust, coke, crack. You can't go to a movie or turn on a TV without seeing somebody

I've either gotten loaded with or screwed. By the way, most actors are lousy lays. They're too into themselves to give a shit about anyone else's feelings, even in bed."

I winced inside and tried not to take umbrage.

She said, "When Marty came along I thought at first he was just another California type, a rich lawyer pushing forty who liked young stuff. Ha! The first time we balled I turned him every which way but loose. He was, as they say, enchanted, and I was pretty smitten myself. He was good-looking, smart, fun to be with, and terrific in the rack, and I knew he wasn't with me just because he wanted to get close to my father. It was my first exclusive relationship. Hard to believe, isn't it, that I was twenty years old and had never had what you'd call a real boyfriend? For the first time in my life I was really in love, and I thought he was, too, so I just figured I'd ride with it. It was great for a while—about six weeks. Then Marty started getting kinky."

I nodded, thinking of Sharon and the kid who wiped off the windshield in the service station, and of the leather bondage outfit Swanner had been wearing when he died.

"It was fun, I guess, mainly because it was so damn off-the-wall. Almost every time, then, it was something different, something new. I'd never known anyone into B and D before. Sometimes he liked me to tie him up and hurt him and tease him. Sometimes he tied me up. Or he'd take me over his knee and pull down my panties and spank me like I was a little girl. And sometimes he'd make me do it to him. And then we got into scenes. Three-ways, you know? Or more than three. One of Marty's favorites was to find some guy—usually he'd pick a young, good-looking one—who'd be willing to tie Marty up and make him watch while he got it on with me."

"Is that what you did with Pepe Morales?"

She looked at me with something that might have been respect. "You've been a busy boy."

I gave a modest little shrug.

"Okay. So I didn't mind it with Pepe. In fact, I like it. He's hung like the bulls he kills." She looked at me to see whether that had shocked me and was disappointed that it hadn't. "I wasn't Marty's only girl, I knew that. You can't expect a man with his sexual tastes and appetites to be faithful. Sometimes we had scenes like that with another woman."

I took another sip of my coffee. I was so intent on the girl's story that it had grown cold.

"Don't get me wrong," she went on, as if anyone ever could. "I'm no lezzie. But if that was what Marty wanted, it was okay by me. Marty always had really good drugs, and he seemed to really care about me, really like me. We were good together."

"So good that Marty had you turning tricks at the Shot o' Gold?"

She frowned, trying to remember. "I'm not sure, to be honest with you. I was really so fucked up I don't even know how I got there. All I know is, I woke up and I was in bed with Delgado, and three of his buddies were there watching, waiting in line. They didn't even take their shoes off. After that they started bringing other guys up. Delgado told me that's what Marty wanted." Her eyes became shiny and her nose got a little red. "When I complained, Delgado hurt me. Real bad."

"How long were you there?"

"I don't know. They kept me blazing all the time."

"Blazing?"

"Stoned, man, coked up. I've been on a real bummer trip." Again she made an effort to dust the cobwebs off her memory. "Was it Saturday? I don't know what day. I don't know. But there's this real sleazoid place in TJ, a hot-pillow hotel or something—Marty liked to get it on in strange places. He had me beat him off under the tablecloth at Le Bistro in Beverly Hills one day during lunch. Anyway, we're in this fleabag and we had a scene going, a B and D number with Pepe Morales. I did some dope, some real powerful stuff, primo, and I guess I did too much, because I flaked out."

I waited as long as I could. "And?"

"And nothing. I woke up pulling a train for the Delgado bunch at the Shot o' Gold."

"Where does Sergeant Ochoa fit in?"

"The cop?" she said. "I don't know, he didn't come around that much. But it doesn't take a genius to figure out that he's been getting taken care of by Iglesias one way or the other, in return for occasionally looking the other way when someone gets beaten up or there's dope to be moved or God knows what-all."

"Who do you know down here that might want Marty dead? Or Iglesias?"

"Walk down the street in Tijuana and swing a big stick, chances are you're going to hit ten people who didn't like one of them or the other. They were pretty famous in that town."

I thought of the reactions whenever I mentioned Martin Swanner's name to Nacio and the bellhop at the hotel and the bartenders and waiters I'd spoken to the day I arrived. I thought of Señor Mendez. Swanner had indeed been famous. Or infamous.

"Did you and Marty and Iglesias ever get into a scene?"

She curled her lip. "You really get off on talking dirty, don't you? I think you'd rather do that than fuck."

"Did you, Merissa?"

She finally decided to answer me and shook her head. "No, but Marty gave me to Iglesias one night. I guess he had something else going for him and wanted me out of the way."

"Gave you to him?"

She shrugged, as though that were simply the way of things.

"Is that how you perceive yourself, Merissa? As a five-foot-six cunt?"

"I didn't make the world," she almost snarled. "The first guy I ever balled asked me if I could get him into free studio screenings before I even got my panties back on. The second one wanted me to introduce him to movie stars. The next guy asked me if I could get him an audition with my father."

"Did you get him one?"

"Sure," she said, and named a popular actor who hung out with the Brat Packers at the Hard Rock Cafe and who had made his big-screen debut a few years ago in a Mark Evering film. "Then I figured that if people were going to want me for myself instead of for my father or my money or my connections, I was going to have to get goddamn good at what I did. And I am good. The best. Any time you want to check that out, just tell me."

"But you were in love with Martin Swanner?"

"You tell me what love means and I'll let you know. He was the most sexual man I've ever met, and after a whole big string of closet fairies and needle-dicks in the Beverly Hills crowd I really grooved on him." She sighed, like Cassius weary of the world. "He's dead now, and I'm really sorry, I suppose, but life goes on. I guess it goes on." She squashed out her cigarette viciously, and I was sure that she was seeing someone's face in the bottom of the ashtray. I didn't know whose, though. It didn't really matter.

She turned away to look at the boats in the marina. For the time being she had dismissed me from her reality. I had one more question that I had to ask her, in order to figure out how to proceed.

"Will you come back to Los Angeles with me, Merissa? Will you come back to your father?"

She didn't stop studying the boats, but I saw her chin quiver. She was struggling with something inside, her own Hobson's choice.

"You don't have to," I explained. "I'm not going to drag you back or force you to do anything you don't want to do. It's up to you, but if you decide to stay here I'll just tell him where you are and let the two of you work it out, if that's the way you want to play it."

"You're a noble little soldier."

"Not at all. That was my deal with your father. I'd find you for him, but coming back to him would have to be your idea."

She leaned her head against the glass of the window, and when she took it away there was an oily mark on the pane. "I don't seem to have too many other options."

"We all have options."

She shook her head, battle-scarred and all used up at an age when most girls are going to school and working part time as checkers or waitresses, dating, standing in line in front of movie theaters, going to rock concerts, maybe married and looking forward to the first baby. Living in worlds Merissa Evering never even knew existed. I guess that's what comes of being born rich and beautiful and having all the advantages. She chewed on a fingernail that was already bitten down past the quick.

"Sure, I'll come back with you," she said at last. "Isn't that where the big bucks are?"

"If that's your choice," I said, and signaled for the check.

"My choice," she murmured. "Shit, I wish I had some coke."

The waiter came and went, and I counted out his tip and left it on the table. "There's one little piece here that doesn't fit,

Merissa. Why was Delgado trying to kill me last night? Why didn't he want me to take you away?"

"How do I know?" she said dully, still staring at the midmorning weekday quiet of the small boat basin. "You're the detective, you figure it out."

And on our short walk back to the hotel through air that prickled with heat and dust, I did.

13

It took me time to get my thoughts together and to make the phone calls I had to make, so by the time my ducks were in a row and I was driving back up the toll road from Ensenada to Pajarito Beach it was that period of late afternoon when the sun fights a valiant but losing battle with the rotation of the earth, turns a breathtaking orange, and takes a header into the Pacific as if to make us regret putting it away for a while in favor of the night's more understated stars and moon. The off-white stucco facade of the Pajarito Beach Hotel had taken on the sun's rosy tint and glowed its hospitality in the waning day as I jostled over the dusty rutted driveway. My mangled car didn't draw any strange looks. Since I was dressed in native fashion, sporting a tan that was relatively intact from a few weeks' unemployment spent, in typical Hollywood actor fashion, in the sun waiting for the phone to ring, those who gave me any more than a passing thought at all must have assumed I was a local driving a car in the usual sorry state of disrepair. At that, the car looked better than most of those on Tijuana's streets.

I went through the lobby, having parked well away from the entrance to avoid curiosity about the bullet holes in the windshield, and into the lounge. Sitting against the window drinking tequila with lemon and salt was a familiar little man I couldn't place at first, but when I searched my memory I recognized him as one of the three men who had assaulted me on Sunday night in the alley behind the newspaper office and had administered a fairly tame beating. I was glad he didn't notice me, because I didn't want to deal with him right now. Unaccompanied by his *compadres* and without the element of surprise on his side he would have been no trouble for me, and I did owe him a smack-ing-around, but I didn't have the time to indulge myself in any vendetta; I had more important things to do. I turned quickly and went back out into the lobby, and then the long way, through the deserted ballroom, around the side of the hotel, and down a rocky path to a large bungalow near the high-tide line. I knocked on the door.

It was the first time I'd seen her in slacks; all the other times we had been together she had worn a dress. They did marvelous things for those legs and hips, and I found myself admiring the cut of those slacks even though I much prefer women in skirts and dresses. Carmen, of course, could push all my buttons even if she were wearing a sou'wester. The slacks and blouse were both a bright pink, the blouse a somewhat deeper hue, and it set off her dark skin beautifully.

That dark skin turned a few shades paler when she saw who it was at the door. "Saxon," she said, "my God, you shouldn't be here."

"Aren't you glad to see me?"

"Don't you know the police are looking everywhere for you? Delgado was killed last night."

"It's part of the police's new master strategy," I said. "Every time someone dies in Baja California they come after me to pin it on." I guess that was a bit petulant, considering the fact that I *had* killed Delgado. "Ask me in, Carmen."

She pulled me in and shut the door, looking around outside first. We were in the sitting room of what was a three-room bungalow almost at the water's edge, detached from the main hotel but still on the grounds, still part of it. The furnishings were a lot nicer than those in Martin Swanner's room, and there were even a few personal touches, like music boxes and original paintings on the walls. They weren't Riveras or Picassos but they weren't the bare breasts on black velvet variety, either. After Carmen locked the door behind me she drew the flimsy white curtains over the windows, blocking out the view of the ocean that made the suite desirable and expensive in the first place, and the curtains were immediately dyed the orange-pink hue of the sun as it sank even farther into history.

"Where have you been?" she asked.

"No es importante," I said. "But what is important is that I know who killed Martin Swanner. And your husband." She didn't say anything. She looked stricken. "Don't you care?"

"I told you," she said distantly, "I am glad he is dead. I can only thank whoever it was."

I looked around the room. There were two bedrooms connected to this central sitting room. One of them was visible through an open door, and seemed frilly and sunny and feminine. The door to the other room was conspicuously closed. "That's a good idea," I said. "Perhaps you'd like to do that now."

"What?"

"Why don't you ask your other visitor to join us?" I strolled over to the other door as Carmen leaned toward me. I tapped once, lightly. "Come on out, matador," I called.

After a moment's pause, Pepe Morales came out, looking as angry with me as the last time I had seen him, at the party in the restaurant at El Conquistador, which was angry enough to do me some serious physical damage. Although I had about forty pounds on him, he was much younger than I and in superb physical condition, which was more than I could say for myself at the best of times, and he probably hadn't been beaten up as often as I had in the last few days. But extreme rage often makes one careless, and that was the only hope I had if he decided to get rough. He stood there in a theatrical pose, as if someone were taking his picture for a poster, wearing a creamy white suit with an indigo shirt open at the neck so the crucifix and all the holy medals shimmered gold against his deep-tanned hairless chest. He was one hell of a good-looking man, I'd give the son of a bitch that much. He was in the throes of the decision-making process, obviously trying to decide whether or not he was going to kill me.

I guess he made his choice, and I could see the effort of will it cost him to get his hatred for me under control, but evidently he managed to do so, because he took a deep breath and bowed quite stiffly from the waist, more Teutonic than Latin, and said, "Señor Saxon, if you do not leave the señora's quarters at once I shall be forced to call the authorities."

"I don't think you want to do that, matador. The police will probably want to ask you a lot of questions about Martin Swanner and Rafael Iglesias, and I don't believe your answers will be good enough. And when the police in this town don't like your answers, they ask you again in a way you will not like. Trust me on that score."

"I don't know—"

"What you're talking about," I finished the sentence for him. "They never do."

"They?" Carmen said.

He drew himself up, shoulders back, flat stomach sucked in even more, as if about to execute a veronica. His eyes glowed like red-hot stones. "You always insult me," he hissed. "Why do you always insult me?"

"Let me ramble a bit, matador, and maybe we can clear things up for you. And for me, too. If I get anything wrong, feel free to jump right in, won't you? I believe this whole thing started about a year ago, when you were still a relatively unknown and struggling torero. At that time Martin Swanner and Rafael Iglesias became your *patróns*. Correct?"

"That is no crime, I believe."

Carmen put her hand on my arm and said, "All bullfighters have *patróns,* you know. That is not unusual."

"Of course it isn't," I said. "And Morales needed a rich and powerful sponsor so he could establish himself as a star. He had the drive to make it, and the talent. *Número uno.* But then I wonder why he didn't move on, out of Tijuana to Mexico City, where the really big money is? Maybe he had another strong drive that was even more powerful than wanting stardom."

"I don't have to stay here and listen to this," Morales said.

"Yes you do, Pepe, because you've got nowhere else to go. As I said, this was a year or so ago—shortly after your little sister had met with a tragic and wasteful death."

His back became even stiffer, he blinked his eyes in a momentary loss of control, and a white line appeared around his mouth from his lips being clamped so tightly together. I felt a twinge of conscience. I hate fighting dirty, but I'd come this far and had to play my hand out, angry and hurting as he might be.

I said, "Forgive me, I know how you must have felt, must still be feeling." Saying that didn't help my conscience as much as I thought it would. I pressed on, "But you did a little investigating on your own. And you found that the coyotes—those of your people who prey upon their own, take advantage of the poor ones who try to get across the border for a better life in my country—those men who took your sister and a bunch of other illegal immigrants out into the desert and robbed and raped them and left them there to die of thirst and exposure, those men were working for the two guys who made most of the arrangements for illegal border crossings in this town: Martin Swanner and Rafael Iglesias."

Carmen put a hand up to her face, as if by covering her own mouth she could somehow shut mine.

"So you ingratiated yourself with them and convinced them to sponsor you, to let you into their inner circle. And that's why you've made no effort to move on to the bigger bullfights, to enhance your career. You were waiting for the right moment to get your revenge. It dovetailed nicely, didn't it? No one ever suspects a star of being a murderer. Not their up-and-coming hero who wears holy medals and goes to church to pray twice a day. And Iglesias and Swanner lavished money and attention and publicity on you and built you the most compelling reason in the world *not* to kill them."

A little white fleck of saliva appeared at the corner of the bullfighter's mouth. I've never seen anyone struggle so hard to swallow their rage, never seen rage quite so bitter.

"So you bided your time, took the money, and made yourself a superman here in Baja. You were waiting until the right moment, whenever that would be, whenever you thought you could get away with murder. And then all of a sudden, last Saturday night, the gods dropped a gift into your lap. Me. A gringo, going all over town mentioning Martin Swanner's name, asking where he was. You being Swanner's fair-haired boy, you naturally heard about it too. When it came to big shots like Rafael Iglesias or Martin Swanner, Tijuana has a pretty impressive grapevine. I don't think I'd spoken Swanner's name five times in public before everyone in town knew who I was and where I was staying. But no one knew why. It was perfect for you, a perfect frame-up, with me as the Mona Lisa in the middle of the frame."

His head quivered.

"You set up one of Martin Swanner's favorite pastimes, a kinky little sex circus, just you and Marty and Merissa Evering, and you got her so coked up she didn't know what she was doing, with Marty all dressed up for the part in his little leather bondage suit and his hands restrained behind him with those cute leather handcuffs that seemed to turn him on so much. And when he was all trussed up and helpless you got your buddy Delgado to take the girl away, and then you hung Martin on a hook behind the bathroom door and you took one of those sharp knives you use to carve up the bulls—probably the *de-*

scabello—and you opened up his stomach and watched him die in agony."

Carmen gave an involuntary little cry.

"But before all that, matador, you were very careful to send me a note at my hotel room, telling me where and when to find Swanner, and you timed it so that I'd walk in on a fresh kill and get nailed by the police, whom you had also called to tell them about the body."

"Liar!" he shouted, but the sweat beaded up on his fine smooth brow and his eyes were shifting wildly so that the whites above and below the pupil showed. I knew enough about body language to know who the liar was here. I also knew he was more frightened now than he'd ever been with half a ton of mad bull wanting to take him downtown.

"Your timing was off a hair, matador," I said. "That's very dangerous in the bullfighting business, as I'm sure you know. But timing is pretty important when you're plotting the perfect murder. The police got there before I did, so much as they wanted to, they couldn't hold me. They were damn suspicious, and they still are, but there wasn't much they could do. I was free and out on the loose, and of course you had no way of knowing I'm a detective and that I'd be trying to get myself clear."

"You can prove nothing!"

"Don't be too sure."

"Filth!"

"Me? No, just an innocent bystander. But like a dumb schmuck I played right into your hands for you. You *comprende* schmuck, matador? Well, just like a schmuck, I started an argument with you and Iglesias the next afternoon at the party in front of half of the population of Baja California. I did it because I had the feeling you knew where Merissa was and I hoped I could rattle your cage enough to find out, but it gave you another idea. You sent three of your groupies to avenge your honor, didn't you? They were the ones that messed me up in the alley. I'm sure it didn't take much coaxing on your part; they adore you, idolize you. There's one of them sitting in the lobby of this hotel right now, grateful to be of service to you, to drive you around and wipe your pretty nose. They'd do anything you asked them to, especially when it comes to your honor. So while they were playing soccer with my head it gave you time enough to get into my room and trash it to make things look suspicious, and to tear a button off my jacket. Then later, when you figured I'd be alone, without an alibi, sleeping off the spanking I'd just gotten, you brought your *patrón* Iglesias to within a few blocks of my hotel, cut him open the way you'd done Swanner, and put my button in his hand. You thought I'd have no one to vouch for my whereabouts except the Sandman. You really left me twisting in the wind, you thought. But I had an alibi, matador."

Carmen looked at me, those big Hershey's Kisses eyes entreating, but I was on a roll now and there was no stopping. I'd come here to have my say.

"Mrs. Iglesias was with me in my hotel room. All night."

Morales looked at Carmen. It was patented look number 287-A, the Wounded Doe. Carmen was unaware of it, though, because she was staring at me.

"So the police kept me overnight, matador, and they hurt me an awful lot. But because of Carmen, my alibi, they couldn't hold me any longer than that. They had to let me go. And you knew I'd eventually put the pieces together, so you sent Delgado and his bozo brigade to make sure I didn't do any talking."

"*That* is not true," he said, and the emphasis made me think that most of what I'd been saying was true but that I'd messed up on one point.

"I think it is," I said, "and since Delgado would move up to fill the vacancy of the number one spot in the racket, he'd be the direct beneficiary of those two deaths, so he was more than happy to accommodate you, too. People have a tough time saying no to you, don't they, matador? One of the perks of stardom. And I wasn't surprised to find you here in the Iglesiases' permanent bungalow, consoling the bereft widow as a friend of the family. Because that was just one more little fringe benefit to killing Rafael Iglesias. It made it that much more sweet, you being in love with his wife."

Once more the tears welled up in Morales's eyes, and I wondered how a man who faced horrible death with such aplomb three times every Sunday afternoon could burst into girlish tears as easily and as often as he seemed to.

"It almost worked," I went on, "but then I went to read your press clippings at the paper and found out about your sister. And if three sad little men hadn't heard on the Tijuana jungle drums that I was somehow connected with Swanner and Iglesias and come to me in my hotel to do a little business, I never would have known how your two *patróns* made their money. I just put it together. It took me long enough, but I finally put it together."

"You don't understand," he said, his voice muted with tension.

"I understand murder, Morales, and I understand I almost took the fall for it."

"My sister was a baby," he said in a small, shaking voice. "A good girl. A virgin, only fifteen years old. Iglesias and Swanner, they took her money that she had worked hard for, cleaning other people's houses, other people's toilets. Money I had made risking death in the ring. They promised her a new life in America, a job, a place to live, they said they could fix it so she could stay there. Then they used her like a whore, their people, and left her in the desert. It took her a long time to die." A teardrop rolled down his cheek. "Do you wonder I wanted them dead? Do you blame me?"

"I'm not here to judge. Not them, not you. But you tried to frame me, matador. And I couldn't let you do that."

Someone knocked harshly on the door of the bungalow, an ugly, forceful, and totally authoritarian knock, and I would have recognized it even if I hadn't known ahead of time whose it was.

"That will be Sergeant Ochoa and Officer Cruz," I said, my skin prickling at my own mention of Cruz's name as I recalled some of the more vivid details of my night in his tender custody. "I took the liberty of calling them and telling them my little story. It made things a lot easier."

Morales was in the middle of the room in his standard toreador pose, proud and straight and invulnerable. But this was not something he could wave away with his *capote*, and all of a sudden he blew it,.the whole image, the whole Latin macho bit, and his entire frame seemed to shrink, to implode upon itself, and I knew that in the movie in his mind the bull was coming, its spittle spraying him, its breath fetid, its eyes red, holding its massive head down, and Morales saw the horns hooking and coming up and he was defenseless. No killing sword, no fancy footwork, and no worshipful crowd olé-ing him on. Just little Pepe Morales from Sinaloa, vulnerable and alone. One audible sob bubbled through his lips, and then he did what no torero ever does—he turned tail and ran. He crashed through the window, the curtains tangling around him and tripping him as he hit the rocky path that wound down to the beach. He was up and on his feet almost at once with that uncanny feline grace that had brought him so far in his chosen profession, and he sprinted down the path toward the ocean, turning at the water's edge where the sand was wet and firm, and running south, parallel with the surf line, his slim form almost a silhouette in the now-damson glow of the sunset.

The policemen outside the bungalow door heard the glass breaking and Officer Cruz smashed in the door with less effort than it takes to open a box of Cheerios. As they blasted past me my spine turned to an icicle as Cruz glared at me just before he went out the window with Ochoa right behind him. I was impressed that a man of his great bulk could move so quickly, but it wasn't going to make us best friends. I took two long steps to the window and watched as the plainclothes cops ran down the beach after Morales. Carmen hadn't moved during all of this. It was almost as though she were frozen to the spot in a grotesque game of Statues in which she was the only player.

When Ochoa had gotten halfway down the path he stopped and blew a piercing blast on his whistle while he still had the breath to do so, and as I watched the beach became overrun with khaki uniforms, all running toward Morales, coming at him from several different directions. I climbed through the window to get a better vantage point, but I stayed up near the bungalow, high ground affording me the best view.

Morales had been running for about two hundred fifty yards, easily outdistancing his pursuers, when one of the uniformed policemen drew his pistol and fired two shots. They were warning shots, aimed at the sky, but Morales didn't know that, and sheer terror at the sound caused him to stumble and fall heavily, rolling over and over in the wet sand, ruining his cream-colored suit. He stopped rolling when the surf splashed him. He simply lay there, cringing and damp but basically unhurt, with one hand covering his face, the way a child covers up in hopes that the monsters from the dark closet won't see him.

When the police got to Morales, big Cruz reached down and picked him up by the waistband of his beltless slacks as easily as he might a small sack of oranges. He set Morales on his feet and twisted both hands up behind him to accommodate the handcuffs. Ochoa was talking to the matador, gesturing with palms upward, and I could almost sense him apologizing to Morales for having the temerity to arrest him for two brutal murders. As I have said, the Mexicans take their bullfighting seriously.

The uniformed cops were milling about on the beach, all dressed up with no place to go, and finally Cruz and Ochoa began leading the manacled Morales back up the sand toward the hotel, and the uniforms came along behind them like acolytes at a religious parade, trying their best to appear as if they had something meaningful to do. Since there was little more to look at, I came back to the shattered window, the glass crunching under my sandals, and stepped inside the sitting room of the bungalow to where Carmen stood, her hand still at her mouth, white and shaken and very small. That queer fluttering feeling I got inside me every time I looked at her came back again and all I wanted to do was take her and hold her and smell her hair and feel the soft contours of her body against me, but this was hardly the moment. So I just looked at her and smiled, trying to make it understanding and reassuring and gentle, and I said, "It's over now." But there was such fear in her eyes, such confusion, that I wasn't sure she believed me. "It's all over," I said again, "and I'm here. I'm here with you, Carmen, and that's the important thing. You're not alone. I'll never let you be alone."

It didn't make me feel any more kindly toward the Tijuana Metropolitan Police when Sergeant Ochoa apologized to me for the treatment I'd received during my night in their scummy jail. I don't believe in apologies anyway; most of them are hypocritical and a waste of breath. I rarely make them myself and even more rarely accept them from others. "Sorry" just doesn't cut it with me.

The good news was that the law was not going to make a stink about Jesus Delgado. They bought my self-defense story, probably because they were as happy as anyone that Delgado would trouble them no more and they were grateful to me for taking him off the streets. If that sounds too easy, rest assured there was a good reason for it. Ochoa had been on the Iglesias payroll, probably not for anything he had to do but for things he chose to ignore, and was no doubt sore as hell that someone had killed the golden goose. I suppose he knew that Delgado, moving into the headman slot, would have eased him out of the picture none too gently because he knew too much. Whoever was going to step in now and fill the gap in Tijuana's illegal-alien-smuggling racket would be more than likely be someone Sergeant Ochoa could get along with.

I knew someone would do it. Nature abhors a vacuum not nearly so much as the weasels abhor a scam that's going to waste with no one raking in the dirty money. Whoever they were, the new group of coyotes wouldn't be any better or worse than the Iglesias-Swanner-Delgado bunch. I imagined that Ochoa would now keep a close watch on things and make the transition easier for someone with whom he had an understanding. He wouldn't be the guy who'd move in at the top level, though. After all, he was an honest cop.

I admit to a few misgivings when he asked me to come back with him to headquarters, since to me it was like returning to the scene of a near-fatal accident. But the police just took a quick statement from me and gave me back my gun. They'd found it next to Delgado's body and run a computer check on it back in the U.S.A., though I think they'd known all along whose it was. I got a tiresome lecture on the folly of bringing unauthorized firearms across an international border, but I think they just wanted me the hell out of town and chose to ignore my arms-smuggling.

It was after nine o'clock at night when Ochoa finally told me I was free to go. He had been polite as hell all day, almost obsequious, ever since I cracked his double murder case for him. Once we got to headquarters he even made sure that Officer Cruz stayed completely out of my sight. However, I decided to forego the pleasure of shaking the hand he offered me when I was leaving. Let him throw me in jail for rudeness.

I went back to my hotel and collected my belongings, including my ruined wardrobe, and checked out. Then from the lobby I called Merissa Evering in Ensenada. There were no phones in the rooms of that cheap little motel, and the time it took me to explain to the desk clerk who I was trying to reach was almost as long as the wait while he went upstairs to get her and bring her down to the office.

"Hello," she said when she finally got to the phone. Merissa had a way of making even a single word sound petulant.

"This is Saxon," I said.

"I figured. No one else knows I'm here."

"Have you had anything to eat?"

"Jeez, thanks for asking—it's almost ten o'clock! Yeah, I went back to that place we ate this morning. I had the camarones." She sounded very far away.

"I'll come and pick you up first thing tomorrow."

"You're going to leave me in this shit hole another night?"

"You think you'll be all right by yourself until morning?"

"I'm a big girl, now, Saxon. You probably hadn't noticed."

As a matter of fact, Merissa's maturity was one thing I had not noticed. Especially when she snickered and asked, "Why aren't you coming back tonight? You got something going in TJ? Is she hot?"

"I'll be by for you about ten in the morning," I said, ignoring her question because she had inadvertently struck truth. "Stay in the room, Merissa. Alone, you understand?"

"Sure," she said. "The grown-ups are the only ones who get to have any fun."

I was about to caution her not to take any drugs, but I remembered I'd only left her enough money for meals. Not that lack of money was any guarantee. Merissa knew very well how to get money or drugs without too much trouble. I didn't want to get her angry, I was hoping for an easy trip back to Los Angeles and I didn't want to drive two hundred miles with a twenty-year-old woman having the sulks, so I kept quiet. I hung up and then phoned the Pajarito Beach Hotel. At least there they have telephones in the rooms.

"Everything is all right," I told Carmen, "I'm on my way back down there. And I'm starved."

"I've eaten, darling," she said, "but I'll come and have a drink with you while you eat."

The drive back down to Pajarito just seemed to take a long time. Maybe it was the anticipation of being alone with Carmen and holding her in my arms, or maybe it was Merissa's talk about camarones—large Mexican prawns in a garlicky red pepper sauce—that made me realize I had once again skipped a meal. That had happened with monotonous regularity since I had crossed the border. I wondered if I was losing weight. I wasn't wearing my own trousers, so it was hard to judge if my waist had grown slimmer. I hoped so, for my acting career if for nothing else. The camera always adds at least ten pounds, they say.

By the time I got back to Pajarito the hungry elf had emerged victorious over the horny one, so Carmen and I went to a little restaurant perched on the side of a cliff overlooking the sea. When dinner finally came, it was a superb meal of seafood stew and prawns and a well-chilled Chenin Blanc, with a lot of hot-eyed looks and hand-touching across the table.

Finally over the coffee she asked me what they were going to do with Pepe Morales.

"I don't know about your Mexican courts," I said. "Up north they'd sentence him to life in prison, give him a great deal of psychiatric testing and treatment, and probably let him go in about nine years. I suppose it will go easy with him down here because he's a celebrity."

She looked very uneasy and I realized the last several days must have taken a tremendous emotional toll on her. After all, Rafael Iglesias had been her husband, whether she'd liked him very much or not. As for Morales, I didn't know what their relationship had been, and I didn't want to know. I've learned never to ask questions I don't want to hear the answers to.

"I want you to come back with me, to Los Angeles," I said, perhaps to forestall any urge she might have to bare her soul. "We'll go to the consulate tomorrow and arrange whatever needs arranging. Have you ever been to Los Angeles?"

She shook her head. "Rafael didn't like to go there. Here in Mexico he was powerful and important, but he said that when he was in the United States he was treated like just another spic.

And my parents never got any farther from home than Mazatlán."

I realized I knew very little about her, that this whole thing had been so sudden the usual steps of getting to know someone had been vaulted. "Is that where you were born? Mazatlán?"

"I come from a little fishing village near there," she said. "My father worked in the fish cannery. He was always tired, but he was gentle and kind and good. I remember when he would kiss my sister and brother and me good night, he would always touch my cheek so softly and sweetly, and his hands would always smell from fish. But it was a good smell because it was his smell."

She went on some more about her father, but somewhere along the line I had stopped hearing her because there was something in my head, some little ferret thing scrabbling to get out, picking at me with insistent, fluttery, sharp claws. I was aware of an acute sense of unease and it was spoiling my dinner, spoiling this moment. I wished the thing would burst through to my consciousness so I could know what it was and deal with it, but it refused to come out. Nonetheless it was a palpable, tangible presence, one I finally made a determined effort to push back away from me, from us. I made myself concentrate on her eyes, on that mane of thick black hair and the coppery skin set off by the white blouse and skirt she wore, on those breasts, which were doing such an incredible number beneath the silk, and I came back to her, to pay more heed to her story, hoping I hadn't missed anything important.

"My father is alone now," she was saying. "The nest is empty. He doesn't work anymore. When I married Rafael I was able to give him enough money so that he no longer had to. Now he goes fishing for pleasure and sits with the other old men in the cafés and drinks strong, bitter coffee and talks about his catches. He has earned his rest." Her eyes shone as she spoke of him. I wanted to ask about her brother and sister and why they had left her father's house, but I was afraid she had already told me and I hadn't been paying attention.

"Where do you live in Los Angeles?" she asked. "By the movie stars?"

I laughed. "I have a little house in a place called Venice, not too far from the ocean. There are lots of old canals there, like in Venice, Italy, and my house is right on the edge of one of them. It's small, cozy. I live there with a young boy I've kind of adopted. Marvel is his name. He had a rough deal, and I'm trying to make things better for him. I'm not a rich man. I do okay; my agency is self-supporting. And sometimes I act in movies myself, or on television. I'm no star, but I make a few dollars. I like my life, Carmen."

I was telling myself that when two people love, wealth or lack of same has no meaning, because that is what one always tells oneself in such situations. The facts are often different. Carmen was a poor peasant girl whose father canned fish, but she had been married to one of the wealthiest men in Baja. I didn't know whether to brag about my life-style or apologize for it. But I admit to a sense of relief when she leaned forward and squeezed my hand and said that it sounded wonderful and she couldn't wait to be there and share it with me.

When we got back to the hotel we made love with an intense carnality we hadn't really known before, almost as two adversaries, and when we were finally done, wrung dry emotionally and physically, panting, our hearts racing too fast, we lay wetly in the ruined bedclothes and let the wind from the sea outside the broken window cool and gentle us. And just as I was thinking that my whole life had been a prelude to this moment, the insistent little thing that had been scratching behind my eyes at dinner started in again. I was allowed to enjoy the sensation of Carmen falling asleep with her head on my shoulder and her hair spread out across my chest, because I didn't close my eyes in sleep all night long.

We awoke early, or rather Carmen did, because in order to wake up you have to be sleeping in the first place, and that was a luxury that had been denied me. Carmen stretched and rolled over on top of me and kissed me. She was wonderful and warm and fuzzy from sleep, and her naked body was beautiful in the diffused sunlight of the morning. We joined together easily and knowingly, and afterward we showered together, which is an intimacy even more meaningful than lovemaking. It's easy simply to screw someone, but showering with a person is somehow an act of giving and of trust, soaping ourselves and each other and feeling the water, first warm and then cold like icy needles. After we had dried off we resisted the impulse to go back to bed, and I ordered coffee and Mexican pastry from room service. Then I sat, transfixed, watching her while she finished blow-drying her hair. There was something so sexy and appealing in the way she tossed her head and bent forward, so that her hair hung down over her face, to dry the fine soft tendrils at the nape of her neck. I watched the wet hair absorb the heat and gain body and form and texture, noting that her long robe would peep open when she raised her arms and threw back her head, moving the pistol-shaped dryer back and forth, her hair rippling in waves under its onslaught, catching the sun and sending off shimmering highlights. I loved Carmen very much at that moment. I was fantasizing, looking forward to a million more mornings of watching her dry her hair. It would be good for me. It would also be good for Marvel to have a woman around the house, something he'd never experienced. The softening influence might help him to come out from behind the wall of self-defense he'd built.

As for Paula—I didn't want to hurt Paula, and I just had to

hope she would somehow understand and forgive and be all right about it. In any relationship one person cares more and gives more than the other, and it was Paula's misfortune to be on the short end of things when it came to the two of us.

Whatever it was that had robbed me of sleep had faded along with the early morning mist from the ocean.

The bellhop brought our breakfast and Carmen quietly disappeared into the bedroom while I let him in and paid him and tipped him. When he had gone I set the tray on the table near the window. Although the shattered glass had been cleared away sometime yesterday and the screen had been put back in by the hotel's management, the window itself had not been replaced, so it was wide open to the morning breeze from the sea, a bright and snappy wake-up kind of zephyr carrying with it the subtle hint of salt and fish. I poured our coffee. I had no idea how she took hers and I yelled the question in to her and jumped as she answered me from just behind my head, having come back into the room without my knowing. We laughed about it. I was pleased she drank her coffee the way I drank mine, black with no sugar, and I shook my head, astounded at my own delight in her. Many people never know in their lifetimes the feelings I was having at that moment, and I feel sorry for those people.

We sat and ate the pastries, looking out over the ocean. At the surf line several early-morning joggers plodded tirelessly over the hard-packed sand. I know many people swear by running, but to me it's the ultimate boredom, and I always look a bit strangely at those who practice it and proselytize others about it with a fervor usually found only in fundamentalist religious sects. These runners were obviously on vacation, but not from their new god, Adidas. A lone horsewoman galloped her mount at the water's edge, and that looked more inviting. I longed to go riding with Carmen, that and so many other joyous and romantic activities, like clambakes and art gallery walks and sailing and long drives up the California coast to the wine country. But first there were things to do this day, important things, and the silly special events that two people in love share were going to have to wait their turn. I stood up, carrying my cup, and went over to where my small overnight case stood and began packing my toilet articles.

"You do whatever it takes to get out of here, darling," I said, aware that the room was being paid for by the late Señor Iglesias. "Pack, check out, find out where we have to go to get you a permit to leave Mexico, and I'll be back in about two hours."

"Deserting me already?" she said.

I grinned over my shoulder at her, at the absurdity of her question. The way she looked, framed in the window with the morning Pacific behind her, I couldn't imagine ever deserting her.

"Fat chance," I said. "I just have to go down to Ensenada for a while. I'll come right back."

"Ensenada? Why?"

"Remember the picture I showed you? The girl I came down here to find in the first place? Merissa? I guess in all the confusion I forgot to tell you. I found her."

There was a small tinkly crash and I turned quickly to see that Carmen had dropped her cup onto her saucer and overturned it, but she wasn't concerned about the spilled coffee. She was staring at me, and the color had fled from her face along with her smile. The muscles at the corners of her mouth were taut and turning the skin around them a livid white.

"What's wrong?" I said.

She didn't answer at once. Then she shook her head, as if by the violence of the movement she could erase what she had just heard, the way one might degauss a videotape. I put down my own cup and went to her and started mopping up her coffee from the tabletop with a napkin, and she stood and moved away from me. Even though I didn't know why, the gesture hurt me more than I could ever have imagined.

Her face was working almost like that of a stutterer trying desperately to get something said but physically unable to do so. Then she turned away to get control of herself, and she wasn't looking at me when she told me she couldn't go back to Los Angeles with me.

I stopped what I was doing. "Why not?"

She shook her head again. "I told you once before, you dig too deep. Now leave me alone. Just forget about me."

"Forget about you? Are you crazy? I love you." I came up behind her and held her upper arms with my hands, feeling the tension in her body and smelling again the fresh-washed fragrance of her hair. "And you love me. You know it, you've said it. What's the matter with . . ."

She turned, and her face was so full of hopelessness and despair that it broke my heart. And with the breaking the tiny thing, the creature in my head with the scratchy, sharp claws, busted loose from where it had been caged and came out to laugh at me.

"Mazatlán," I said dully. "Mazatlán. In the state of Sinaloa. Oh my God, you were there that night. With Pepe and Merissa and Martin Swanner in the El Portal Hotel. You were there. You must have been in on all of it."

She ran from me and hurled herself onto the bed in the other room, that bed where so recently we had reaffirmed our love in soft feathery touches and tropical heat. She sobbed and cried and moaned, and all at once I became removed from it, like a spectator at a high school play, and from outside looking in I saw it as one hell of an act. There was a big hole in my chest where my heart had been, and if an empty place can ache, then mine did. I went back to the table and soaked up the remainder of the spilled coffee, and then I sat down and stared out the window. Her sobbing was a rhythmic counterpoint to the grumble of the ocean.

I don't know how long she stayed in the bedroom. Time had little relevance then, and I didn't look at my watch. I was in no hurry to go anywhere. By the time she came out I had a headache that showed every sign of never going away. I didn't look at her, willed myself not to. I was afraid if I looked at her I'd be lost. She sat down on the sofa and sighed loudly. I didn't say anything.

"I've told you that my family was poor," she said to the back of my head. "In this country that is not so unusual. What is very special is that we could all read and write. My father taught himself to read Spanish and English and then after my mother died he taught us. We knew there was more in this world, my sister and my brother and me. We didn't want to live and work and die in the same little village with our backs bent, worn out before we were thirty, our hands smelling of the fish. It was our dream, and our father's dream for us, that we go to America. So he worked for us and he saved, and we worked too, doing whatever we could. My brother went to the cannery when he was twelve years old. My sister sewed until her fingers bled, blankets and serapes to sell to the tourists. I cleaned the bathrooms and greasy kitchens of the rich. We finally got enough money together to fulfill the dream. They would go together to America and get good jobs and make some real money and then they would send for my father and me. It was all arranged. The money was paid, there would be a man in Los Angeles to help them get green cards so they could work there. They climbed into the truck and they waved good-bye and *vaya con dios,* my brother and sister and some other people from our village. One of them was little Guadalupe Morales."

I knew I had to hear this, that I wouldn't have any peace until I heard every bloody detail of it. I turned to her, but she wasn't looking at me. She was staring off into her own private vision of hell, and I couldn't have stopped her from talking if I'd wanted to. It was her catharsis, something she finally had to say, as if the saying of it would make the doing of it all right.

"After they raped my sister and left her and my brother to die in the heat," she went on, "then my laughing, gentle father became a very old man—all of a sudden, almost before my eyes. His back was bent just a little lower and those eyes were now without life, without seeing. And I knew it must be up to me to get *venganza.* I took what little money I had saved and I came to Tijuana. I asked questions. I made believe I wanted to go to America too. I bought some nice clothes and I went to all the expensive bars and restaurants and people noticed me. That was how I met Martin Swanner."

There was a golf-ball-size lump in my throat and as she spoke it grew to the size of a tennis ball. I didn't know it would be a basketball by the time she finished.

"You know enough about Martin Swanner," she said, "to know he wasn't going to ship anyone like me away. Not for a while. It was not easy for me. I knew what he was, I knew what he had done, and I wanted to vomit every time he touched me. I am thankful that he tired of me after a while, so he gave me to his partner and friend Rafael Iglesias. Yes, he gave me, the way you give someone a book after you've read it. I hated Rafael more than Martin. Martin was a gringo, but Rafael was worse because he exploited his own people. But he was easier to handle, because he was old and sometimes very tired, and with Martin I had learned ways to make a man not tired. And so he fell in love with me. I made him fall in love with me, Saxon. And I talked him into becoming Pepe Morales's *patrón* because Rafael would do whatever I asked of him."

"You and Pepe," I said, my tongue thick. "You were lovers too?"

She shrugged. "I've known Pepe since he was born. He's been in love with me since he was five and I was nine. I came to see him when I got to Tijuana. We shared a common heritage, and a common grief. It just—happened. He is a boy, an immature puppy thing with the face of an angel and the body of an animal. I needed him."

"What for?"

"My revenge. It was always in the back of my mind, whenever I was being pawed by Martin or Rafael or even Pepe. Revenge is what has kept me going all these months, like gasoline in an automobile. That's why I said yes when Rafael asked me to marry him. It was going to make my revenge that much sweeter. And it was going to—it *has* left me very rich."

She began crying again and I let her. I couldn't do much about it anyway, because I felt myself turning to smooth, cold stone. After a while she sniffled and held her breath for a time to get herself under control. "You were right about a lot of things, Saxon," she said. "We heard you were looking for Martin, and we did set it up so that you would come to the El Portal and be blamed for the murder. The note, the hotel. Yes, I was there. So was Pepe, and your Merissa. Martin wanted us to tie him up and make him watch Pepe with both of us. He liked doing that, it excited him. We had done it before, the four of us. Rafael never knew. He was too busy making money, too stupid and too vain of an old man's power to pay that much attention to me. So just before nine o'clock we gave Merissa a big dose of 'ludes and I took her away while Pepe—did what he had to do."

"Why in hell did you take her to the Shot o' Gold?"

"It was the only place I knew that was safe. Delgado ran it. He was only too glad to help and to keep his mouth closed. He knew that with Martin and Rafael out of the way he was going to have it all."

"All the rackets, the alien smuggling?"

"Everything. And he thought he was going to have me, too."

"Where'd he get that idea?"

"I told him," she said simply. "You see, he was also part of my revenge."

My mouth was clamped so tight my jaw muscles throbbed. "Christ!" I said. "Delgado too."

"It meant nothing to me," she said, her voice a whisper without any emotion anymore. "Just a stepping-stone to what I really wanted. Swanner and Delgado and Rafael—all of them dead. Like my sister and brother."

I was literally finding it hard to breathe.

"When I met you that night in the bar I had no way of knowing who you were. I knew that I wanted you, that for those few moments what had come to pass with us was very special and very beautiful. But there was nothing I could do about it. Rafael was asleep here in the bungalow. Then the next day at the corrida I found out who you were. I knew you had gotten to the hotel a few moments too late. And I still wanted you."

"So much that when your frame didn't work you decided to hang another murder rap on me."

She made as if to put her hand on my arm and then changed her mind. "We didn't plan to, you must believe that. For the moment it was just to be Martin who died. But then when you quarreled with Rafael in public at that party it seemed to fit in very well with our plans."

"You think pretty fast," I said.

"I had to. Pepe has dressers and handlers that worship him like a young god. They heard you insult him; it was their idea to follow you and beat you. Pepe and I just—used it. We used the time to go into your hotel room and take the button from your jacket to place in Rafael's hand after he was dead."

"You're quite the user, aren't you, Carmen?"

"Don't say that! Oh, please, don't say that to me."

I went on like a school kid reciting his multiplication tables. "Then you came to my room and slept with me to make sure I didn't have an alibi while Pepe was killing your husband."

She nodded meekly. Deep inside the stone statue that had once been me there was an exquisite pain, white-hot, like a toothache. And I've always been one to worry a toothache with my tongue and make it hurt worse. For me Carmen had been like the promise of a part in Mark Evering's new film—a carrot on a stick dangling inches before the nose of a very stupid donkey who would keep plodding after it, never to attain it.

I said, "There's one thing I don't understand. I was in custody. They had me dead to rights for killing Rafael, or they thought they did. And then you came and got me out; you gave me the alibi you'd tried to take away from me in the first place. Why? Nothing would have kept me from swinging for murder. Why did you save me?"

"You fool!" she said, her eyes blazing life for the first time since she'd begun her story. "Don't you know I loved you? From the very start? And after we made love together I knew I could never let you go."

"It doesn't seem like making love is so important to you," I said.

"Not before. There have only been five men for me. Martin Swanner was an animal, scum, interested only in filth. Rafael was a fat old pig whose manhood needed all sorts of help and encouragement in order to perform. And Delgado was . . . cruel. Pepe is just an unskilled child with a horse's parts, and he hurt me worse than any of them. But when you touched me it was with tenderness and with caring and love. I had never . . . enjoyed a man—love—before you. And I did love you. I still love you."

I must have been pretty far gone. She wasn't even getting to my ego—especially when all the other little pieces began falling into place.

"But by bailing me out you were leaving Pepe to take the rap for both killings."

"I don't love Pepe!" she screamed, her balled fists striking the fronts of her thighs. "I love you. You are my future."

"What about Merissa's future? Was she going to be used by every sleazebag with a twenty-dollar bill in his pocket until she was an old lady at twenty-five?"

She shrugged again, once again listless and lifeless, her eyes turned up at the corners, giving her a slightly Oriental look. "Merissa was no better than a whore to begin with. And she was the only one who could have tied Pepe and me to Swanner's murder. It was Delgado's idea to keep her at the Shot for a while. For fun. Then he was going to collect a ransom to bring her back home. He wasn't going to call it that, of course. One of the things he wished to take over was Martin's job of supplying young girls to Merissa's father. But he was going to collect a big reward. And if that didn't work he had another plan. He would take money from Merissa's father for keeping his mouth shut about Merissa's being at the scene of a murder."

"So Delgado was in on the whole thing too. How were you planning to keep him quiet afterward?"

"I wasn't planning on letting him live very long," she said, so simply and directly that it didn't sound as though she were talking about killing a man at all. "Delgado was one of the pigs who took my sister. If I had to I would have cut his throat in his bed."

"So that's why Delgado tried to kill me when I wanted to take Merissa away?"

"I suppose so. I didn't know anything about that. I didn't even know you'd found out where she was. I swear that to you,

Saxon. You must believe I wouldn't have let anything bad happen to you. Not then."

"Why is it so important that I believe you?"

"Because. I never loved anyone before you."

I ran both hands through my hair, trying to sort out all the facts, separate the lies from the truths. I was reeling, on the ropes, practically a TKO victim. I said, "How did you know Merissa wouldn't blow the whistle on you when she finally did get back to Los Angeles?"

"Who would believe her? Drugs do funny things to the mind. She wouldn't have remembered it all, anyway, and if she had, everyone would have thought she'd been on some sort of bad drug trip. Besides, if she had said anything, it would have been very embarrassing for her father. He would have seen to it that she kept quiet."

I went to her, looming over her, and she looked up at me at such an angle that her eyes seemed bigger and browner than ever before, even red-rimmed and puffy as they were from crying. "One other thing," I said. "Pepe Morales is in jail right now, and no one knows better than I how Ochoa and Cruz deal with a murder suspect, matador or not. What makes you think he's not going to crack? To spill his guts, the whole story, your part in it, everything?"

A small feline smile flickered around her mouth, one she made no effort to suppress. "Pepe would never do anything to hurt me," she said. "He'd let them kill him first. He loves me."

"You seem to have that effect on men."

She covered her face with her hands and began crying again. I wanted to reach out and touch her hair; it took all the willpower I had not to. Instead I turned to close my suitcase.

She said to my back, "Are you going to the police?"

I braced myself for a knife between the shoulder blades but

did nothing that might have prevented it. Frankly, my dear, I didn't give a damn. The voice coming out of my mouth might have belonged to someone else, someone I didn't know. "Three very bad, very cruel men are dead," I said. "I killed one of them. Self-defense is what the authorities are calling it. The man who took a sword to the other two and watched them die slowly is now in custody, a confessed murderer. I have nothing to say to the police, Carmen. It's none of my business anymore."

She threw her arms around me from behind, her face pressing into my neck, her breasts against my back. "Take me with you," she said. "Take me back to Los Angeles, Saxon. I am a rich woman now. You'll never have to work again. We can be so happy. I can *make* you so happy. I love you so much! I can be a good wife to you, and you can teach me so many things. You'll be so proud of me, Saxon! And we can forget about all this ugliness."

I quietly disengaged her hands from around my waist and set my overnight case down on the floor. "You're probably right," I told her. "You would be a good wife to me and you would make me happy. I would never get tired of you, Carmen. I could never get tired of looking at you or touching you."

She stretched out her arms like the girl in a Jontue commercial, but I extended my hand palm out, like a traffic cop, and stopped her in her tracks.

"But forget about it? I can't, Carmen, because one day you might want *me* to do something, some little something I might not want to do, like killing somebody for you. Or you might want someone else to do it, and you'd fuck him and hate every minute of it because it's me you really love. And I'd wind up in the paddy wagon, like Pepe. Or I'd wind up like your other three lovers. And you would be telling the next guy how wonderful it will be . . ."

"Don't you understand that I *love* you?"

"And I love you too. I really do. But somewhere along the line there is a little piece missing in you, Carmen, somewhere in the vicinity of your value system. I understand your wanting revenge and I don't blame you. What I can't deal with is what you're willing to do to get it. Murder two men, let an innocent man go to prison, let Pepe take the rap for it. Use people. Manipulate them. You have all the moral values of a rattlesnake." And I hope I never again have to say anything as difficult as it was for me to say, "And only a crazy man cuddles up to a rattlesnake."

I took my bag and went to the door. When I turned and saw her standing there in front of the window, the sun reflecting from the water and shining through her long silken robe, her Hershey's Kisses eyes huge and sad and uncomprehending, she looked more the abused little girl sullied against her will by an unfeeling world than Merissa Evering had ever been. And when I went out the door of the bungalow into the bright midmorning of Pajarito Beach I left a lot more of myself in that room than I had ever thought I could spare.

I collected my passenger in Ensenada. She had metamorphosed as if by magic from drugged-out whore to innocent-in-the-mud to her final butterfly stage. She was now the spoiled daughter of a rich and powerful man, her nose pointing skyward, disgusted to find herself on El Camino Libre in Mexico instead of on Rodeo Drive in Beverly Hills, chin quivering with disdain in the best Katharine Hepburn fashion, regarding my once-new convertible, now battered and bullet-ridden, as though the magic coach had changed back into a particularly seedy pumpkin.

I took her arm and led her over the uneven ground from the hotel to the car, but she was in a nasty and antagonistic mood. I think I liked her better when she was freaked out on drugs.

"What are you, on vacation or something? You said you'd be here at ten o'clock and it's almost noon! What's the big idea? Don't think I'm not going to tell my father you left me cooling my heels all alone in this fleabag."

"I know," I said, "some dirty old man might have goosed you going up the stairs."

"Where the hell have you been?" she demanded.

"I had things to do."

"*I'm* your things to do," she reminded me. "My father's paying you a hell of a lot of money, I imagine. You're supposed to be taking care of *me*. Not leaving me sitting here in some rathole God forgot while you're off getting your whistle tooted somewhere!"

I opened the car door, my hand still on her elbow, and slung her into the front seat with more physical force than I had really intended. "Shut your fucking mouth," I said.

And she did. Somewhere between Newport and Long Beach she said, "Can we stop somewhere? I have to pee." Other than that she didn't say a single word to me all the way back to Beverly Hills. I was enormously grateful for the silence.

Mark Evering was involved in what he called a "story conference" when we arrived at his house. He was wearing another silk lounging caftan, his glasses perched high on his forehead. There were two young guys sitting in his living room with scripts open on their laps. One was wearing a three-piece off-white suit like John Travolta's and the other sported a pink linen sports coat with the sleeves rolled up, a black shirt, and a skinny white tie, the knot about four inches shy of his neck. There was a bowl of cocaine on the coffee table. Evering said to Merissa, "You've given us quite a scare, young lady. I'll talk to you in the morning." If the two young men, both of them obviously members of the new corps of USC film school graduates who were now writing most of the scripts in Hollywood, had come up with an ending line like that, Evering would have sent them home for rewrites. It was not quite the emotional reconciliation scene I'd been expecting.

Since he was so busy he had Brandy Evering write me a check, including a staggering amount for auto repairs and wardrobe, but he broke away from his meeting long enough to give me an unpleasantly wet kiss on my cheek and to express his undying gratitude. Then he reminded me again to have my agent call, told me to please keep in touch, and assured me I was now like a part of the family. Mrs. Evering gave me a familial kiss, too, in the atrium, indicating she was even more grateful than her husband, and threw in a little dry-hump just for fun. From Merissa Evering there wasn't even a curt nod, a small wave, or a kiss-my-ass; she simply went upstairs to her room in the sullen fashion of a teenager who's just found out she has a twelve o'clock curfew on prom night.

I drove wearily home from the Evering place in Bel Air to my own little bungalow in Venice. Negotiating Los Angeles traffic at night was tricky at best, and trying to do so through a demolished windshield was almost impossible. I had a headache by the time I got there, and left my car parked in front instead of garaging it. I almost dragged myself into the house, which was reverberating with the unmistakable trumpet sounds of Miles Davis. When Marvel first came to live with me I introduced him to the wonders of jazz to save myself from the cacophony of punk rock and heavy metal, and he turned out to have a great ear for early bebop. But like most of his peer group, he persisted in listening to it with the volume pot full up.

He was sprawled across the sofa in one of those classic teenage positions that made it appear he had eight arms and legs, like a spider. He was reading a comic book, but put it aside when he saw me.

"Look like shit," he said. Marvel often eschewed articles and personal pronouns in his speech.

"Feel like shit," I answered. "Aren't you going to ask me how was Mexico?"

"I sees how was Mexico," he said. "You need doctorin'?"

"I need sleep, pal," I said.

He got up and turned the stereo down to almost normal. He was a good kid. I was going to have to make those missed ball-games up to him.

I went into my den, where the red light on my answering machine was blinking. I was really too tired to care who had called, but my curiosity got the better of me, so I poured myself an industrial-strength jolt of Laphroaig, rewound the tape, and sat down to listen to the messages. A few were from bill collectors, a few were from friends, and two were from Paula. I felt disoriented and guilty about her, but I couldn't think about that right now. I was going to pull a Scarlett O'Hara and think about Paula tomorrow. The most recent message, however, was from Jo, who sounded a bit on edge and suggested I contact her at my very earliest convenience.

I dialed her number and her husband Marsh answered. Marsh Zeidler is one of those tiresome people who answers the question "How are you?" with the truth.

"It's been tough," he said. "I'm writing a movie for this independent producer. It's all on spec, of course, but he swears the money is there as soon as he has a script to show the backers. Anyway, I'm totally blocked. I'm stuck. Did you ever have writer's block?"

"No," I said, "I come from a wealthy family and my mother had me vaccinated. Can I talk to Jo, please?"

He was still explaining his writer's block to me when Jo took the phone away from him and I was rescued.

"Are you all right?" she said.

"Define all right for me, Jo. I'm alive. And I'm home. And oh, Auntie Em! Auntie Em! I'll never go away again. Because I've learned that—"

"I hate to have to tell you this," she said.

My God, it chills my very bone marrow when someone opens a conversation by saying that. It effectively dashes any hope I might have for a nice, hassle-free talk.

"Gently, please, Jo."

"Mark Evering's first two checks have bounced higher than a handball at the YMCA."

"*Gently,* I said!" I took a sip of the Laphroaig. Then I drained the glass. Laphroaig is too good—and too expensive—to drink all in one gulp, but the niceties of genteel sipping were beyond me right then. I didn't say anything for quite a while. I wasn't sure if anger was stilling my tongue, or exhaustion, or some other emotion that ran a lot deeper. Jo didn't intrude on my thoughts.

Finally I said, "Jo, I want you to take your boy genius into the bedroom, put on a pair of black nylons, and get him unblocked. Don't worry about Mark Evering. I'll talk to you in the morning."

The mother in her was taking over. She sounded as if her five-year-old had just found his pet gerbil dead in its cage. "Are you all right?" she said again.

"Amendment: I'll talk to you in the morning if you swear never to ask me that again. Otherwise this is our last good-bye."

I put my finger on the disconnect button. I have one of those modular phones that hangs up automatically when you put it down anywhere. It also chirps like a canary instead of ringing. Then I lifted my finger, waited for a dial tone, and punched up Mark Evering's number. The Filipino eunuch answered, and after telling me the *tuan* was busy he put me on hold for a long time. It was bad judgment, because by the time Evering got on the line I was well past annoyance and on my way to furious.

"Look, Saxon, I said keep in touch but I didn't mean tonight. You know I've got people here."

"I happen to be people too, Mr. Evering. And at the moment I am one pissed-off people!"

"I don't think I care for your tone," he said warily, once more the mongoose. "What's got your back up?"

I informed him that his checks bore the unmistakable odor of burning rubber and he told me to hold on to them for a few more days and then redeposit them, and that's when I really lost it and told him exactly what I thought of him. I have rarely been as eloquent. I used some of the expressions I'd picked up from Jesus Delgado in the alley behind the Shot o' Gold, I threw in some of my own old favorites, and I don't believe I left anything out.

There was a shocked silence at the other end of the line. Obviously no one had ever spoken in such a fashion to Mark Evering before, not *the* Mark Evering, he of the two-of-the-top-twenty-biggest-grossing etc.

Finally he said, "Saxon, you insolent prick! Just for that you're not going to be in my new picture!"